Forked

Special Edition

Melanie Harlow

USA TODAY BESTSELLING AUTHOR

Copyright © 2014 by Melanie Harlow

All rights reserved.

No part of this book may be reproduced in any form or by any electronic or mechanical means, including information storage and retrieval systems, without written permission from the author, except for the use of brief quotations in a book review.

A heart which has loved as mine cannot soon be indifferent. We fluctuate long between love and hatred before we can arrive at tranquility, and we always flatter ourselves with some forlorn hope that we shall not be utterly forgotten.

— HÉLOÏSE D'ARGENTEUIL

Chapter One

This moment called for some whiskey.

I pulled out the bottle of Two James Grass Widow Bourbon I kept stashed in my bottom desk drawer and poured myself two fingers. It was only three o'clock, but it was Friday and I had no clients coming in this afternoon, so I took a sip for courage and crunched the numbers.

Sixty-two thousand dollars.

That's what I needed if I wanted to put twenty percent down on the house and get a mortgage payment I had a prayer of making. *Fuck.* I took another sip.

Thirty-one thousand dollars.

That's what I needed if I wanted to put ten percent down and struggle each month. Goodbye lattes, La Mer, and Laphroaig.

Then there were closing costs, bank fees, taxes, and moving expenses. Plus the arm, leg, breast, eyeball, elbow, and ass cheek it was going to cost me to renovate the hundred-year-old place.

I took a third glug of bourbon and propped my forehead in one hand.

Twenty bucks.

That's what I needed to buy a hammer at Sears and pound my head in, which was going to happen if I didn't get out of my parents' house soon. I'd moved back home eight months ago to save some money for a down payment, but living with your parents and Lebanese grandmother at age twenty-eight is a special kind of torture. They were perfectly nice people, but they had an opinion about everything, from my wardrobe to my hair color to my love life, and they weren't shy about sharing it.

That skirt length isn't really right for you, is it?

Why is your hair blue at the bottom? Was there an accident at the salon?

Don't worry, habibi. Plenty of girls don't get married. In my day we call them old maids, but I bet there is nicer name now.

I cracked open the whiskey a little early that day too.

Tucking one side of my bottom lip between my teeth, I checked my savings account balance. The crazy thing was this flutter of hope I had in my belly, as if maybe it had grown overnight on its own, magic beanstalk style.

Nope—less than fifteen grand.

I released the breath I hadn't realized I was holding, my shoulders slumping in defeat. There was no way I could afford this house. And yet there was no way I could let go of the idea of living there, either. It was *my* house, dammit. I knew it the moment I walked in, even if it did smell like cat pee circa the Kennedy administration.

Twisting my brown hair with blue tips (*not* an accident, thank you very much) into a knot at the top of my head, I stuck two pencils through it and looked again at the numbers I'd scribbled on my note pad. My real estate agent had just called to tell me someone else was going to make an offer on the house. If I wanted it, she said I'd have to act fast, as if indecision was my problem. I was totally willing to act fast.

When it came to something I wanted, waiting around was not my style.

But act fast and do what? Get a second job? Rob a bank? Sell my eggs?

Don't think I wasn't considering it.

I took a bigger swallow of booze and contemplated asking my parents for the other seventeen thousand I needed to put ten percent down, which is what my agent thought I should do. They had plenty of money, and they probably wouldn't even make me pay it back, at least not right away. But they'd think offering their financial help meant they got A Say in what I bought, and I could just imagine all the arguments we'd have over my buying a hundred-year old, five thousand square foot fixer-upper by myself.

Redo the kitchen? That's absurd. You've never even picked up a hammer!

A yard? Don't be silly. You don't know how to mow a lawn.

A house like that needs a man.

I slugged the last of my Two James and eyed the bottle, seriously considering pouring another, even though the numbers I'd scribbled were beginning to swim a bit.

"I'm heading home." Mia poked her head into my office and grinned. "Gotta start packing my bags."

Grateful for the distraction, I popped up from my chair and rushed over to embrace her. "Eek! This is so exciting! I wish I were going with you!" Mia was leaving on Tuesday for France, where she would be married two and a half weeks later. Erin and I would fly over six days before the wedding.

Mia let me squeeze her slender frame and laughed when I didn't let her go. "Me too. There's so much to get done before the eighteenth. And I wish I spoke French; it would make things so much easier." She sniffed. "Have you been drinking?"

Releasing her, I put one hand in front of my mouth. "Just a little." But then I couldn't resist taking her by the shoulders, shaking her gently. "God, Mia. I can't believe you're getting married in two weeks—to Lucas! At a villa! In Provence!" Both of us jumped up and down a few times.

"I know!" She bit her lip. "But don't jinx me, Coco. I don't want anything to go wrong this time." Mia had been engaged once before, but her asshole fiancé had called off the wedding a week before it was supposed to happen.

"Stop it." I squeezed her upper arms. "Nothing is going to go wrong this time. This is totally different. You and Lucas are made for each other, the wedding is going to be the most beautiful thing we've ever planned, and every little detail will be perfect."

Mia closed her eyes, as if saying a quick prayer. "I hope you're right."

"I am. Want me to come over and help you pack?"

She shook her head. "It's OK. I've got my lists made already."

"Of course you do."

She pinched my arm. "Don't make fun of me. It's my wedding; I get to make lists. And you're on your own here for the next two weeks. I'm sure you've got things to do."

"Yeah, like obsess over the house I can't afford."

Mia frowned. "Which house?"

"The one in Indian Village. I can't stop thinking about it."

"The old one? Coco, are you drunk? They're asking over three hundred grand for that place! It's huge! And it needs so much work!"

Fidgeting, I admitted, "It would be a project, I know. But I love old houses! And when I walked through it, I got a feeling." I shivered as I recalled moving through rooms with high ceilings, creaky wood floors, lead glass windows. Maybe there were a few cracks in the plaster and some smelly carpet —not to mention a kitchen that hadn't been remodeled since 1975—but there was an old newspaper covering a broken windowpane and it was dated September twenty-sixth, which was my birthday. It was clearly a sign.

"A feeling?" Mia asked dubiously, her upper lip curling.

"Like I was supposed to live there. Like it's been waiting for me. And that newspaper in the kitchen—it was a sign!"

"A sign that that window has been broken since your twenty-first birthday."

I held up my hands. "I know it sounds crazy, but I felt a connection to the place. I can't explain it completely. I mean, we were in that neighborhood looking at another house entirely."

"Yeah, one you could afford."

"I know, but then I saw that one and fell in love. I think it was fate." I clasped my hands over my heart and rose up on tiptoe. "I want it, Mia. And my agent just called and said there's going to be an offer on it. She said I better be prepared to act soon."

"Of course she did. They all say that." She shook her head. "Don't let her push you. Buying a house is a huge investment and you need more time to think it through. You need a plan."

My heels returned to the ground. "I gotta get out of my parents' house, Mia."

"I can understand that." She shrugged. "You could stay with me and Lucas for a while. We have a spare room."

I gaped at her. "What? You'll be newlyweds! No way." Not only would it be a gross intrusion on their privacy, it would serve as a painful reminder that everyone else on the planet was having sex and I wasn't, even if the drought was self-imposed. I wasn't looking to get married, much to my grandmother's chagrin, but it would be nice to meet someone attractive, fun, and fucking stable to hang out with. The last couple guys I'd dated either had prior records, vicious exes, or Mommy Issues. I was done with that.

"Fine, then with Erin."

My chin slid forward and I stubbed the toe of my red wedge sandal into the floor. "I want that house. I need it."

"Coco…" Mia's voice held a warning note.

"What?"

"You can't afford that house. Promise me you're not going to do anything rash while I'm gone."

My eyes shifted to the left. "I'm not, I promise."

"Coco!"

"What?" I leaned down and fussed with the straps of one shoe to avoid meeting her eyes.

"You are the worst liar in the world. Listen to me." She grabbed my arm and brought me up to eye level. "I know how you get when have a *feeling* about something. But you can't buy a house with a feeling."

"I had a feeling about you and Lucas, remember?" I asked brightly. "Look how well that turned out!"

"Coco." Her voice was stern and her grip tight. "Yes. You are a very intuitive person. But you're also very impulsive. We just got your finances in order. Your credit card balance is down and you have a good amount of cash saved up. You just need to stop the crazy spending."

My eyes slid left again. "I don't crazy spend."

She let go of my arm. "Oh no? What about the four-hundred-dollar sets of Le Creuset cookware you bought for all of us last year?"

I twisted my fingers together. "Well, it was Christmas…almost."

"And the two-hundred dollar Beachwaver curling irons?"

I threw up my hands. "That was a limited time offer on QVC! I can't be expected to pass those up."

"Uh huh. And the trapeze lessons?"

I opened my mouth but nothing came out. Yeah, I couldn't really defend that one. Exhaling, I shook my head, my spirits wilting like a week-old wedding bouquet. "But this isn't like that—this feels different!"

Mia spoke in a calmer tone. "Look, after the wedding, I'll sit down with you and we'll make a list of all the other houses we've seen and discuss pros and cons of each of them." Either she didn't see me wrinkle my nose or she ignored it. "And if you still don't feel like one of those is right for you, we'll keep looking, OK?"

Grimacing, I tried to resign myself to the fact that she was right, and I was stuck living with my parents for the time being. Endless nights of cribbage and criticism loomed in front of me. My shoulders slumped. "I think I need another drink."

She patted my head. "What you need is a little boost. Tell you what. Any business that comes in while I'm gone is all yours—the entire twenty percent commission."

I gasped. "Really?"

"Really."

Throwing my arms around her, I squealed. "Thank you! You're the best friend ever!" With any luck, I'd book a wedding or two in the next week. If they were big enough, I could count on earning at least ten grand. Granted, I wouldn't see that money for a while, but with it guaranteed to come in, maybe I'd revisit the idea of borrowing from my parents.

Please God, send me a bride. A sweet, lovely angel bride with exquisite taste and deep pockets.

As if on cue, I heard a voice. "Hello?"

Chapter Two

I let go of Mia and peered around her to see a short young woman in my office doorway. She had long, impossibly platinum blond hair blown perfectly straight, and she wore skinny black jeans, a zebra-print tank top, and a *lot* of eye makeup. A tangle of gold necklaces rested between breasts unnaturally large for someone her size, and a tiny white dog peeked out from a Louis Vuitton bag she carried under one arm.

I smiled at her. "Hello. Can I help you?"

"I don't know. I'm looking for Devine Events." For an angel, she had a very shrill voice. And an amazing tan.

"You found us. Please come in." Mia held out her hand. "I'm Mia Devine, and this is my partner, Coco Thomas. I'm on my way out, but she'll take good care of you."

Instead of shaking Mia's hand, the girl handed her a business card. "Angelina Spackatelli."

My heart raced. Even her first *name* was seraphic! But she placed a little extra emphasis on her last name, and my stomach tightened up when I realized why. She had to be the daughter of Tony Spackatelli, sometimes called Tony Whack. Officially he ran a sanitation company, but unofficially he controlled Detroit's arm of the mafia. Mia must have recognized this too, because she glanced at me behind Angelina's back, eyebrows raised.

Maybe this wasn't my angel.

"Nice to meet you." I took a card as well, gesturing to a chair in front of my desk. "Please have a seat." Her card was hot pink with white print. On one side was a picture of her and her little dog, both wearing tiaras, and the other side listed her name and social media information. The fancy font was hard to read but under her name I thought her title said Italian American Princess.

Interesting. I didn't know we had those.

The bottle of Grass Widow beckoned from its place on my desk next to the empty glass, but I quickly tucked them back into the drawer before sitting down. "What can we do for you, Angelina?"

After lowering herself into the chair, she snapped her gum and set her dog-in-a-purse down by her feet. "Well, first I wanna make sure—are you the ones that did that wedding on TV this year?"

I smiled. "Yes, we are." Earlier this spring Devine Events had been chosen to design Detroit's Wedding of the Year, and it had been a huge success. We'd gotten a lot of great press out of it. "Are you looking for someone to plan your wedding?"

"Not yet. But I want you to plan my engagement party." She flashed her ring at me.

As prompted, I cooed appreciatively at the crab-apple-sized diamond set in gold. "Wow. Congratulations. What kind of party would you like?"

"A blowout." She made a little exploding motion with both hands. "For five hundred people."

Five hundred people for an engagement party? Jesus, how big would her wedding be? And more importantly, if I did a good job planning the party, would she let me do the wedding too? I glanced over at Mia, and she gave me a thumbs-up.

"That sounds like fun." Lifting my eyes to the ceiling, I said a quick thank-you to God for sending me this miracle and pulled up a blank contract on my laptop. "So when were you thinking? Something later this year?"

"That's the thing. It's a little bit short notice."

"Short notice?" Mia, who was still lingering in the doorway, looked a little panicked. *Short notice* was her least favorite expression. "How short?"

Personally, I didn't care how short the notice was—I needed this gig. Flashing Mia my best I Got This grin, I shooed her out of my office. "Go on home, babe. You have lists, remember? I'll talk to you later."

"But—"

"I'll take care of everything here. You be on your way now." I did everything but put my foot on her butt and shove her out the door.

She smiled. "You're right. Sorry." Lifting her hand in farewell, she disappeared into the hallway and might actually have cleared earshot if Angelina spoke at a normal volume.

"It's next Saturday. It has to be then because of the TV people. I'm gonna be on a reality show."

I could practically hear brakes screeching in the hallway. Glancing at the door, I expected to see Mia pop back into the frame and brace herself against it, her eyes wild with panic. I held my breath.

No Mia.

But my phone pinged with a text.

NO NO NO NO NO

"Wow." Swiping my phone off the desk and into my lap so Angelina wouldn't see it, I turned off the sound and cleared my throat. "That *is* short notice. And what's this about TV people? You're on a reality show?"

"I'm not exactly on it yet. But I'm being considered for this show called Italian-American Princesses. They're looking for girls to star in the premiere season, see. So I applied, and they think I might be the perfect fit. Some producers are coming to scout the location and meet me and everything, and I figure what better way to show them my star potential than to throw myself a big party? Right?"

"Right." While she was talking, my phone buzzed in my lap, three times with only a second in between.

TV PEOPLE???
DON'T DO IT!
NOT ENOUGH TIME!

"Look, I can pay extra or whatever," said Angelina. "I already sent the invitations. And I know exactly what I want, so all's you have to do is arrange it." She made it sound like she'd already done all the hard work, and I'd just have to make a couple calls. In reality I'd have to bust my ass to pull off an event that big in such a short time because I was guessing her list of exactly-what-I-want was long, specific, and ridiculous.

Which meant expensive.

Bring it on, princess.

My phone continued to blow up with texts from Mia as I broached the subject of cost. "Angelina, I'd like to help you, but parties this big can get expensive. What's your budget?"

5 REASONS YOU SHOULD NOT TAKE ON THIS PARTY

She pursed her frosty pink lips. "I don't care what it costs. The important thing is to make a good impression. A *big* impression. Unforgettable, you know?"

1. HER TWITTER HANDLE IS @SPOILEDROTTENBITCH

"Unforgettable, yes. OK, well, ballpark it. What are you comfortable spending?"

"I dunno." She shrugged. "Fifty thousand maybe? A

hundred? I got no idea what this shit costs but my dad said he'd pay for whatever I wanted."

2. CREEPY LONG FRENCH MANICURED TOENAILS + FROSTY PINK LIPS WITH DARK LINER = BAD TASTE.

I blinked at her. Twice. Had I heard right? Fifty to a hundred grand? For an *engagement party*? Visions of myself mixing up cocktails in my cat-pee-free dream house danced in my head. "Uh, for that kind of money, you can have more than big."

She smiled and snapped her gum again. "Good because I want ginormous. But it has to be perfect."

3. SHE CARRIES AN ANIMAL IN A PURSE. IT WEARS A CROWN.

"Ginormous it is." As long as she didn't expect me to don a tiara, I didn't give a crap what she put on her dog's head.

"Ginormous *and* perfect." Her voice was slightly sharper. "You'll get all the things I want, right?"

At this point, I experienced a frisson of doubt. I had faith in my ability to design an amazing event, but Angelina might be a difficult-to-please client with over-the-top taste. As if Mia was mind-melding me, which she sometimes did, her next text said,

4. SHE WILL CHANGE HER MIND EVERY FIVE MINUTES AND BLAME YOU FOR NOT KNOWING WHAT SHE WANTS.

My hand shook as I typed in the date on the contract. "Of course I will." *Crap.* Maybe I should have asked what all she wanted before saying I'd do it, but it was too late now. "Shall we talk details?"

"Sure."

"Venue?"

"Easy. My parents' house. Outside on the lawn." She gave me a tony address on Lake Shore Road and I wrote it down. It actually wasn't too far from where my parents lived, which would be helpful. So far so good.

5. HER FATHER'S TRUNK IS PROBABLY FILLED WITH BODY PARTS OF EVENT PLANNERS WHO GOT THE DETAILS WRONG.

At this point, I turned my phone off and dropped it into my purse. "OK. I assume the yard is big enough for a couple tents?"

She stared at me. "Uh, yeah."

Of course it was. At that address, you could probably set up the Ringling Brothers Circus on the front lawn, and I wouldn't be surprised if that was on her list of requests. Grabbing my note pad and pen, I elbowed my laptop aside and glanced at the page with the real estate numbers on it. Suddenly they didn't seem so depressing. Smiling, I flipped to the next blank page and jotted Spackatelli Party at the top. "All right, what else do you have in mind?"

"I want a champagne fountain, a big dance floor lit underneath by sparkly colored lights, a band and a DJ, fireworks, a ice sculpture of me and Lorenzo, and—"

"Wait a minute." I held up one hand and paused my frantic note-taking. "You want an ice sculpture? In August?"

"Yeah. I saw it on Bridezillas once."

God help me. "I'll see what I can do. How about food?"

"Ciao Bella's gonna cater dinner. The owner is a friend of my dad's."

"Great," I said, relieved. "I've worked with them a lot. That makes it easy on me. Are they doing dessert too?"

"Yeah, they're doing a cake and some pastry trays. I love those anus cookies they have there."

My pen froze mid-word, and I looked at her without raising my head. Had she said...anus cookies? I glanced over my shoulder toward the door, half expecting to see a cameraman there, filming us. This had to be a joke. "I'm sorry...what kind of cookies?"

She looked annoyed. "Anus or something? Or maybe it's

Annuss? I don't know how you say it. But they're really good. They taste kinda like licorice."

"Oh, *anise*." Relieved, I sucked my lips between my teeth so I wouldn't laugh and lowered my chin in case my eyes gave me away. Fucking *anus cookies*. I couldn't wait to tell Mia about that one.

We went over more details, including tables and chairs, flowers, bringing in the bar, hiring servers and bartenders, arranging for bathroom trailers, and we discussed a few local bands. To my relief, other than the ice sculpture and maybe the fireworks, nothing Angelina wanted seemed impossible, especially with her huge budget. Outlandish, maybe, but not impossible, especially once I explained to her that the city probably wouldn't let her have caged tigers on the property (apparently her fiancé was a rabid Detroit Tigers fan). I held my breath as she took in the disappointment, but she handled the news OK. While she was there, I made some calls and was able to book vendors I knew and trusted for all rental items, a florist, and a DJ. We put in a call to the talent agent I used for live music, and touched base with the woman in charge of catering for Ciao Bella.

Holy shit, I might actually pull this off. A smile tugged at the corners of my mouth as I noted the vendor names on the contract. No, not might. I would *absolutely* pull this off by myself, and it would be fabulous. Huge without being impersonal. Fun without being tacky. Elegant without being stuffy. Mia would be proud of me, we were bound to get good buzz if this reality show took off, and with the estimated total cost —at which Angelina didn't even bat a fake eyelash—I'd make enough money to put ten percent down on the house. I could make an offer next week, even.

See? Stop worrying. This was all meant to happen. It's fate.

And then.

"Oh! I almost forgot. I want that Italian chef, Nick Lupo, to do burgers at midnight," announced Angelina. "Right after the fireworks."

The floor dropped a few feet, or maybe it was my stomach. I gripped the edge of my desk. "What did you say?"

"I want that Italian guy. You know, the one who won first place on that reality show about hot chefs last year, Lick My Plate? He's from here and he has a restaurant downtown called The Burger Bar. He's there like every night. I saw him in there this week."

"Yes, I know who he is. I just…" *Haven't seen him since he snuck out of our hotel room in Vegas seven years ago.* "…think he might be difficult to get."

Angelina blinked at me. "Why?"

"Well, because he's, um…" *My ex. Famous now. The best sex I ever had and the worst mistake I ever made.* There were any number of ways I could've finished that sentence, but finally I went with "probably not available."

"I want him." Angelina poked an index finger onto my desk. Unlike her pink and white pedicure, her fingernails were painted corpse gray. "Get him."

"Uh, I don't think Nick Lupo does private parties." I hadn't said his name out loud in years, and the sound of it, the feel of it on my lips brought back powerful memories—the taste of whiskey and apple pie. A warm, muscular body moving over mine. The crunch of leaves beneath my back. A wide, lush mouth closing over my breast as he filled the hollow ache inside me—

I crossed my legs and squeezed my thighs together. *Don't.*

"This isn't just any private party. Tell him who it's for," said Angelina, like *duh.* "Tell him who my father is. He'll do it."

My insides churned. "I guess I could try."

"Do it. Or I'll get someone who can." Her loud voice was razor sharp, and I suddenly got the feeling God wasn't the one who'd sent her.

Fuck.

"I'll do it." My throat was bone dry, my words barely audible.

"What?"

"I'll do it," I said more forcefully. "I'll get him."

"You promise?" Angelina sniffed.

"Yes."

Fuck. Fuck. Fuck.

We finished up, and after she left, I dropped my head onto my desk and banged my forehead against the wood until it ached.

Nick Lupo. I had to face Nick Lupo, after all this time.

Even Mia didn't know the complete truth about my most impulsive decision ever. I'd been too ashamed to tell her.

When he'd left me sleeping in that room at the Bellagio seven years ago, I'd been wearing a wedding ring. That he'd put on my finger the night before.

He'd left his ring on the nightstand along with a note.

This was a mistake.

Chapter Three

I needed a plan. Automatically I pulled my phone from my purse with the intention of calling Mia, but as soon as I unlocked my screen I saw one last message from her.

Please tell me you said no to that party.

Crap. I couldn't ask her for help. What's more, I was going to have to lie to her about taking the Spackatelli gig. She had enough to worry about—packing and planning and dealing with multiple families. Both her and Lucas's parents were divorced, and figuring out where to house and seat everyone had given her hives over the last couple weeks. Being less than honest with her about the business we shared made me feel squeamish, but in this case, I felt a little truth-avoidance was the kinder way to go, even if it was a bit self-serving. Thankfully, I wouldn't have to do it in person—Mia wasn't kidding about my being the worst liar in the world. And just in case I was so bad she could hear the falsehood in my voice, I decided on a text.

No worries! She agreed to move the date. Have fun packing!

I pressed send, ignoring the voices in my head screaming,

You just lied to your best friend! You're a terrible person! You deserve to fail!

Dropping my phone back into my bag as if it had bitten me, I squeezed my eyes shut and took several deep, slow breaths. Seven of them, to be exact—one for each year Nick and I had been apart. Years I'd spent grieving him, nursing my broken heart, hating myself for my stupidity and Nick for his callous behavior. Years during which I'd come to terms with the fact that he and I were wrong for each other, that my first love wouldn't be my last, no matter how romantic the notion, and that some betrayals just can't be forgiven. Years I'd *suffered* for him.

But that was the past. Ancient history.

I could let all that go, couldn't I? For the cause? I was older now. Wiser. And I was totally over him.

Wasn't I?

Fuck yes, I'm over him. I'm over him, and I can handle this.

That would be my mantra.

I called Erin and asked her if she'd meet me at The Burger Bar around seven. She was way more level-headed than I was, and I needed someone there who wouldn't let me do anything stupid like throw a plate at his head or grab his ass.

"The Burger Bar? Isn't that the place owned by your college boyfriend, the hot chef?" Erin hadn't gone to MSU with Mia and me, but she'd heard enough about low-down good-for-nothing cheating bastard Nick Lupo to sound shocked at the idea of putting myself in his path.

"Yes," I said through clenched teeth.

"Why would you want to go there?"

I gave her the lowdown, and she gasped. "Are you serious? And you said yes to this without telling Mia? Coco, this sounds like a very bad idea."

"I had to, OK? Mia said I could keep the commission of any event I booked while she's off. And I need money for a down payment so I can get the hell out of my parents' house.

This looked like a golden opportunity! How the hell was I supposed to know she'd want my ex flipping fucking burgers at her party?" I was yelling at her by the time I finished, but I couldn't help it. The thought of seeing Nick again after all this time had my intestines in knots. I'd avoided watching Lick My Plate for fear I'd backslide and get mopey about him again, but I'd seen his photo online enough times in the last year to know that he was still ridiculously attractive. The boils and baldness I'd wished upon him had not materialized.

"OK, OK. I get it. But why not tell Mia the truth?"

"Because she was panicking about the timeline, which isn't that big a deal. It's not the *when* that's the problem here —it's the *who*, Erin. Please tell me you'll come with me tonight to talk to him." Erin could sweet talk anyone into anything. She could probably even make him think it'd been his idea in the first place.

"I'm sorry, I can't. It's my mother's birthday and I promised her I'd have dinner with her. How about tomorrow night?"

"No, I gotta get there tonight. I'm short on time as it is."

"How do you know he'll even be there?"

"I don't, not really. I'm just hoping."

"I could probably meet you later if you need me to, unless she guilts me into a movie. But text me, OK?"

"OK. And please don't tell Mia I lied. I'll come clean with her in France, I promise."

She agreed to keep it between us, although I'm sure she thought that was a Very Bad Idea. But I'd worry about Mia later. It was after six o'clock, which gave me just enough time to brush my teeth in the office bathroom, take my hair down from its messy knot, and assess my appearance in the tiny mirror over the sink. Did I look good enough to face an ex without a wingman? I took a quick inventory.

Hair a bit tousled but otherwise OK. Had I known about

tonight's errand I might have washed it this morning, but too late to worry about that now.

Eye makeup good, lips needed a new coat. I dug my go-to color, MAC's Russian Red, out of my purse and reapplied, then stuck a finger in my mouth and slid it out to avoid getting any color on my teeth.

You shouldn't do that in front of me. You know it turns me on.

Nick's voice slid into my head without warning. In the mirror I imagined seeing him come up behind me, wrap an arm around my waist and bury his face in my hair.

You smell so good.

Stop it, you'll muss me up and we're already late.

I don't care.

It's your own birthday dinner. We're in your parents' house.

I don't care.

I shivered, feeling his breath on my neck, one palm easing down my belly, his eyes on mine in the mirror, his cock stirring against my back.

We were late that night. We were late a lot.

Desire surged through me, and I cleared my throat and my head. *Stop it. None of that.* I eyed my reflection suspiciously. *You want one thing only from him, and it doesn't involve an erection so just keep focused on the task at hand.*

Breath? I exhaled into my hand and sniffed fast, feeling a little like a seventh grader at a dance but satisfied with the outcome.

Now for the outfit review. I was wearing a dress since it was July and I have a strict no-pants policy between the months of June and September. Not only do dresses keep my legs cooler, but I've always felt they're more flattering to my hourglass figure. Today's choice was one of my favorites—a curve-hugger with cap sleeves, a gathered bust, and a slim pencil skirt. The print was tiny red roses on a cream-colored background, and the material was stretchy and starchy at the same time, some miracle of modern engineering. I love vintage looks, but I will be the first to admit that my closet is full of contemporary knockoffs, which are sturdier, easier to clean, and just as pretty.

I locked my office door and took the wide central staircase down to the foyer of the renovated Victorian mansion in Brush Park that housed the Devine Events offices. Mia and I each had offices on the second floor that used to be bedrooms, and we shared a room between them which might have been a dressing room at one time but now served a dual purpose as a small conference room and lobby. There was a powder room and bathroom at the end of the hall, which we shared with the interior designers who rented the rooms on the other side of the stairs, but at this hour on a Friday, the entire house was empty.

The dark, shiny wood of the banister and beautifully refinished plasterwork on the ceiling reminded me of my dream house in Indian Village. I ran my hand along its satiny finish and refocused my attention on what mattered—getting the house. If all went well in the next few days, it could be mine within in the next few months. My insides danced with excitement. All I had to do was get Nick to do me this one favor. And he owed me, didn't he? He *so* owed me.

So what if I'd ignored all his attempts at apologizing after the fact? So what if I'd divorced him without speaking to him? So what if I'd refused to acknowledge his existence on the planet for seven years? After what he did, that was my right.

But I still had no idea how to approach him. Should I be friendly? A how-are-you-old-buddy-old-pal kind of thing? After all, we'd had some good times together. Some very good times. Times that involved midnight drives and blankets under the moon and pants around knees and a skirt around my waist and the stars falling from the sky beyond his head like sugar into my mouth while he whispered in my ear,

You know how I love you...don't ever leave me... and his body rocked into mine with deep, steady strokes.

When I came to, I was standing with my feet on two different stairs, my fingers clenching the banister, my toes curling in my shoes.

Nick, you bastard. You did love me. I know you did. And I loved you. But it wasn't enough. Why wasn't it enough?

Swallowing against the lump in my throat—which surprised me, I hadn't cried over Nick in years, nor any man since—I exited the building, locking the front door behind me. On shaky legs I walked to my car, a red Volkswagon Beetle, and slid carefully into the driver's seat. Pretty much everything had to be done carefully in this dress. *Careful, that's a good word for tonight too.* I'd be careful not to rip my dress, careful not to let my emotions get the best of me, and careful not to let the past impose itself on the present.

Or his hand impose itself on my ass.

The thought popped into my head before I could help it, the kind of dirty little joke Nick would have made himself if he could read my mind, which I often thought he could. He got my mostly-classy-yet-secretly filthy sense of humor perfectly, and I'd missed the way he could make me laugh.

What? No. N-O. I'm over him, and I can handle this.

But the danger in approaching Nick Lupo without a game plan was apparent, and I could see myself falling back under his spell if I wasn't prepared.

A script, I thought as I made my way to Corktown, where The Burger Bar was located. That's what I needed, a script. Nothing left to chance, no awkward silence upon meeting again into which one of us might be tempted to insert an inside joke, a remember-when, a penis.

Oh my God. Stop. It.

After some hard thought, I came up with five different opening approaches.

First, there was Coy, which would be delivered with

fingers steepled over the heart: *Oh, is this your place? I didn't realize!*

Then there was Chummy, served best with an elbow to the gut: *Hey, you! Congrats on all your success! I've been wanting to come in here, but I've been so busy!*

Perhaps Nostalgic would work, accompanied by a little eyelash batting: *Gee, remember that night I gave you my virginity out in your family's orchard? Yeah, that was sweet. Is it too late to ask you for something in return?*

Then there was Honesty, which would come with foot shuffling and a wry smile on top: *Look, I know we fucked things up really badly between us but Tony Whack's daughter wants you to cater midnight snacks at her engagement party and if you say no I'm dead.*

Finally, I had Desperate: *I need you. I'll do anything you want if you'll do this for me.* This would most likely be accompanied by a panty-drop and a side of 69.

God help me.

Despite the heat of the night, and the fact that my windows were down—I'm not a big fan of AC—I shivered. In all honesty, I wasn't even sure what Nick's reply would be to something like that. Did he still think about me that way? Once upon a time, he couldn't keep his hands off me, but that was B.V. Before Vegas. I couldn't even guess what he'd been thinking that weekend, let alone how he'd feel now.

I locked the car and dropped my keys into my purse, my shoulders stiff with tension. Thinking about the past had me all worked up—I'm the kind of person who remembers things vividly, with every sense. For me, memories are visceral, evocative things, full of tastes and smells and sounds, and for years I'd been careful to keep certain ones sewn up inside me. But today I felt my memories of Nick Lupo pushing at the seams, their contents threatening to burst—the sound of his voice, the smell of his skin, the taste of his kiss, the feeling of him inside me.

My stomach went momentarily weightless, and for the millionth time I wondered if Nick really had been *that* good at sex or if I only thought so because he was my first and I had no one to compare him to at the time. I mean, how good could a twenty-one-year-old guy actually be? Probably my memory was just doing that thing where the farther back in time something is, the rosier it seems in your mind. I bet there were plenty of times where he put his own pleasure first and ignored my needs.

I just couldn't think of any.

Looking both ways, I crossed Michigan Avenue, stepped up onto the curb and put a hand over my chest, a vain attempt to calm my fluttering heart. I had to stop thinking about sex with Nick; it wasn't helping. I needed to focus on the present. Stick to my goal. Remain calm. Cool. Unemotional.

The Burger Bar's vertical neon sign hung to my right, and I forced myself to put one foot in front of the other and move in its direction. As I got closer, I heard the music being played inside and smelled grilling meat and frying potatoes.

Five more steps and I'd be at the entrance.

Four.

Three.

Two.

One.

Taking a deep breath, I pulled the glass door open and stepped inside.

Chapter Four

The cool rush of air conditioning hit me as I removed my sunglasses and looked around, taking in the details as my eyes adjusted. It was smaller than I'd expected. White honeycomb tiles on the floor, a bar to my left and small booths lining the wall on my right. Dark wood. Chrome. Chalkboards on the walls. "Folsom Prison Blues" playing on the jukebox in the corner. I almost smiled.

He still likes Johnny Cash.

The place was crowded, every booth full and every seat at the bar taken. The vibe was young and fun, unfussy but authentic. Somehow it felt both urban and country—the kind of place where you knew you'd get real food and have a good time, see and be seen, feel both hip and virtuous since the chalkboard nearest the door boasted about Nick's farm-to-table philosophy. The one right next to it said *If you are racist, sexist, homophobic, or an asshole, don't come in. Otherwise, welcome.*

At least it didn't say "or my ex-wife."

Servers moved quickly, carrying trays laden with baskets lined with blue and white striped tissue paper, on which rested thick, delectable hamburgers and piles of thick, seasoned fries, making my mouth water. Despite everything, pride bloomed in my chest. Lick My Plate was a ridiculous show—who really cares if chefs are hot as long as they know what they're doing?—but it had given Nick a huge boost. He'd always wanted this, his own place, things done his way. Looking around, I could see that he'd put himself into every detail here, from the design to the menu to the music. When I heard the door open behind me, I took a few tentative steps forward so I wouldn't be in the way of entering customers.

"Coco Thomas."

I spun around to find Nick Lupo just inches from me, so close I could see the tiny crescent moon scar above his left eyebrow, a remnant of his scrappy childhood. He looked the same—thick dark hair, although threaded with a few surprising strands of gray at the temples, light brown eyes framed by ungodly long lashes, that wide mouth hooking into a grin at my expense.

I wanted to say something, but at the sight of him my lungs had ceased functioning, holding on to the breath trapped inside them as if it were the last one they'd ever get.

Damn. Why'd he have to look so good?

Nick was dimple-cute when he smiled and sexy-as-sin when he pinned you with that stare, the one that said Fuck Dinner, The Only Thing I Want To Eat Is You And I'm Starving. He could go from boyishly charming to hot and demanding in a heartbeat, and right then I wanted that heartbeat to be mine.

His dark, expressive brows rose. "Speechless, cupcake? That's a first. Or have you run out of names to call me?"

"Hi," I managed. One word, but it felt like a huge victory.

"Hi."

When I couldn't get another word out, he laughed. "OK, come on." Taking my arm, he steered me over to the bar, every eyeball in the place trained on us. "It's about time you came in here. Let's find you a seat."

He's touching me. He's touching me. He's touching me. Inside my head, a voice repeated the phrase over and over again. I'd seriously underestimated the impact his physical presence would have on me after all this time. My skin prickled with awareness of him, as if my body remembered the insane chemistry we had and it was just waking up from a seven-year sleep.

Nick led me around the far end of the bar, where there was an empty stool I hadn't been able to see from the door. "Sit down right there and let me look at you."

I slid onto the seat and crossed my legs, placing my purse on the bar. I kept my movements slow and deliberate, so as not to betray how flustered I felt. "Thank you." There, two more words. Hallelujah.

Planting his feet wide, Nick crossed his muscular, tattooed arms and shook his head. "Damn if I don't have the hottest ex-wife on the planet." He spoke loud enough to attract the attention of other patrons, on purpose, of course. Nick loved a good show. Immediately I noticed more heads turning in my direction. Cell phone cameras aimed. Whispers and stares. I imagined the headlines on TMZ: **Hot Chef's Secret Past Revealed, Ex-Wife Disappointing.** I patted my hair self-consciously.

"Ex wife?" said the guy on the stool next to me, a hipster type with a receding ginger hairline and huge, bushy Abe Lincoln sideburns. He swiveled his stool to face us and lifted his thick glass beer mug toward Nick. "I didn't know you were married."

"I was, Lou. I was. To this vision right here." Nick gestured to my face. "Tell me, do I not have the most beautiful ex-wife in existence? I mean, how many guys can say that? Wait." He put a hand on my shoulder. "Wait. Are there more of us? How many husbands have you collected so far?"

I smiled with tight lips. I would not let him provoke me. "Just one."

He touched his chest, which was hugged by a tight black Burger Bar t-shirt, sleeves tight around his biceps. I noticed he wore a silver Shinola watch, which momentarily distracted me because I'd always been really turned on by Nick's thick strong wrists and forearms. "Whew. For a moment there, I didn't feel special. I mean, since you left me, you've had time for…" He checked the watch. "At *least* thirty more marriages as long as ours."

Fuck it, I was provoked. "Left *you*! You left me, remember? In a hotel room in Vegas? On our wedding night?"

Lou's eyebrows rose above the rim of his mug, and he looked at Nick as if waiting for an explanation. But I wasn't about to give him a chance to defend himself. Fuck calm, cool, and unemotional—he wasn't pinning this on me. "Or have you forgotten the note you left me on the nightstand, right next to your ring? 'This was a mistake.' That ring a bell?"

"I apologized, didn't I? You're the one who filed for divorce and left for Europe without talking to me, like a stubborn teenager."

"Stubborn teenager! You apologized in a text message, Nick. Two words—*I'm sorry*." Briefly I put my hands over my ears and took a deep breath. It was seven years too late for this, and I hadn't come here to fight. "Look, it doesn't matter anymore. Yes, I filed for divorce and left for Europe without talking to you. Because you were right—the marriage was a mistake."

Nick shrugged. "For what it's worth, I disagree. And I tried to tell you that but you divorced me too fast."

I fisted my hands in my lap so tight it felt like my fingernails might slice my palms. "We would have divorced anyway, Nick. We were young and stupid."

"*I* was stupid. *You* were just mad. And I don't blame you for that."

I cocked my head. "But you blame me for other things?"

The air between us grew charged. Nick leveled me with his eyes. "In the end, it was you that decided we were done."

"You cheated on me."

"You lied to me."

"You lied to me first."

"That wasn't the same."

"Wait, you guys lost me." Lou picked up his beer again and turned to Nick. "Let's start with you. What did you lie about?"

"He lied about sex, for one thing." I crossed my arms, grumpy at the memory. "When we were freshmen in college, he told me he was a virgin like I was."

"I had to, or she wasn't going to sleep with me." Nick threw his hands up. "I had to have her, Lou. I'm sorry I lied, but I was in love with her and I had to have her. At least I came clean when it was over."

Lou nodded, as if he was the arbiter of what was fair in this fight. "OK. Sort of a douchey move, but possibly understandable, given the…circumstances." He gestured vaguely toward my chest. "And what did you lie about?"

"Wait a minute, what circumstances?" I sat up taller, narrowing my eyes at him.

"I think he means the circumstances protruding from your ribcage." Nick's grin lit up his face.

"The legs too," added Lou. "And the face. Did anyone ever tell you you look like young Lauren Bacall?"

"Exactly." Nick shook his head. "I was nineteen and in love with the most beautiful girl I'd ever seen. I could not be expected to behave."

I blushed, but anger won out a moment later. It was just like Nick to make me mad and then flatter me right into forgiving him. "Oh, for fuck's sake. That does not excuse you."

"Well, you lied about Paris." He turned to Lou. "Her

junior year she told me she hadn't been accepted to this exchange program she'd always planned on doing. But she's such a bad liar, I figured out the truth."

"I didn't want to go that year. You didn't have a problem with me staying behind at the time." *Probably because you spent a good part of that year screwing me from behind.*

"Then the following year she told me she hadn't even applied, another obvious lie. But she stuck to it, and I had to hear the truth from her friend Mia."

"Because I didn't want to leave you, asshole." I'd been angry at Mia for weeks about that, but she said she'd only caved and confirmed what Nick suspected when he promised her he'd encourage me to go. Mia thought I was crazy to forego the opportunity to study in Paris for a guy.

"Leaving me wouldn't have necessarily meant breaking up. We could have stayed together."

"Ha!" I poked him in the chest. "You cheated on me every summer we were apart. You think you'd have been faithful with an ocean between us?"

Nick's chin jutted. "I didn't cheat every summer."

I rolled my eyes. "Two out of three. And I bet there was a spring break I don't know about, and maybe a Christmas vacation, and probably even a Martin Luther King Day too." I turned to Lou and sniffed, feeling superior. "He can't keep his hands to himself, he never could."

As if to prove my point, Nick's hand clutched my thigh. "Coco, come on. Two times I kissed other girls, that was all. And you broke up with me so often, I never even knew when we were together and when we weren't."

I removed his hand. "That's because you were such a flirt."

"That last year, I was totally faithful to you. I swear it."

"Uh huh, right up until Mia told you about Paris. Then you ran out and screwed someone else."

Nick looked away without denying anything or defending

himself, and the night of his confession came back to me like a knife to the gut. I'd screamed myself hoarse, slapped his face, and shoved him out of my apartment. Then I threw every gift he'd ever given me out the window into the parking lot. I remembered how he'd watched, silently huddled on the hood of his truck in the dark.

Lou drained his beer. "Wow, this is really sad, you guys. So then what happened?"

"We broke up," I said, teeth gritted. "But the next night he showed up at my apartment with a bottle of whiskey." *And I didn't say no, like I should have. Like I never could where he was concerned.*

Nick's eyes met mine. "We got back together."

I lifted my chin. "We got drunk is what we got."

"We caught the red-eye to Vegas."

"We got tattooed, and we got married. Two idiot decisions."

Lou watched us, his head moving from side to side like a spectator's at the French Open. "And then?"

We stared at each other a moment longer, each of us reliving the pain and pleasure of that insane weekend. What could we say? No matter what, Nick couldn't deny that he was the one who'd been unfaithful that spring—the act of betrayal that started the whole chain of crazy events. And in a whiskey-tears-and-sex-filled craze, I'd forgiven him, even married him—but then he'd abandoned me in that hotel room. No apology could make up for the hurt, and I sure as hell hadn't wanted to listen to any explanation.

For God's sake, why should I listen to him say that he didn't love me enough to stay?

With my parents' help, I'd quietly taken the necessary steps to divorce him quickly and left for Paris. The three of us agreed to keep it quiet; I wasn't even sure my grandmother knew.

Later that year I'd had the small tattoo of his name and

our wedding date on my left shoulder blade made into a swallow taking flight. Briefly I wondered what he'd done with the large tattoo of my name he'd had inked on his chest.

It doesn't matter now.

"And then he left," I said. Deep breath. "But I forgive him now." The lie rolled off my tongue with surprising ease, especially for me. I'd never forgive him, of course. Did it show on my face?

Nick cocked his head, and I could tell he didn't believe me. "Why?"

"Wh-what do you mean, why?" I blustered. "You asked my forgiveness and I'm giving it."

"I asked for it then. You didn't want to give it, and now you do. There must be a reason you're here after all this time." The mischief was back in his cocky Elvis half-grin, and I felt like punching him. But instead I saw the opening and took it.

"If you must know, there is."

"I must know."

"Me too," said Lou, raising his hand for the bartender to bring him another beer.

"Fine." I glared at both of them before focusing my full attention on Nick. "I need a favor."

His grin widened. "Sexual, I hope."

"No." I sat taller, ignoring the wickedly pleasant sensation between my legs at the thought of a sexual favor from Nick. "A cooking favor, actually."

"A cooking favor? Hmm. Decidedly less exciting, but I'm intrigued nonetheless. Tell you what, cupcake." He glanced at his watch. "Let's go down the street for a drink at Two James. You can ask for your favor, I can stare at your face—and maybe your other circumstances—we can have some whiskey for old times' sake, and maybe we can work something out."

Oh fuck. I knew what I'd feel like working out after "whiskey for old times' sake" with Nick Lupo, and it had nothing to do with cooking. Could I be trusted to stick to the plan? I looked at his mouth, the first mouth I'd let anywhere near the parts of my body that were warming and tightening up right now. How many nights had I dreamed of those firm, full lips on my skin, just one more time? How many fantasies started and ended with that mouth on mine? How many orgasms had I given myself with his body, his voice, his name in my head? Too many to count, and I'd probably do it again tonight.

Goddammit, he still *got* to me.

My mouth opened, and my mantra escaped. "I'm over you. And I can handle this."

Nick burst out laughing, his mouth wide, head thrown back, and my entire body warmed. I'd forgotten how much I loved making him laugh. "Ah, God. I've missed you," he said, tapping my leg. "Come on, let's go."

I can handle this, I repeated, grabbing my purse and scooting quickly toward the door so he wouldn't be tempted to guide me with a hand on my back. The first part of my mantra was becoming fainter in my brain.

Channeling my inner Mia, praying she existed somewhere in there, I made some rules for myself. *No sitting too close, no touching, and no overdoing it on the memories or the whiskey.*

When we reached the door, Nick moved ahead of me to open it, and I glided by him, catching his scent on the warm air that greeted me. It was so familiar—musky and masculine but summery, like fresh-cut grass, with a hint of something savory too, like maybe he'd been chopping herbs in the kitchen earlier. Pretty soon I'd add whiskey to the mix, and the combination might be lethal.

I glanced at him over my shoulder. "Thanks."

"My pleasure." His lips curved into a slow, sexy smile and I added a few more rules to the list.

No smelling him, no looking at his mouth, and absolutely no kissing.

Great. At this point I was going to have to ask the bartender at Two James for a blindfold, a nose plug, and a muzzle along with my whiskey. And I'd have to sit on my hands until my senses were dulled.

Guess I'd make that first shot a double.

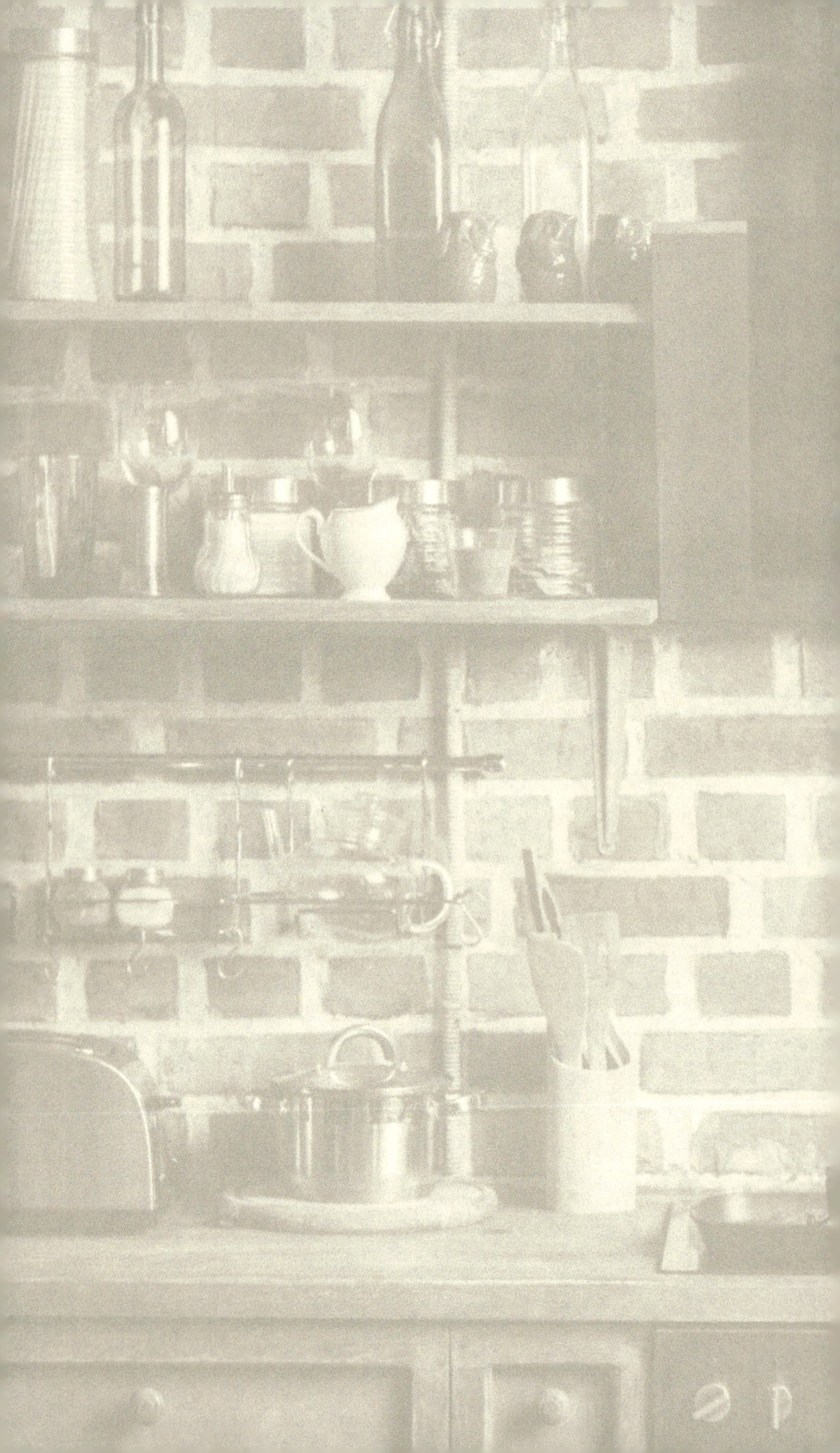

Chapter Five

To distract myself from the fact that Nick Lupo was walking beside me, that we were actually *walking somewhere together* after all these years, I began counting the steps it took to get to Two James. This is something Mia taught me to do when I really, really want to buy something but I know I don't have the money. I count the steps it takes me to leave the store, turn a corner, put it out of my sight. Usually it works, but today the strategy was doomed to fail since the object of my desire was following me. Handbags, hot tubs, and high heels just don't do that.

But I tried. That counts, right?

Twenty-nine, thirty, thirty-one. Keeping my eyes down, I watched our shoes hit the cement. Nick's black suede oxfords with bright blue laces seemed to move in slow motion compared to my hurried, anxious steps, and I remembered how he was never the sort of person to rush. It used to drive me crazy, especially when we were running late. We would bicker about it, and one time we got into this insane philosophical discussion about time, and he accused me of always looking at it as running down, like sand in an hourglass. Finite, and slipping away from me.

But time *is* finite, I'd argued. And it *does* slip away, if you're not careful. You only get so much of it and you have to make choices about how you want to spend it. I don't believe in putting things off until the next day, waiting for things to go on sale, or driving around looking for a better parking spot just to get ten feet closer. I don't sit around hoping something will go my way when I can be doing something to *make* it go my way or get where I want to go, faster.

I'd accused him of looking at time like an ocean—it seems infinite, like it stretches out in front of you forever, but it doesn't. Somewhere on the other side is the other shore, and furthermore, the water level is probably shrinking.

He'd laughed and tackled me, sending me over backward onto the blanket we used to drag outside to drink whiskey and look at stars whenever we were visiting his grandmother's farm. I hadn't thought about that argument in years, but his next words came back to me clear as the sky had been that night. "Listen," he'd said, stretching his long, lean body over mine. "When we're out here in the country, and I'm looking up at that sky full of stars, somehow I just know that you and me and time and everything in the universe goes on forever. So don't try to tell me different because I won't listen."

Every cell in my body had vibrated with life and feeling as I looked up at him. *He said forever. He said forever.* "Forever, huh?"

He rubbed his whiskey-flavored lips on mine. "Forever."

And then for some reason I got scared that he would die young, because he was an idiot and could be reckless and foolish like only a twenty-one year old guy could, and I clutched him to me, opening my mouth and my legs and my heart as wide as possible, like taking him inside me would protect him.

I should have been worried about protecting myself.

My heart ached for a moment, remembering how much

I'd loved him that night, how much we'd loved each other. I'd wanted so badly to believe he could be right.

I'd wanted forever.

"Here we are." Nick pulled open the door to the distillery, which was housed in an old garage on Michigan Avenue. The circular bar in the center of the tasting room was busy, but one of the bartenders waved hello to Nick and gestured to some empty space in front of him. As he cleared the glasses and wiped the counter, I walked over and took a seat, dropping my purse by my feet. Nick slid onto the chair next to me.

"Nick." The bartender, a heavily bearded guy in a blue button-down, reached across the bar and shook Nick's hand. "Good to see you."

"You too, Sebastian. This is my friend Coco."

"Nice to meet you, Coco." Sebastian reached for my hand, and I took it.

"My pleasure," I said. "I'm a huge fan of Two James."

He smiled. "What can I get for you?"

"How about the five-spirit tasting flight?" Nick looked at me. "You up for sharing that?"

"Sure."

Sebastian left us, and Nick swiveled his seat to face me, dropping his folded hands between his thighs. "So."

I glanced briefly at his wrists, which happened to be resting near his crotch, causing another unwelcome yet pleasant tickle between my legs. I pressed my knees together and forced myself to meet his eyes. "So."

He said nothing, just continued looking at me for a moment, and then he tucked his full bottom lip between his teeth, like he wanted to say something but wasn't sure if he should. *Very* unlike him.

"What?" I squirmed in my seat.

"What, what?"

"You're staring at me."

He shrugged. "Can't help it. You're beautiful. Even more

beautiful than you've been in my thoughts, which shouldn't be possible."

Feeling heat in my cheeks, I looked down at the bar and busied myself folding the napkin Sebastian had set there into ever smaller squares. "Don't."

"Come on, you have to let me look at you a little. It's been so long."

I nodded, refusing to meet his eyes, scared that if I did, somehow time would begin rolling backward. "It has been."

"Seven years."

"Seven years," I echoed.

"Seven years, two months, five days, fourteen hours..." He looked at his watch. "And six minutes."

My mouth fell open, my heart thudding in my chest. Had he really been keeping track of exactly how long it had been since he'd seen me? "Wait a minute. You seriously know that?"

He grinned. "Nah, I'm just teasing. But it's probably close, right?"

I slapped his leg. "Ugh, I believed you for a second, you asshole. God." Rolling my eyes, I turned back to the napkin, unfolding it and starting over.

Nick laughed gently. "Sorry, couldn't resist." He paused, shifting in his seat. "You know, I can't decide if it feels like it's been seven years or seven hours since I last saw you. In a way, it's like no time has gone by at all."

I wondered if he meant that it seemed like I hadn't changed *physically* or if he meant that his *feelings* for me hadn't changed, that they were rushing to the surface in the uninvited and uncontrollable way mine were. "I know what you mean," I said, trying to keep my voice neutral. "And then in other ways, it's clear how much time has passed." Unable to resist teasing him, I reached over and flicked a finger through the few gray hairs above his ear. "Old man."

"Very funny." He grabbed my wrist and we grappled for a

moment, his eyes lighting up as I struggled and failed to get my arm back. My heart started to race as I realized the last time he had my wrist circled like this he was probably fucking me. I froze. Glancing at my arm, he noticed the tattoo I had running from my inner wrist toward my elbow, a quote from a book I'd loved as a child. "Nice. Is it new?"

"No, not really. I got that one in Paris." Our eyes met as unspoken history flowed between us.

"What does it say?" He studied the French script.

"It says, 'Here is my secret. It is very simple: one only sees clearly with the heart. What is essential is invisible to the eye.' It's from The Little Prince."

Nick looked at the tattoo again, so tenderly that for a second I was terrified he would kiss it and I'd be lost. But he didn't.

"I'm sorry," he said.

"For what?"

"For everything."

Slowly he brushed his thumb over those words, and the entire room seemed to go still, the air compressing all around me. It was the barest of caresses, but it sent a powerful wave of longing through my body, and called up other memories of his hands running over sensitive skin. *He's got to stop touching me. I can't take it.*

I sat back in my chair, grateful he allowed me to reclaim my arm. When I spoke, my voice was strained. "No problem. Like I said, I forgive you."

A pause, and then he sat back as well. "Aren't you going to apologize too?"

I shrank from him. "Am *I* going to apologize? For what?"

"For divorcing me so fast. You didn't even let me explain my decision to leave that night."

"Why should I? It was obvious—you didn't love me enough to stay." Saying it out loud before he did was important.

He shook his head. "That wasn't it at all, Coco. I was crazy about you. Believe it or not, I had what I thought at the time was a pretty good reason."

I continued to gape at him. "Nick, you can't be serious. That decision defied explanation. No reason was good enough to leave me there like that, especially if you loved me."

"You're not even going to let me tell you what it was *now*? After all this time?"

I hesitated, wondering at both his reason for wanting to offer an explanation at this point and at my reluctance to hear it. "What's the point?"

He shrugged. "It will make me feel better. Wouldn't it make you feel better?"

That was actually a good question. *Would* it make me feel better to hear his "pretty good reason" for leaving me that way? What if it was a lame excuse and I just ended up hating him again? Or—and this could be worse—what if I found his reason decent enough to understand? What if I could be persuaded to see things from his point of view? What if I fell for him all over again?

No. Just... No. It was bad enough that I was still so attracted to him. I didn't want to revisit the past, reconsider our actions. No matter what our reasons were for any of the decisions we'd made back then, we'd moved on. *I'd* moved on. We could be friends going forward, perhaps, but no good would come of going back. Too much damage had been done, too much time had passed, and too much effort had been put into forgetting him. Forgetting the forever he'd promised me. I couldn't live through it again.

"I don't think so," I said slowly. "If it's OK with you, I'd like to leave the past where it belongs, let bygones be bygones and all that. Start over as friends."

"Friends, huh?" His mouth hooked up. "You think we can be friends?"

"I think we can certainly try." A note of false hope crept into my voice. "You know, we've never really been friends. We jumped right into a relationship practically the day we met."

"True. We did." He grinned, looking sheepish and charming, just the way he had the day he'd followed me into History 140. It was the second week of classes, and he'd caught my eye as we entered the lecture hall together, my pulse racing when he slid into the row in front of me. How had I not noticed him before? He'd brought nothing to class with him—not a backpack, not a laptop, not even a pencil. But he was so adorable with those big brown eyes and long, thick lashes and that beautiful mouth, I didn't mind when he kept turning around.

Hey. I'm Nick.

Can I borrow a piece of paper?

Do you have an extra pen?

Somehow I managed to focus and get through the lecture, but I spent a good amount of time staring at the back of his head and texting Mia that the hottest guy I'd ever seen in my life was sitting right in front of me in Western Civ, and I really, really, really wanted to lick his neck.

When class was over, he stood up and handed me back the pen and piece of paper. "Here you go. Thanks."

Confused, I stared at the paper, which was folded in half.

"Don't you need this? I mean, doesn't it have your notes on it?"

He shook his head. "Nah, I didn't take any notes."

"You didn't?"

"No. I'm not even in this class."

"Then what are you—"

"I saw you walking across campus and followed you in here. I wrote my number down on that piece of paper."

My mouth falling open in disbelief, I unfolded the paper and read the phone number written there before looking at him again. Students streamed by us, but everything beyond his face was a blur. "You sat through a two-hour lecture on the Reformation just to give me your number?"

He smiled. "If you call me, it was worth it."

I couldn't take my eyes off him.

We went for coffee that afternoon, and I found out he worked in one of the dining halls. That night I dragged Mia across campus to it for dinner, and even though it had only been a couple hours since I'd seen him, I practically ran the entire way there. When we caught sight of each other over plates heaped with colorless chicken divan, our matching grins could have lit up Spartan Stadium at midnight. Mia said she'd never seen anything like it.

Later that evening, we went for a drive in his truck and parked out on some country road. I didn't lose my virginity that night—I held out another six weeks on that—but I did have my first non-self-induced orgasm, thanks to Nick's patience, skill, and amazingly supple tongue.

My core muscles clenched at the memory, and I was glad when Sebastian arrived with our tasting flight, five shot glasses filled with about an ounce each resting on a wooden tray. I half-listened as he gave a spiel about the five different spirits, resisting the urge to grab the nearest one and shoot it straight down my throat, hoping it would numb the desire for Nick that was reawakening in me.

It's not desire. It's just nostalgia.

"Which would you like first?" Nick asked.

"Hmm, the gin maybe?" I accepted the glass of clear liquid he handed me and watched him choose the rye.

He held it up and smiled. "To friendship."

"To friendship."

We clinked glasses and took a sip, leaving enough so both of us would have a chance to taste them all, and for the next half hour, we chatted about safe topics and sampled the whiskey, rye, gin, and bourbon. We inquired after immediate family, laughed about Lick My Plate, and discussed the rebirth of Corktown with businesses like Two James and The Burger Bar. With each passing minute, I felt more at ease, more like I really was hanging out with an old friend and not a former lover. Part of that was likely due to the alcohol, but I thought as long as we kept the chatter casual and focused on the present, I could remain in possession of my wits, at least outwardly. I picked up the absinthe, which reminded me of Mia.

"Oh! Remember Mia?"

"Of course I do."

"She's getting married in two weeks. To this French guy who—"

"Lucas, I know. He owns The Green Hour."

I pouted, feeling both robbed of the opportunity to deliver big news and somehow offended that he knew about something big happening in my life. I didn't know anything about his life anymore, although it struck me right then that I wanted to. *It's a shame we went so long without speaking. We should have done this sooner. I was too stubborn.* "You know Lucas?"

Nick shrugged. "Sure. He's been in The Burger Bar a few times, and I've gone in The Green Hour too. Someone introduced us at some point. I saw Mia in there once."

I froze. "You've seen Mia? She didn't tell me." *And I might have to kill her.*

"Well, when I came in, she ducked out the back door so fast, she probably hoped I didn't notice her. We didn't talk, in other words."

"Oh." *I love you, Mia. Best friend ever.*

"Lucas is a great guy. And The Green Hour is doing really well, I hear."

I sipped the absinthe and handed it to Nick. "He is a great guy. And he's crazy about Mia. They're great for each other."

"Nothing like us." Nick's eyes twinkled over the rim of the absinthe glass.

I smiled ruefully. "Nothing like us."

Nick took a small sip. "This is nice, being friends."

"It is, actually."

"So, *friend*." Nick set the glass down in the tray and propped his head in his hand. "Ask me a favor."

My heartbeat got loud and clunky for a few seconds, so I silenced it with one more shot of rye. "All right." Turning in my chair to face him, I braced my hands on my knees, took a deep breath, and gave him a brief rundown of the scene in my office today, complete with a description of Angelina, her reality show dreams, and her family connections.

Nick's chin came off his hand, and he pretended to be shocked. "Wait a minute. You want me to cater a party at *Tony Whack's* house?"

"Yes."

"I don't know, Coco. Hoffa's probably buried beneath that guy's pool. This could be dangerous."

"Don't tease me, Nick. I really need you."

"Hmmm. Sounds like it." He leaned on the bar again. "So when is this party?"

"Next Saturday night. August fourteenth."

Nick's eyebrows shot up. "Next Saturday night! Give a guy a little notice, why don't you? I might have big plans next Saturday night. A date with a hot blonde. Maybe several of them."

"Blondes aren't your type," I said without thinking.

"How do you know what my type is? Maybe I've changed."

He was joking with me, but I wasn't interested in playing around, not until he agreed to do the damn party. "Look, I know it's short notice, and I'm sorry about that. She just came in today, and with Mia gone it's only me to run things, and I told her I'd get her what she wanted without knowing she wanted you."

He grinned. "Bet that was a real pisser, huh? When you heard my name? God, I'd have loved to have seen your face."

"It was a bit of a shock," I admitted.

"What happens if I say no?"

I shrugged. "Best case scenario, I lose a lot of money and Devine Events suffers shit publicity. Worst case, I end up next to Hoffa."

"Do you need money, Coco?" The smile was gone, and his voice had lost its playful tone.

For a moment, I hesitated, wondering if I should let him in on my plans to buy a house. It was kind of personal, but then again, if we were going to be friends and I was asking for this big favor, I supposed I could be up front about why I needed the money so badly. "Yes, but it's not what you think. I'm saving for a house, and there's one that I want in particular. There's going to be another offer on it, so my agent thinks I need to make an offer myself. I need the money for a down payment."

"A house, huh?" He looked interested. "Where? In Grosse Pointe, near your folks? I'm surprised they don't just buy one for you."

"No, in Indian Village, actually. And I don't want them to buy it for me, thank you very much." I sighed and squeezed my eyes shut for a second, telling myself not to acknowledge his dig at my privileged upbringing. No need to scrape away the dirt over that old argument. "The house is a big old thing that needs lots of work and costs way more than I can afford, but for whatever reason…" I looked at him and lifted my shoulders. "I have to have it. I know it's not practical. But I have to have it. And I want to do it myself."

Nick eyed me, toying with the small glass of bourbon in his hand. After a moment, he tipped it back and set down the glass. "I think I can help you."

My heart raced. "You'll do it?"

He nodded. "Yes. But—"

Without thinking, I jumped off my chair and threw my arms around his neck. "Thank you, thank you, thank you!" I was completely breathless, either from excitement or the way our bodies were suddenly pressed together. He might have been a little stunned too because it took him a second to return the hug, but eventually his arms wrapped around my lower back and his knees widened so he could pull me in closer, my hips now cradled between his legs.

Erin's voice rang in my ears, telling me this hug was a Very Bad Idea, and yet I couldn't peel myself off him. Not when his hands began sliding up and down my sides. Not when he turned his face into my hair and inhaled. Not even when I felt his chest pushing against my aching breasts and realized it was because he was breathing heavy. *God, he feels good. And smells good. And I bet if I turned my head just so, put my mouth to his neck, and then licked that spot below his ear that used to make him crazy, he'd taste good too.*

What? No. No licking.

Friends do not lick one another.

Somewhere inside my head, common sense spoke up—the voice I depend on to tell me I don't need a second piece of tiramisu or a fourth pair of red heels. I released my hold on Nick. "Sorry," I said bashfully, backing up to my chair again. "I'm a little carried away. You have no idea what this means to me." My heart was still beating overtime, and I couldn't keep a smile off my face.

"No complaints here." Nick fidgeted in his seat, adjusting his jeans, and I laughed silently, thinking that I'd probably just made the fit a little more snug in the crotch. "But don't get too carried away yet," he went on. "You don't know what I'm asking in return. Maybe you'll think the price is too high."

"What do you mean? Angelina won't care what your price is—she said she'd pay whatever."

"Not my price for her. My price for you." On the word *you*, he poked me in the sternum.

I crossed my arms. This was *just* like him, or at least the old him. Clearly he hadn't changed much in seven years, gray hairs or not. "OK, Nick. I'll play along. What's the price?"

He leaned forward so that we were nearly nose to nose, his expression that of a child who just got away with stealing another cookie from the jar. "You have to spend the weekend with me."

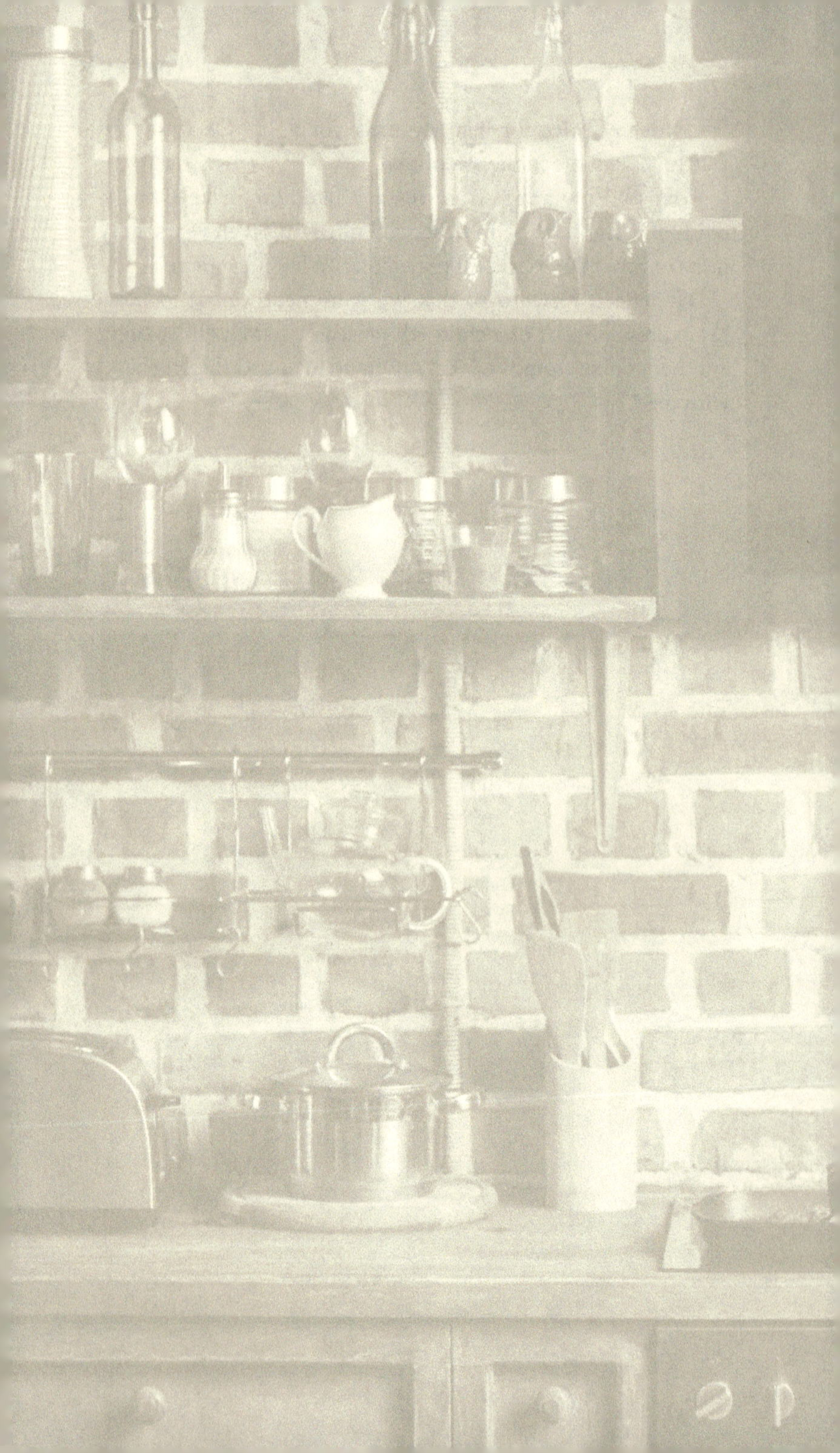

Chapter Six

I was so distracted by the nearness of his mouth, I didn't fully comprehend what he'd said. My voice came out in a whisper. "What?"

"Spend the weekend with me."

I shrank back. "Spend the weekend with you! Are you crazy? No!"

"Why not?" he asked, like it would be perfectly normal to spend a weekend with someone you hadn't seen since he ditched you in the Bellagio bridal suite seven years ago.

"Because it's ridiculous! I can't even believe you're asking me to…do that." I gestured wildly between us, totally hot and bothered.

"Do what?"

"*That.*"

"I just want to spend time with you," he said, his face the picture of innocence. "You're the one who's reading into it."

I dropped my hands in my lap and cocked my head. "Really. You ask me to spend the weekend with you and you're telling me you're not thinking about sex?"

"Well, now that you mention it—"

"I'm not mentioning it. I'm vetoing it. Unequivocally." I

looked at the glasses on our wooden tray, desperate to find some drop of alcohol we'd overlooked. The absinthe was the only thing left, and even though it wasn't my favorite, I took a less-than-advisable sized swallow. And then another, grimacing as the alcohol burned its way down my esophagus.

"What's the problem?" he asked.

"You. Trying to get me in bed after all these years."

"I'm not trying to get you in bed, Coco. I mean, I wouldn't kick you out of it, but I was serious about wanting to spend time with you. Look." He put his hands on the tops of my legs and leaned into me, the bastard. "I know you don't really forgive me for leaving you in Vegas. And maybe you're right —maybe getting married so young was a dumb idea, maybe it would have failed anyway, but leaving the way I did was wrong, and I've spent the last seven years feeling horrible about it. We spent all that time together, and I don't even know you anymore. I'd like to know you again. As a human being. As a friend. That's all."

It was exactly what I'd been thinking earlier, but somehow it didn't sound plausible coming from him. "This would be a little more convincing if your hands weren't on my thighs."

"But I like your thighs."

My brain struggled to move beyond the feeling of his palms through the fabric of my dress. I had the crazy feeling that if I lifted my skirt I'd see his handprints burned into my skin. "Is this how you get to know all your female friends? Invite them to move in for a weekend?"

"Not all of them. Just the hot ones."

"Funny." *He still thinks I'm hot.* Warmth flooded my veins. I was starting to get that dangerous feeling, the one I get when I really, really want something, and no matter how impractical the shoe or fattening the cheesecake or expensive the scotch, I just can't bring myself to walk away. How easy, *how delightful* it would be to jump back into his bed. But then what? Could I trust myself not to fall for him again?

No way.

"The answer is no, Nick. We can have a drink, go for coffee, watch a movie or something. *That* is what friends do."

He shrugged. "But that's boring. And I really don't have that much free time. In fact, I have to be in L.A. on Monday, then New York for a while, and after that, Chicago."

"Wow. That's a lot of traveling." My chest caved a little. For some reason, the thought that he wouldn't be around much made my heart ache—what the hell was that? And why was he still touching me? Did he know how it clouded my senses?

"Yeah, I'm looking for space to open another restaurant. And I still have to do events for Lick My Plate. I'm under contract for another year."

"Oh." My eyes dropped to his chest and arms, admiring the way he filled out his t-shirt, the way tattoos sleeved one arm to the wrist, the other to the elbow. Immediately I wondered about the rest of his body, how much ink he had, and what and where. If I spent the weekend with him, I could find out.

Common sense made a last-ditch effort.

You barely survived the first time he left you. What will you do the next time? Because that's what he does—fights with merciless charm for what he wants from you until he gets it, and then does something to fuck it all up. He hasn't changed.

But as my gaze wandered to his hands on my thighs, I thought about the ring I'd placed on his finger. About the one he'd placed on mine. And about our sad, silent ending, which stood in such ugly contrast to our relationship, which had been volatile, yes, but also vibrant and passionate and fun. We hadn't even had a goodbye fight.

Sighing, I covered his hands with mine, feeling like this moment had been inevitable, no matter how hard I'd tried to forget him. Maybe we needed this. Maybe this weekend would be our chance for closure, a way to put the past behind us and start over as friends.

"Nick."

"What? Say yes." Those huge dark eyes willed me to give in. That voice, low and sweet.

"I want to," I hedged. "But—"

"I'll cook for you."

I groaned. Nick's cooking made my clothes fall off. "You bastard. You know how I feel about your cooking. This is so unfair."

He sat back in his chair, finally taking his hands off me. "It will be fun, I promise. And I have to go see Noni tomorrow. You can come with me."

The name brought a smile. "Really? How is she?" Nick's grandmother was an adorable spitfire of a woman who baked the best pies in the world, never let five minutes go by without asking, "Are you hungry, honey?" and always referred to me as Nicky's *lesbian* friend when she meant *Lebanese*. If Noni was involved, I could definitely say yes.

"She's great. It's her ninetieth birthday tomorrow, and my family is having a party for her."

"At the farm?"

"At the farm."

"The farm where you plucked my virginity from me as easily as a ripe apple from a tree?"

His jaw dropped in mock outrage. "Easy! I had to work hard for that apple! For months I had to pet the tree, kiss the tree, sweet talk the tree—"

"You *lied* to the tree."

"I did. I did lie to the tree." He looked not at all contrite. "But I'm not sorry, because it was the most delicious apple I've ever had in my entire life. I've never had one better."

I narrowed my eyes. "Never had one better? Not ever, not even with all the... fruit you've eaten with fancy reality TV people?"

He shook his head. "Not ever."

I pursed my lips, not really sure whether I believed him, but not really sure I cared if he was lying, either. And bantering with him like this felt so natural, so good. I'd missed the playful way we used to tease each other when things were good between us. "OK, Nick. If I say yes, there are some rules for the weekend."

He grinned. "So you'll do it?"

"I'll do it." I held up three fingers. "On three conditions."

"Which are?"

"Number one. No talking about the past. I don't want to spend two days arguing with you over who was right and who was wrong and who cheated and who lied and what we could-have should-have done differently. Let's leave the past alone."

"Next?"

"Nick!" I slapped his shoulder. "Do you agree to no talking about the past?"

"Jeez, you're always hitting me. I forgot about that. Fine, no talking about the past. Although there were plenty of good times too."

"Yes, there were, but we're going to leave the memories alone. Now, number two. This weekend is not to be seen as an opportunity for a second chance. We are friends hanging out and going to see Noni."

His full lower lip protruded a little, but he shrugged. "I can handle it."

"And number three." I pinned him with a cold, hard stare. "No. Sex."

He laughed. "OK, if you think you can stick to that."

I slapped his shoulder again. "God, you're so arrogant. Of course I can stick to that. It's *my* rule." *Please, please, Lord, help me stick to that.*

"Relax, Coco. I'm kidding. God, next you'll say No Scrabble and the whole weekend is shot."

I lifted my chin. "Scrabble is permissible. In fact, I'd enjoy the chance to obliterate your ass at Scrabble again."

"When did you ever obliterate my ass at Scrabble?"

"All the time! Is that gray hair affecting your memory or what?" I went to ruffle his hair but he ducked, grabbing my wrist again.

"Look at you, you can't keep your hands off me," he said, laughing as I tousled his hair with my other hand. He *hated* when anyone messed with his hair.

"Ha! Can too." But I knew I'd be battling the urge to touch him all weekend long.

"Then it's a deal." He offered his hand, and I took it, giving it one solid pump before letting it go. The less physical contact between us, the better. "But from here on out," he went on, "*I* get to make the rules. After all, you're the one who needs me to do the favor."

"Fine," I said. "But no tricks."

"I'm offended you'd even suspect it."

I rolled my eyes. "This from the guy who tried to claim zyzzyv was a word."

"Excuse me, it was zyzzyva, and it was totally a word. We looked it up, remember?"

I held up a hand. "Please. Before we looked it up, you did not know it was a tropical snouted weevil or whatever, and you snuck the 'a' on the end when I wasn't looking."

Nick looked smug. "Doesn't matter. It was a word. I won."

"You cheated. Once a cheater, always—"

He held up a finger and clucked his tongue. "Ah, ah, ah. You just broke rule number one. No talking about the past. Two and three can't be far behind." He winked at me. "Come on, let's go back to my apartment and bake a cake for Noni. I'll let you lick the beaters while I watch."

"Nick." A warning. "You promised."

"I know." His eyes glittered with mischief. "That's why

there will be no frosting put on your body and licked off. Absolutely none."

"Nick!"

Ignoring me, he signaled Sebastian and pulled his wallet from his back pocket. "I should check in at the restaurant before we go. Are you hungry?"

I was turned on, that's what I was, and if he was going to keep flirting with me like this, I was in so, so much trouble. In fact, I actually felt light-headed. Was it him or was it the booze without dinner?

"Yes, I am hungry. Can I grab a quick bite there?"

"Absolutely. I've got a burger on the menu I bet you'll love. You inspired it, in fact."

"Oh yeah? What's it called, the Bitch Burger?"

He smiled as he pulled a few bills from his wallet and laid them on the bar. "No, it's called a Beirut Burger. It's got ingredients in it found in Lebanese cooking."

My heart fluttered. "Really? Sitty would be so pleased."

"How is she?" Nick took my arm to help me off the chair. He also reached down and picked up my purse, handing it to me as we walked toward the door.

"Thanks." I slung it over my shoulder, remembering how I'd always liked Nick's manners. He might have been a flirt, but he was always quick to open a door, pull out my chair, give me his jacket when I was cold. "She's the same as ever. Quiet and observant but always ready to cut you to pieces with a remark carefully crafted to make it seem like she's just confused about something when really she's being critical." I affected my grandmother's accent and tone as I rubbed at the words tattooed on my wrist. "Oh, sorry, habibi. I thought it was dirt."

Nick laughed. "My mother feels the same way about mine, but never says anything. Just sort of stares at them, like they might disappear if she concentrates hard enough."

I rolled my eyes. "Don't even get me started on my

mother. Hey, thank you for the drinks, by the way. I'll get the next round."

"You're welcome." He pushed open the door for me, and we walked back down to The Burger Bar. The sun had set, and more people were lingering out in front of popular places like Slows and The Sugar House. The Burger Bar had a line too.

"There might not be a seat for me," I said as we entered. The music seemed louder, the crowd noisier. "This is a popular place."

"Oh, I think I can squeeze you in somewhere. Give me a minute." He patted my shoulder before disappearing into the kitchen, and I stared at his ass as he walked away, thinking that I'd like to squeeze *him* in somewhere. A couple places, actually.

I chewed on one side of my lower lip. Had I really made a no-sex rule? Perhaps I'd been too hasty. Perhaps there was some...*wiggle* room allowed when good friends spent the weekend together. A moment later Nick re-appeared with an extra bar stool, which he fit in at the end of the bar, flirting shamelessly with the woman whose chair he had to move in order to make a spot for me. Years ago I'd have been furious at the way he made another woman blush and giggle, but now I sort of liked the way she eyed me with jealous appreciation after seeing how solicitous Nick was of me, how eager to please.

While I waited for my food, I watched him move through the restaurant, greeting customers, taking pictures with fawning women, and stopping to chat with tables here and there. I had no doubt his down-to-earth nature and friendly accessibility was part of what made his place so popular. As cocky as he was, it didn't seem like he'd let his success go to his head. He worked as hard as the servers, no task beneath him—he delivered meals, poured beers, mopped up spills, replaced napkins, checked the restrooms. I smiled at his disheveled hair when he brought me my burger and fries. After setting it in front of me, he stole a fry from my plate.

"You could ask first." I laid my napkin on my lap.

"Just testing the doneness. I want it all perfect for you, cupcake."

"Right." I picked up the burger, trying to look pretty since he was still standing there behind the bar, watching me take the first bite. But it's hard to look feminine and eat a big thick burger dripping with fixings—kind of like trying to look graceful while giving a really good blow job—so I gave up on grace and went for gusto. I was rewarded with a huge bite bursting with flavors—I tasted the cinnamon and pine nuts and parsley my grandmother cooked with, and the minty cucumber yogurt sauce was the perfect match for whatever was giving it a kick.

"And?" Nick looked eager to hear my opinion. "What do you think?"

"Delicious," I said, setting the burger down to wipe my mouth. "Sitty would be proud. What's giving it the heat?"

"Harissa. You like it?"

"I love it."

Nick grinned, pleased with himself. "I'll let you eat. Sure you just want water to drink? We have some really good local beers."

I nodded. "I'm sure." I had to drive home eventually, and I wasn't much of a beer drinker anyway. But maybe I'd pack a bottle of something good in my suitcase for the weekend. I couldn't believe Nick and I were going to the farm—I had thought I'd never see that place again.

Immediately I imagined that old blanket under the stars.

God, I missed that kind of romance. I mean, certainly I hadn't been celibate the past seven years. There had been a fair amount of sex, some of it good, some of it bad, none of it amazing. And I'd dated one guy for a decent amount of time two years ago, but I couldn't recall doing anything like Nick and I used to do—midnight skinny dipping, sex in the orchard, naked Scrabble. At the time, I'd told myself that we'd been crazy romantic because we were just kids—not even out of our teens when we met.

But what if it went deeper than that?

What if we were supposed to be together?

What if all this party nonsense with Angelina was just a great big ruse the universe had arranged to put us back in each other's orbits?

What if I'd never gotten over Nick because no matter what I did or who I dated or where I went in the world, every possible avenue just led me right back here to him?

A chill rattled my bones, and I wanted to believe it was the air conditioning, but part of me knew better. I believed in fate, believed in it absolutely. I believed in *feelings* and *signs*. But I had a much easier time dealing with them when they weren't indicating I should let a wolf play with a lamb.

All right, maybe not a lamb. I wasn't totally innocent here, not with the way I kept looking at his butt. But who could blame me?

I sucked up the last of my ice water through a straw and watched Nick pose for a picture with a young woman who then asked for a hug. A familiar jealousy gnawed at me when I saw her arm wrap around his waist and his arm circle her shoulders.

Get over it. You're only friends now, remember?

Right. Friends.

But damn, his ass looked mighty fine in those jeans. And I knew—*I knew*—what it looked like naked. That's what made this even harder. It wasn't as if Nick was some unknown quantity, some guy I met who was attractive but off limits for whatever reason. I'd known every inch of his body intimately, and he'd known mine. I knew the exquisite pleasure of being ravaged by that mouth, those hands, that cock. *Fuck yes, that cock.* My panties grew damp as I remembered what it felt like between my breasts, between my lips, between my legs. I knew the sound of his voice telling me he wanted me, loved me, needed me. I knew his gasps and moans and silences. I knew the throb of his heart against mine, the whisper of his breath against my forehead, the pulse of his orgasm deep inside me.

I knew his taste.

Setting the empty glass down, I admitted the truth.

I'd never forgotten him. I wasn't over him. And I wanted to taste him again.

Tonight.

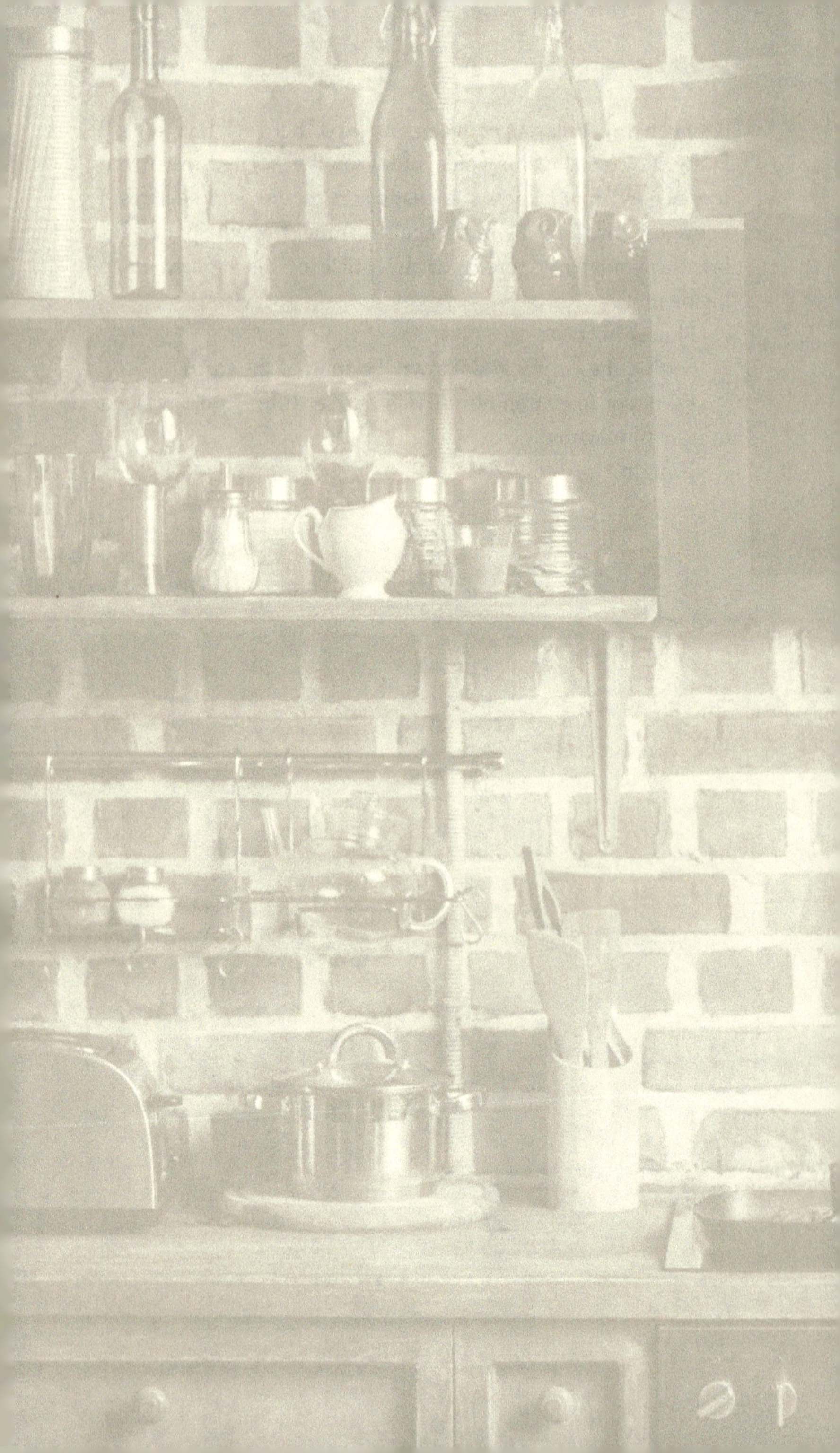

Chapter Seven

The trouble was, I knew that one taste would never be enough.

One taste of Nick would be like my trying to eat just one Kettle brand Country Style Barbeque potato chip. No way in hell. I eat one of those things and I need that whole damn bag of chips so just GIVE IT TO ME NOW BEFORE SOMEONE GETS HURT.

Sighing, I tore my eyes off his body and took a few slow breaths, trying to calm down.

Damn, I wanted him again. Badly.

But he didn't need to know that.

If we broke a rule, we broke a rule, but I wanted it to be Nick that initiated it. I wanted it clear that it was Nick who couldn't resist me; it was Nick who wanted it more. Since he was the one who'd left, my pride demanded it.

And just to be clear, the only rule I was willing to break was the last one. I still didn't want to hear his reasons for leaving me, and I definitely wasn't viewing this as a second chance. Just a good time with a hot guy who made me laugh and happened to give me the best orgasms of my entire life. Plus he said he'd cook for me.

I nearly came just thinking about it.

I had to go home and pack a bag, so we agreed to meet at Nick's apartment downtown. When I pulled out my phone to put his address into Google Maps, I noticed I had missed a call from Erin. She'd texted me too.

I don't think I can meet you tonight, I'm dirty.

Smiling, I texted her back. **Really? You bad girl. Go get some.**

"Get a text from your boyfriend?" Nick asked. He'd walked me to my car and stood leaning against it, arms folded.

"No. Just my friend Erin. She was going to meet me tonight but couldn't and Auto Correct turned her 'I'm sorry' into 'I'm dirty.'"

Nick smiled. "Have I met her?"

"No. She and Mia grew up together, but she's a year younger than we are and didn't go to State, so even I didn't meet her until after college. But the three of us are really close. She's smart and sweet and kind of proper, but Auto Correct is always turning her texts into smutty thoughts."

"Nothing wrong with smutty thoughts."

I looked at him, eyebrows raised. "Ahem. Address please."

He gave it to me and I typed it in before unlocking the car door. When he pulled it open, I hesitated a moment before getting into the car, half hoping he'd hug me, or even just peck me on the cheek. When he didn't, I tried not to let my disappointment show. "Well, thanks for dinner," I said brightly, sliding into the driver's seat. "And for walking me out."

"You're welcome. Sure you're OK to drive?"

"Yes." My earlier buzz had gone away completely, which made the urge to kiss him a bit more unnerving. I pulled the door shut, started the car, and lowered the window. "I'll be there in an hour or so. Just have to pack a bag and tell my parents what I'm doing." Embarrassed, I explained, "I've been staying with them to save money."

He grinned. "Ooooh. Are they going to let you sleep over at a boy's house? Better not tell them it's me."

"Very funny." I started to put the window up.

"Hey," he said, knocking on the glass.

"Yeah?"

"*Do* you have a boyfriend?"

I peered up at him. "If I did, I wouldn't be spending the weekend with you. I'm faithful like that."

His face contorted. "Ouch. You said no talking about the past."

"OK, fine. What about you? Girlfriend?"

"Several. Did I forget to mention they'd be joining us?"

Scowling, I put the car in reverse and pulled out, but I could still see him laughing at me in the rearview mirror as I drove away.

Nick actually had a point about my parents. They weren't huge fans of his, and it wasn't because he didn't have money, like he'd always thought. They liked him fine back then; they just weren't overly excitable or affectionate people. But that was B.V. Since they knew about the whole marriage and morning-after episode, I was glad when I got home that they appeared to have gone out for the evening. I didn't really want to explain what I was doing spending the weekend with the guy who broke my heart—not that I really knew what I was doing—so I figured I'd just leave a note, make something up. That was much better for me than having to lie to their faces about it.

Upstairs, my grandmother's bedroom door was closed,

and I tiptoed past it down the hall to my bedroom over the garage. From beneath my bed, I pulled a small vintage suitcase that Mia had found at a flea market for me. It was yellow with three brown stripes, rectangular and hard shelled, the kind people used to cover with travel stickers. This one had only two—one for the Cunard line, and one that said Hotel Pierre, Paris.

Into the case I put two sundresses, a romper, my bathing suit, pajamas that were comfortable and pretty but not too sexy, and a pair of flats. I packed running shorts, a sports bra, and a tank top as well as my running shoes, remembering how nice it was to run on the dirt roads around the farm. Last, I packed some undergarments, carefully choosing pretty, feminine things that were girlish and even a little modest. No thong underwear or crotchless panties or anything that said Obvious. And anyway, I preferred retro-inspired boy shorts and matching bras, which provided good coverage and support where I needed it and complemented my curvy shape. If there was satin and lace and a sheer panel here and there, well, so be it. I wanted to be *prepared* to break the no-sex rule without looking like I'd *planned* on it.

I threw in my toiletries and hair dryer, and was tucking my birth control pills into a side pouch when my grandmother spoke from the doorway.

"You going somewhere?" She wore a robe and slippers, her shrewd black eyes drifting over the contents of my suitcase.

Frantically, I slammed the top and snapped the latches. Had she seen the pills? My heart jack-hammered as I tried to make my voice sound normal. I was twenty-eight and shouldn't have cared if my grandmother knew I was on birth control, but I did. "You startled me, Sitty. Yes. Um, I'm going somewhere with Erin for the weekend." Sitty had actually been fond of Nick, and hadn't really said much when I'd told her we'd broken up—a heavy sigh followed by "Well, you're still young. You could find someone else" (which she *never* said to me anymore, by the way). But if I told her I would be with Nick this weekend, she'd tell my parents, and that was not a situation I wanted to deal with. Not that they could tell me what to do, of course. Despite their tendency to treat me like a child, I was an adult that made my own decisions, but I *was* living under their roof at the moment, which gave them the *opportunity* to make my life unbearable, if not the *right*.

"Where are you going with Erin?" Sitty asked.

"Where? Uh, her cottage. I mean, her parents' cottage. On Lake Michigan. They invited us. For the weekend." My choppy sentences were awkward, obvious lies, but I was careful to keep my head down so she wouldn't see my face.

"I thought her parents got divorce."

"They did. Yes. Um, they're not going to be there. Just Erin and I will be. They invited us to use it. I mean, her mom did. She owns it now." Rising to my feet, I knew I should get out before I made it worse. "Well, I better go."

Sitty stepped aside and let me pass. "OK, habibi. You go for your weekend. With Erin. With fancy underwear. I think it's nice."

I stopped moving halfway out the door and looked back over my shoulder. Her eyes told me she was no fool, even if she pretended to be one. "Thanks. Can you tell my Mom and Dad?"

"I will tell them. You have fun. But don't get another one of those scars."

I rolled my eyes. "They're tattoos, Sitty. Not scars."

She sniffed. "What's the difference?"

I almost answered the question but realized she could keep me there arguing with her twisted old lady logic forever. There was no way to win an argument with her. "OK, no new scars this weekend."

I rushed down the stairs and out the door, hoping I was right.

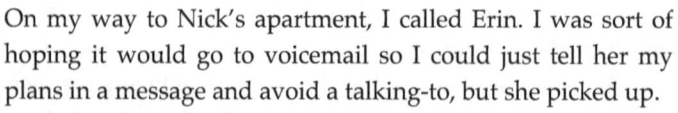

On my way to Nick's apartment, I called Erin. I was sort of hoping it would go to voicemail so I could just tell her my plans in a message and avoid a talking-to, but she picked up.

"Hello?"

"Hey. Are you at the movies?"

"Yes, waiting in line for snacks. Where are you? Did you see him?"

"Yeah."

"And?"

I filled her in on my evening so far, leaving out the wet panties, urges to lick him, and various other sordid details that would make what I was doing a Very Bad Idea. But Erin wasn't stupid, and sure enough, when I got to the part about spending the weekend with him, she gasped.

"You didn't say yes, did you?"

"I had to! He wasn't going to do Angelina's party otherwise."

Silence. "I don't think you need me to tell you what this sounds like."

"I *know* it's a very bad idea, Erin. I'm just choosing to ignore that."

"Oh for God's sake. So you're doing it?"

"I'm doing it. But my parents think I'm away with you this weekend. And if Mia asks, tell her I went to Cleveland to see my brother." Jesus, this was a mess. It made my stomach hurt, it was such a mess. Somehow I just had to put the lies from my head for now—I had more immediate problems to deal with, like how to keep myself from tearing Nick's pants off for two days.

She laughed. "You really are a teenager again. Telling lies. Sneaking out with your boyfriend."

Frowning, I exited the freeway at Mack Avenue and headed toward Grand Circus Park. "He is *not* my boyfriend."

"Any chance you guys would get back together?"

"No," I said emphatically. "This is strictly a business arrangement." With possible meetings conducted in the buff.

"OK. Keep in touch—I'll worry if I don't hear from you."

"I'll text you, I promise. But right now I gotta figure out where to park down here, so I'll let you go. Tell your mom I said happy birthday."

"I will. Bye."

I tossed my phone into my purse just as I reached the entrance to the parking structure adjacent to Nick's apartment building. Formerly offices and retail space, it had been built in the 1920s and renovated in recent years, transformed into luxury residences.

As I searched for a parking spot, I wondered what Nick drove these days. In college he'd driven a rickety old pickup truck that always had a taillight out or squeaky brakes or a window that wouldn't go down. It was rusty and dented and not terribly reliable, but Nick had loved it to death because it was the first big purchase he'd made with the money he'd earned busing tables in high school. Given that his income had increased substantially, he probably drove something much nicer now, although he'd never been the kind of guy who craved luxury brands or designer labels.

In fact, he used to make fun of me for driving the BMW my parents had bought for me when I turned sixteen. It wasn't new or anything, by far not the nicest car owned by my group of high school friends, so I never understood why he gave me such a hard time about it. Or why he refused to drive it. We went everywhere in his stupid old truck, and actually I wouldn't have been that surprised to see the old monstrosity parked in here somewhere. I pulled into the first empty spot I found and grabbed my suitcase from the back, thinking that if whatever he drove now wasn't as nice as my little Volkswagon, I'd convince him I should drive to the farm. It would be fun in a convertible.

Nick lived on the twenty-third floor, and I found his apartment without any trouble. His door was slightly ajar when I arrived, but I knocked self-consciously without entering. "Hello?"

I heard footsteps, and a moment later, the door swung open all the way. Nick stood there in his jeans and a white tank undershirt, a blue plaid button-down in his hands. "Hey," he said softly. "You came."

Not yet, but the sight of your arms and chest might do it for me in the next minute or so. I forced myself not to stare through the thin cotton to see if my name was still inked there. "Did you think I'd ditch you?"

"It crossed my mind. But I'm glad you're here."

Stop being sweet, I felt like telling him. *You're too shirtless to be sweet right now.* Nick wasn't bulging with muscles like a bodybuilder, but he was toned and tight and solid through the core, a boxer's physique. He'd trained a little in high school, and he'd done some recreational boxing just for the hell of it during college, but his time for sports was limited because he'd always had to work. We'd sometimes run together, although he was faster than I was and had much better endurance. After three miles, I'm ready for a frozen margarita and a plate of nachos, not another lap around the track. Nick actually enjoyed running, but honestly, if I didn't love food and drinks so much, I'd happily toss my Nikes out the window.

"Come on in." Nick stepped aside so I could enter, and closed the door behind me. "I wanted to change out of my work shirt, so I left the door open in case I was upstairs when you got here." He slipped his arms into the sleeves of the plaid shirt but didn't button it.

Setting my purse and little suitcase down, I took in the huge airy space, marveling at its two-story ceilings, gleaming wood floors, red brick walls, and massive floor-to-ceiling windows arched at the top. It was beautiful—and almost completely empty.

No couch, no chairs, no tables. Just a huge flat screen TV mounted on a brick wall, and an enormous white fluffy thing in the middle of the floor. "You're a Minimalist, I see. Is that... a bean bag?" Curious, I moved closer to it. "It's huge!"

"It's amazing."

I glanced sideways at him. "Couldn't you afford a couch?"

"This is *way* better than a couch," he scoffed, rolling up his sleeves. "Go ahead, try it."

I was tempted—it actually did look plush and comfortable, and it had to be six feet across—but for the life of me, I could not think of a graceful way to sit on it. My dress was so fitted, I'd have to sort of just fall backward and plop into it. "Maybe later," I said, strolling toward the windows to admire the twinkling lights of nighttime Detroit. "Wow, your view is incredible. This whole place is incredible, actually. It just needs some furniture."

"Thanks. I like this apartment too; I'm just not here very often, which is why I haven't bought much." Nick came to the windows and stood next to me. My body responded to his nearness involuntarily—a tightness in my chest, a shortness of breath. "And I'm not really sure how long I'll be here."

I turned to him. "You're thinking of moving?"

He looked at me, his hands in his pockets, and something about his body language suggested he was keeping them there for a reason. "I'm thinking of doing a lot of things."

Me. Too.

What would happen if I took a step closer? Would his hands come out of his pockets? Would they pull me in or hold me at length? Suddenly I had to know.

Before I could think it through—and this is the problem with me—I swayed toward him, lips parted.

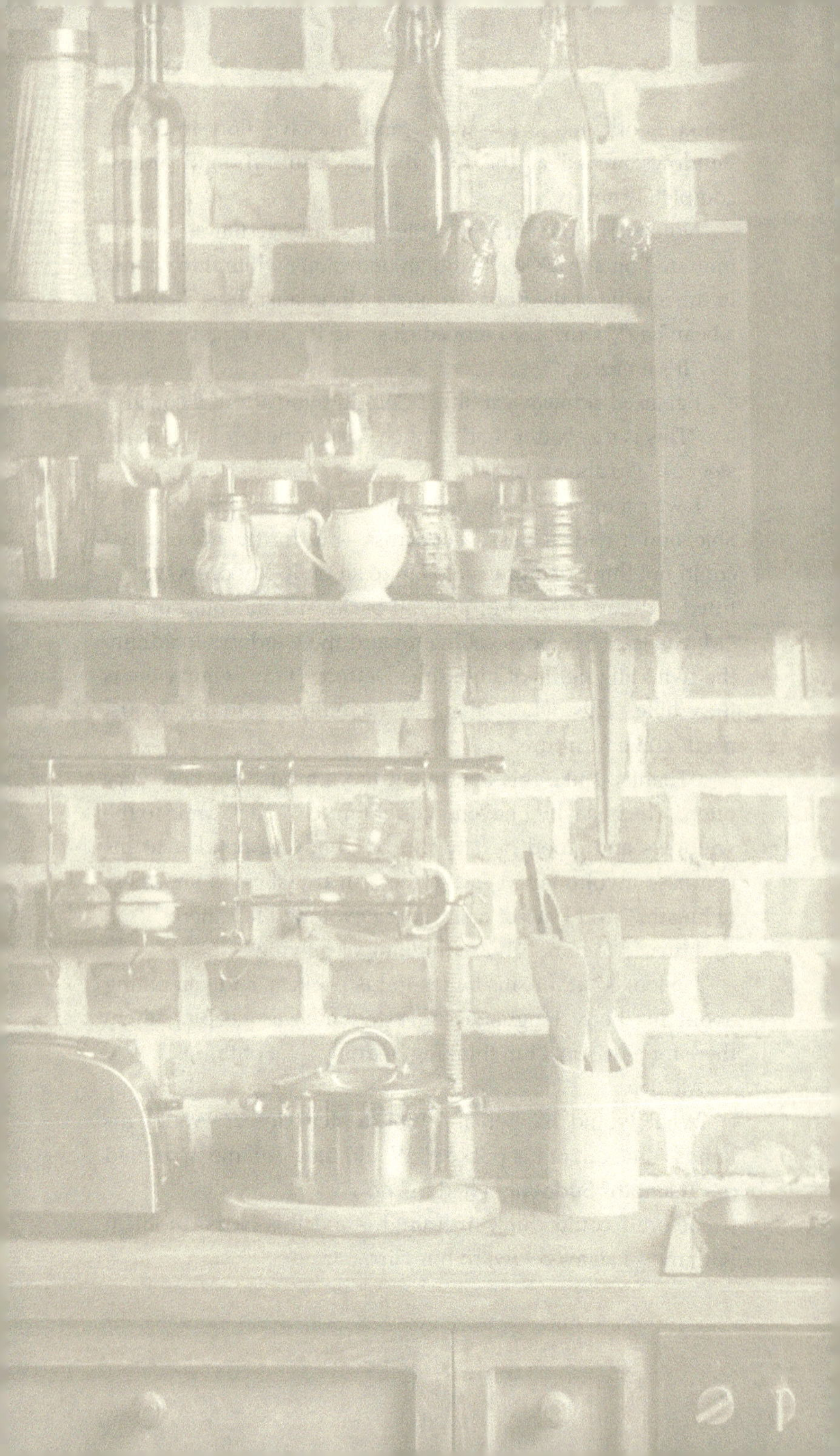

Chapter Eight

Nick cleared his throat and took a step back. "Want something to drink?"

Disappointed and trying not to show it, I rocked back on my heels and smiled too brightly. "Sure." *What the hell are you doing? You made the rule—you have to stick to it!*

While he went over to the kitchen, which took up one entire side of the apartment, I peered up at the open loft above it, which was accessed by a wooden staircase with no back slats and appeared to be suspended from the ceiling by wires. Is that where he slept?

Don't even think about it.

Moving over to the island, I slid onto one of three stools—the only real seating in the entire place—propped my chin in my hand, and looked around the kitchen. In contrast to the rest of his apartment, it appeared to be fully appointed, as if he'd moved in here with only his clothing, his pots and pans, and his spice rack.

It was beautiful, of course—stone counters, stainless appliances, glass tile backsplash. The cabinets were a deep brown wood, the hardware chrome. Above the island hung a gorgeous bronze Art Deco light fixture with frosted amber glass shades. "I love that," I said, gesturing toward it. "Was it here when you moved in?"

"Yeah, it was. It was salvaged from the original building, they told me. It's what sold me on this place." Turning his back to me, he retrieved two old-fashioned glasses from a glass-paned cabinet.

"That's so cool." The fixture lent a little touch of glamour to the overall feel of the kitchen, which was luxurious and masculine at the same time. Nick looked perfect in it. "You've done really well, Nick. I'm happy for you."

"Thanks." He poured a few fingers of scotch into each glass. "You've done well, too. I hear Devine Events is very successful and you're excellent at your job."

"Oh?" I arched a brow. "And how did you hear that?"

Sliding a glass toward me, he said casually, "Lucas told me."

"You asked Lucas about me?"

He shrugged, like it was no big deal. "Maybe once or twice."

"I see." I made a mental note to ask Lucas *exactly* how many times Nick had asked about me, what his *exact* words were, and what *exactly* had been said to him in return.

Nick picked up his scotch. "Try this."

I lifted mine and inhaled the aroma. Part sweet, part spice. My mouth watered. I glanced at the bottle to see what it was. "Auchentoshan Virgin Oak?"

"Yeah, I've got a thing for virgins."

"Don't I know it." I sipped, closing my eyes and letting the scotch roll seductively over my tongue before swallowing. "Mmmm. Delicious. I love it."

"I thought you would." He took another drink before turning away to switch on one of his double ovens.

I put my glass to my nose and breathed in again, half annoyed and half flattered that he'd know my taste in scotch, or even that he *thought* he would. While I sipped again, Nick pulled out a battered black binder from a drawer, its pages spilling out.

"What's that?"

"It's Noni's old recipe book. It has the cake recipe in it that she used to make for all our birthdays. She gave the book to me a few years ago but she made me promise not to tell my aunts or cousins." From another cupboard he took out a mixing bowl, measuring cups and spoons, and an old hand mixer, which surprised me.

"Don't you have one of those fancy KitchenAid things on a stand?"

"Nah. I like this one." He pulled the beater attachments from a drawer and nudged it closed with his hip. For some reason the movement sent a spike of lust straight through my core. "I need it to do the frosting on the stove anyway."

"You're even making the frosting from scratch? I'm impressed."

He smiled as he attached the beaters to the mixer. "Good."

Curious, I got off the chair and wandered around to Nick's side of the island. "Can I look at the book?"

"Sure." He pushed it toward me and I opened it, careful not to lose any of the scraps of paper and recipe cards stuck in the front. Gingerly I began turning the pages, keenly aware of the fact that Nick had moved behind me in order to look over my shoulder, definitely standing closer than a *friend* would. I could smell him.

Chewing my bottom lip, I tried hard to focus on the recipes and not on the proximity of my ass to his dick. The *other* voice in my head, the one that liked to speak up when I was watching QVC or trying to decline the dessert tray at Andiamo, said, *If you arched your back just a little, pretended like you were stretching, you could totally "accidentally" rub your butt on his crotch. See if he's hard.*

I willed that voice to shut up and go away, since I didn't need any additional temptation where Nick was concerned. I turned a few more pages, smiling at the names of Noni's favorite dishes. "This is amazing. Some of these look really old." The pages were yellowed and brittle, the recipes painstakingly written out in spidery cursive on notebook paper stained over time by splatters and spills. "Kitty's Deviled Hamburgers. Bride's Pie. Papa Joe's Gravy."

"Yeah, that one's old for sure. Papa Joe was my Great-Grandpa Lupo, which would have been Noni's father-in-law. He was a great cook, ran an Italian restaurant downtown for years."

I glanced back at him, and my forehead nearly hit his chin, he was so close. "Really? I never knew that. I thought your family was from Bay City."

"Noni's family was from up there. But she was a Bosco who married a Lupo. The first Lupos in this country lived in Detroit, near Eastern Market. They ran a restaurant." Nick took another sip of his scotch before stepping away from me to pull ingredients from the fridge—butter, sour cream, eggs.

"Really? What a coincidence. Or maybe not—guess it's in your blood, huh?" I sat down again, admiring the smooth, confident way he moved around the kitchen, remembering how he used to cook for me at my apartment in college. The best meals were the eggs and bacon he'd fry up at three AM after several good bouts of hot, sweaty sex. If there was anything better than bacon after sex, I had yet to discover it.

"Actually, the Lupo history is pretty interesting," Nick went on. "Papa Joe was a bootlegger during Prohibition. Ran whiskey from Canada."

I gasped. "Stop it. Really? That's so cool! I can't believe you never told me about that."

"I wasn't really interested in family history back then, but I love it now. My mom found some old photos for me, and I'm having prints made to hang at my restaurant. You know, people even say I look like him. My great-grandfather, I mean." He opened a high cupboard, taking out flour, baking powder, baking soda, and salt.

"Yeah? Got a picture I can see?"

He carried the dry ingredients over to the island. "I do, actually. On my iPad, which is upstairs. I'll get it." He kept talking as he made his way over to the steps. "I think it's a wedding picture."

I clapped my hands and took off after him, too impatient to wait for him to come down. "I want to see!"

Nick climbed the staircase ahead of me, and despite the insubstantial look of them, I was happy to note that they did not sway or jiggle. I followed him up, which gave me a nice eye-level view of his ass. At the top of the stairs, he switched on the light and pulled his iPad from a black leather messenger bag on the floor next to his bed.

While he looked for the photo, I glanced around at the sleeping loft. The head of his platform bed, queen-sized from the looks of it, was pushed up against the brick wall and neatly made up with plain white sheets. *He makes his bed now. That's different.*

It's been seven years, Coco. He's probably matured in a lot of ways, just like you have.

But I bet he's still phenomenal in bed.

Heat rushed my face. Blood rushed my core. I crossed my arms and my legs, squeezing my thighs together against the ache that was building there.

"OK, come here and look. I found it." He went over and sat on the bed, holding the iPad on his lap, and I walked over and lowered myself beside him, careful not to sit too close.

"Oh my God," I breathed, putting a hand over my heart. "You *do* look like him. And what a gorgeous picture. When was that?" It was indeed a wedding photo, black and white and pretty old from the looks of it, although the digital copy appeared to have been restored. The groom, whose wide mouth, full lips, and dark eyes were eerily like Nick's, wore a black suit, and his diminutive bride stood next to him. She wore a simple but lovely white lace dress with a high neck and short sleeves, and a sash around her small waist.

"I'm not sure. Nineteen twenty-something? My grandfather was born around nineteen twenty-five, I think, so they must have been married by then."

"Look how little she is." I pointed at the petite woman, whose skin was so fair it looked translucent. She had wide eyes and a lovely heart-shaped face. Her lips were dark, as if she wore deep red lipstick. Immediately I felt she and I were kindred spirits. She was smiling—they both were, which seemed unusual for such an old photo. Most of the time, people in old photographs look pretty miserable, but this couple was truly happy, you could just tell. Something like grief squeezed my heart, which was ridiculous. What did I have to be sad about?

"Yeah, she was little. Her nickname was Tiny. I don't even know what her real name was. She died when I was just a few years old."

I looked at him. "You don't know your great-grandmother's real name? That's not right. We have to find out, I want to know about her."

He smiled, his eyes still on the picture. "Why?"

"I don't know. Because she wears red lipstick. Because they look so happy. Because I think it's interesting," I said as he laughed at my reasoning. I thumped his leg. "Have you forgotten I was a history major? I eat this kind of stuff up."

His eyes, light and shining, met mine. "I haven't forgotten anything about you, cupcake."

My heart stopped.

I willed him to lean closer, to whisper my name, to touch my lips with his...but he didn't.

"We'll ask Noni about her this weekend," he went on. "And speaking of Noni, we better go make that cake. It's after ten already."

I swallowed. "OK."

But he didn't move, and I didn't either. I couldn't. My stomach muscles were clenched so tight it almost hurt. He looked at my lips, so I licked them, let them fall open. Tipped my chin up, ever so slightly. *Come on, Nick. Kiss me, already.*

He smiled. "You totally want me to kiss you right now."

Shrinking back, I slapped him on the shoulder. "I do not!"

"You did, you so did," he said, laughing as he stood up. He tossed the iPad onto his bed. "You licked your lips."

Steaming mad, I clenched my fists at my sides and trailed him down the steps and back into the kitchen. He was so fucking infuriating! "That doesn't mean I wanted you to kiss me. Because I don't."

"Oh no?" He whirled around and grabbed me hard by the shoulders. His lips hovered over mine. "Then tell me not to kiss you," he said, his breath warm and soft on my mouth. "Say it's against the rules. Say you don't want it."

Oh God, oh God, oh God. Why did he have to play these kinds of games? I knew what he was doing—he wanted me as badly as I wanted him, but he wanted it to be *my* idea so he wouldn't look like the asshole. So he could say that *I* was the one who broke the rules. That *I* was the one who wanted him more.

No way.

He was either going to take me the way I wanted to be taken or not at all. I wasn't going to offer him a fucking invitation, not after what he'd done.

"I don't want it." The lie slid out through clenched teeth.

He paused before letting go of me. "Good. Because I don't want it either."

Before I could stop myself, my hand shot out and grabbed his crotch. Beneath his jeans, his cock was thick and hard and totally erect.

I smiled wickedly. "Liar."

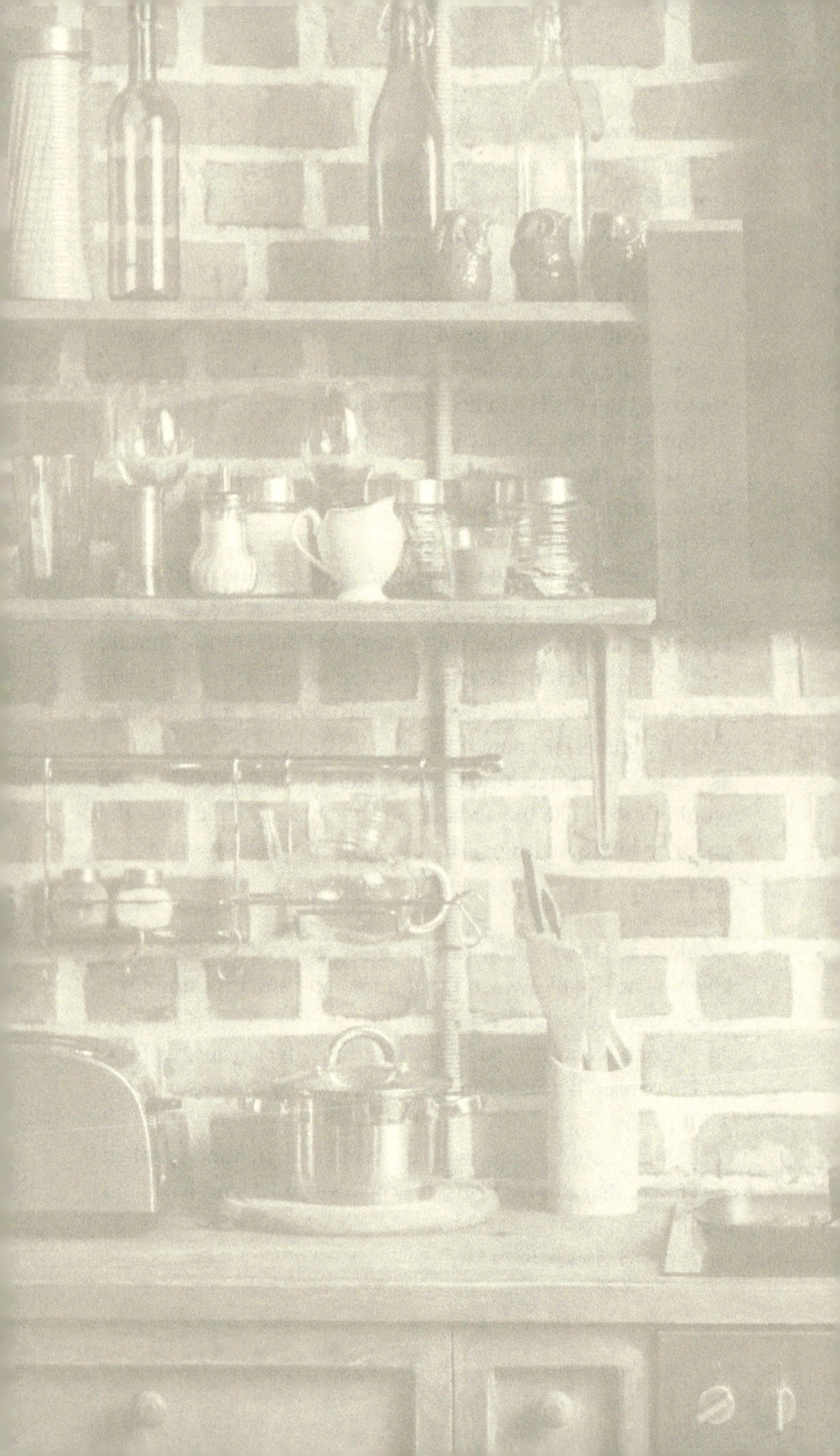

Chapter Nine

Satisfied with his awestruck expression, I removed my hand and turned to the ingredients lined up on the island. "Well, don't just stand there. We've got a cake to bake, remember?"

"Coco." He said my name with enough force to make me wonder if he was angry at what I'd done. I faced him again and saw his hands fisted at his sides. And there was something other than shock in his eyes. They were darker than they'd been a moment ago, making my nether regions tingle. And was it the oven making it so hot in here?

I felt for the counter behind me. "Yes, friend?"

Rushing toward me, he wrapped his hands tightly around my head. "Don't." Then he crushed his mouth against mine, igniting a fire within me that consumed any lingering doubts or desire to play the coquette. I threw my arms around him and molded my lips and body to his. Later we'd probably argue over who started this, but right now all I could think about was getting closer to him.

We kissed like it was the first time, like we were back in his truck and we couldn't believe we'd just met, like we'd better get our fill of each other because such insane chemistry couldn't possibly last—surely it would burn out as quickly as it sparked.

But God, *God*, it felt good.

"Nick," I whispered as his mouth, that incredible, luscious mouth that had taught me so much about pleasure, moved down my throat. He closed his fingers in my hair, sending needles prickling across my scalp and down my spine. I tugged at the blue shirt, impatient to feel his skin against mine, to wrap myself around him, to get him inside me.

He dropped his arms and I shoved the shirt from his shoulders, but as it dropped to the floor, he did too, sinking to his knees in front of me. Breathing hard, I watched him slide his hands up the outsides of my thighs, pushing the dress to my hips. "Christ, this body," he whispered, resting his forehead against my white lace panties. His hands flexed on my hips. "I've dreamed about this."

"You have?" My fingers threaded through his thick dark hair.

"Yes. And this." He kissed me through the lace. "And this." He dragged the panties down to my knees. "And especially this." He slid his tongue between my legs, which nearly buckled at the first firm, wet stroke.

At the second stroke, they began to tremble.

By the third, I wasn't even sure I had legs.

"It feels so good, Nick," I whimpered. "I don't think I can stand."

"Fuck standing." He yanked my underwear all the way down and I stepped out of them, holding onto his shoulders for balance. As he stood, he reached behind me and hitched my legs up around his hips, my dress riding all the way up to my waist. Our mouths and tongues collided, and I locked my ankles behind him. God, I'd missed this. I'd missed everything about him.

He set me on the edge of the island and I clawed at his white tank, breaking our breathless kiss only to whip the shirt over his head. At first I was so ecstatic to feel his hot skin under my palms, I thought of nothing but running my hands all over his chest and torso and back. Every curve and line on his body begged to be touched, kissed, licked.

Oh yes. There would be licking tonight. I didn't care if we were just friends, I was going to lick this man up, down, and sideways. I was going to trace his tattoos with my tongue, savor every inch of him, drink every last drop—

And then I remembered.

Taking him by the shoulders, I held him away from me slightly so I could look at his chest, which rose and fell with ragged breaths.

I inhaled sharply.

My name was still there.

My throat tightened. I reached up and ran my fingers over it, black cursive letters on smooth golden skin. Other, unfamiliar tattoos marked his body—animals and symbols and words I'd examine later in delicious detail—but for now, the only one I saw was the one he'd gotten on our ill-fated wedding day. "You still have it."

"Of course I do."

"But you could have had it removed, or covered it, or changed it into something else."

"I've never even considered it."

I swallowed hard, guilt oozing between the layers of desire. I'd transformed my wedding day tattoo into something that symbolized my freedom, rather than be stuck with a permanent reminder of him, of what we'd done. "Why not?"

"Because I like it." His voice was soft but gruff. "It reminds me of you."

I had no idea what to say. *Damn you, Nick. I just want sex. Don't make me feel things.*

As if he could read my mind, his lips curved into a sexy grin. "Bet you never thought you'd see it again."

That made me laugh a little. "You're right about that." I trailed my fingertips down his muscular abdomen, anxious to stay in the moment. "But I'm glad I did."

He slid his hands up the insides of my thighs and brushed his thumbs against my pussy, still wet from his mouth. "Me too."

My breath hitched at his touch, and I reached down to unbuckle his belt, unzip his jeans, and slide my hand inside them.

Yes. This.

I wrapped my fingers around his hot, hard cock, adoring the way his body shuddered as I began working my hand up and down its solid length. *This is what I want. This is safe.* His mouth reclaimed mine, his hands returning to my head, holding it steady as his tongue stroked between my lips. The tip of his cock grew wet, intensifying the hollow ache inside me. Widening my knees, I shoved his jeans down at the sides and placed him between my legs, moving the smooth head over my clit.

He pulled back to look at me, a question in his eyes.

I knew what he was asking. "I want this, Nick. I don't care what I said. I want this. I want you. Now." I slid both arms around his bare torso and pulled him close, his erection sliding up between my slick folds, pressing against me. "Now," I whispered against his mouth. "I want you inside me *right now*." His cock twitched.

"Fuck." Suddenly he reached behind me and swept an arm across the island. Everything clattered to the floor—measuring spoons, cups, mixing bowls, our glasses of scotch, sugar and flour spilling across the dark wood floor. Nick didn't even look down.

Laying me back onto the cool granite, he spread my knees with his hands. My entire body trembled as he licked his way up one inner thigh and down the other. His hands slid under my calves and lifted them to rest on his bare shoulders, and I crossed my ankles behind his neck. Picking up my head, I saw my red shoes behind his dark hair and nearly lost control at the sight of it. He looked me in the eye before lowering his mouth to my pussy, his tongue gliding up the silky seam at my center and tracing soft circles on my clit. My head fell back against the hard stone, but I barely felt it.

"Mmm, I missed this. You taste just the way I remember." His words, his breath on my skin, sent a shiver through my body, and I moaned with pleasure as he devoured me.

"I do?" I panted, my lower body tightening and my hands seeking to grab on to something. Finding nothing on the island, I reached for his head, weaving my fingers into his hair. My legs slipped off his shoulders and dangled over his arms.

"Yes. Like fucking perfection." His hands reached under my legs to pull me closer to him, and I gasped when his tongue slid inside me before returning to the small, humming bundle of nerves and flicking it lightly, electrifying my entire body.

I closed my eyes, letting the rapturous pressure build. "Oh my God, it feels like the first time. In your truck. Remember?"

"Are you kidding?" He slid a finger into my slick, swollen wetness. "I jerk off to that memory all the time." When I moaned, a second finger joined the first, twisting so they moved against some secret place in my body only Nick had ever been able to find. What miraculous relief to be with someone who knew the terrain of my body inside and out, who remembered all its hidden pleasure spots. He sucked my clit greedily as his fingers worked me into a frenzy, and I rocked my hips against his mouth, panting loudly. Jesus, it had been so long...it really did feel like my first time, and oh, my, God—"Yes!" I flattened my palms on the counter. My insides were seizing up, clenching his fingers, and my head dropped to one side, my face contorting with pleasure so intense it was almost painful. *Oh my God oh my God oh my God, he's so fucking good, and I haven't felt this way in forfuckingever, and my body is on fire, and I'm going to come so hard right here on his goddamn island, and then he's going to fuck me on it...*

Knowing it would be just moments until Nick was inside me again finally sent me over the edge, and I cried out as the orgasm tore through my body with powerful, rhythmic surges that throbbed around his fingers and pulsed against his tongue. I savored every lingering aftershock, open-mouthed and gasping.

The second my body relaxed, Nick straightened up. "Don't move."

Before I could protest, he raced out of the kitchen and up the stairs. Propping myself up on my elbows, I nearly called out to him to forget the condom, I was on the pill, but I bit my lip instead. It was smarter to use the condom. Even when we were a couple we'd used them, terrified of my getting pregnant.

We'd only done it three times without one, all on the same night.

Our wedding night.

My stomach flipped as I heard Nick bounding down the stairs. Half a second later he appeared in the kitchen, shirtless and messy-haired and unbelievably gorgeous, condom in hand.

"Let me." Sitting all the way up, I took it from him, tore it open and slid it over his swollen cock within five seconds.

It was like no time had passed.

Yet it was like we'd never done this before.

Spreading my knees wide, I inhaled sharply when he grabbed me by the hips and slid in, deep and slow. "Yes," I whispered, grabbing his shoulders as he began to move, his hips undulating lazily between my legs. "Yes, like that."

"Tell me you've thought about this." Nick's voice was deep and gravelly.

"Oh God, I have. I do. All the time."

"Yeah?" His fingers dug into my flesh as he rocked into me, his movements unhurried but steady. "About my cock inside you?"

"Yes." I squeezed my eyes shut, appreciating every thick, hard inch of him gliding in and out of my body. "All the time."

"You miss the way I fuck you. My mouth on you. My hands on you. All the ways I make you come."

"Yes," I whimpered, the tempest swirling inside me again.

"Tell me." He began to move faster, driving into me harder and deeper. "I want to hear you say it."

"I miss the way you fuck me." My toes pointed. "Your mouth on me. Your hands." My nails dug into his shoulders. "Your cock. I miss it inside me." Barely able to speak, I gasped when his hands slid beneath my ass and he lifted me off the island. "All the ways you make me come," I panted. I wrapped my legs around his waist, tilting my hips to take him deeper. "All the ways…you make me come." Nick cursed and held me tight to his body, grinding me against him so the base of his cock rubbed my clit. "Oh, God, do it, Nick. Don't stop. Don't stop. Don't stop!"

Clutching him to me, I buried my face in the curve of his neck, sighing long and hard as the shimmering waves of my second orgasm paralyzed me with pleasure. He groaned as I grew even wetter, stumbling through everything he'd thrown on the floor, and slamming my back into the refrigerator door. Pounding into me hard and fast, he cursed and grit his teeth, fucking me against the heavy stainless steel appliance so violently the entire thing shook. Reaching over my head, I hooked my fingers over the top of the fridge and held on for dear life—my back would be bruised to hell tomorrow. We both cried out as his orgasm peaked, his cock swelling and throbbing deep inside me. I clenched my core muscles around him, desperate to feel every twitch and tremor in his body.

Desperate to cling to the physical intensity between us rather than the emotional.

Desperate to think of some way to convince myself that what we were doing was OK.

Desperate to suppress the wellspring of romantic hope beginning to bubble up inside me.

I can't love him again.

I can't.

And I won't.

I just had to keep telling myself that.

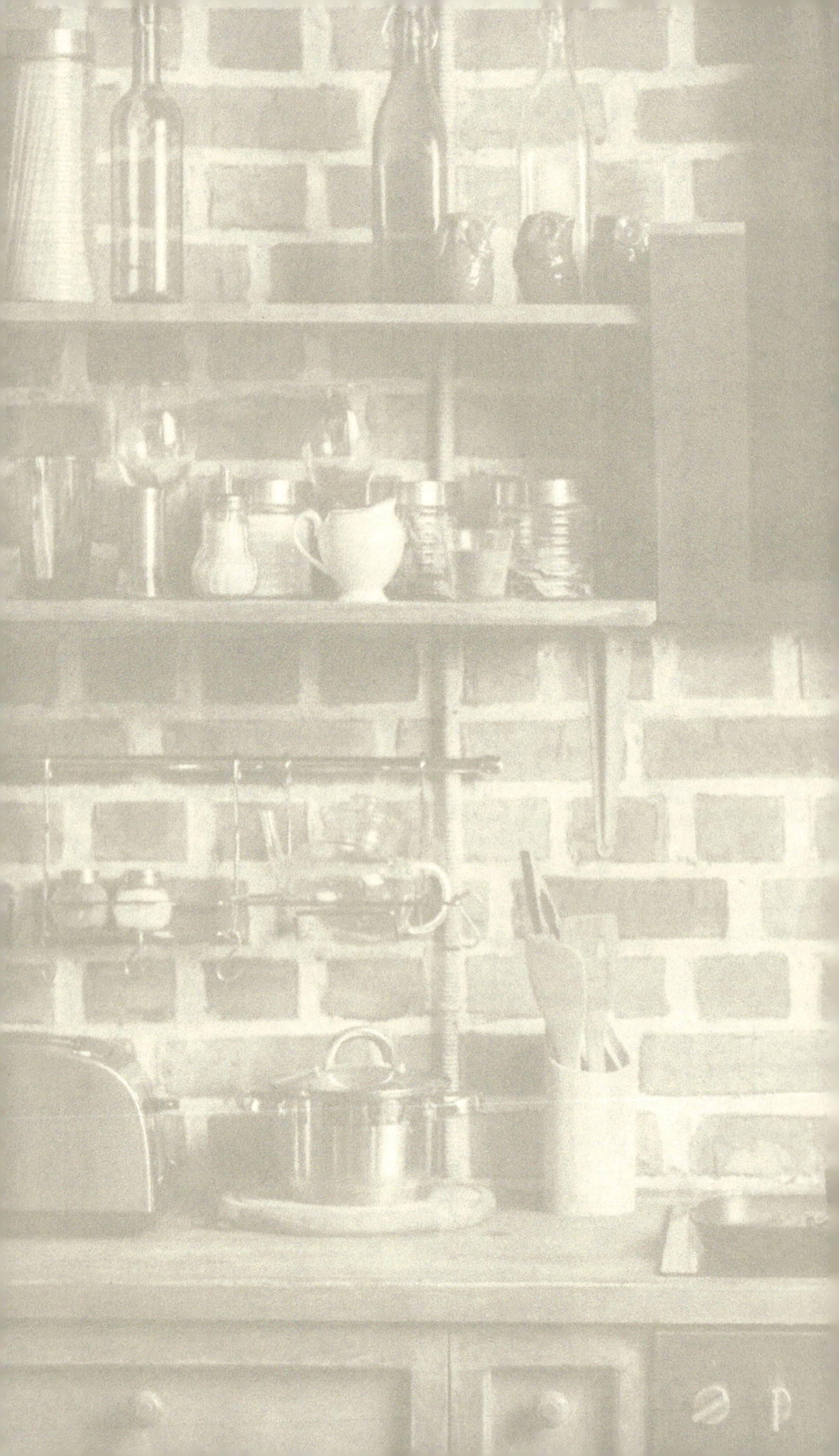

Chapter Ten

When his body had stilled, Nick picked up his head from my shoulder. "Oops."

I smiled, still grasping the top of the fridge. "Oops."

"It's hotter than fuck in here. Is the oven on?"

"Yes. We were supposed to bake a cake, remember?" I let go and held on to his shoulders as he swung around and set me on the island again, the mixing bowl banging into a cupboard when he accidentally kicked it.

"Oh yeah." He kissed me on the temple. "This was a better idea. Good thinking."

"It wasn't *my* idea, Mr. Let's Be Friends."

He pulled back slightly to look at me. "You didn't want to be friends either, Coco. Admit it. Friends don't grab each other's business the way you did."

"Can we please not have an argument right now? You're still inside me, for fuck's sake."

One side of his mouth hooked up. "Sorry. Want to call it a draw?"

"I guess we could. Just this once."

Amazingly enough, somehow getting the whole will-we-

or-won't-we question out of the way made me much more relaxed than I'd been when I'd knocked on his door earlier tonight. Even though I had no idea what this would do to our "friendship," it felt unbelievably good to quit pretending we weren't still attracted to each other. It was a relief, really. And as long as we didn't break rules one and two, I felt certain that I could keep my emotions in check even if I let my sex drive run a bit wild. This weekend was like a little vacation from reality—a trip to the past, that's all. I could handle it.

Fucking time travel.

How cool was that?

Nick showed me where the downstairs bathroom was, and I cleaned up and washed my hands, observing my red cheeks and mussed hair in the mirror over the vessel sink and waterfall faucet. But I felt no guilt, none at all. After all, we were single, friendly, and familiar with each other. It was like watching my favorite movie again or rereading my favorite book. Pure pleasure—nothing more.

When I was done, I looked for my suitcase by the door, but it was gone. Had Nick taken it upstairs? I went up to the loft, reaching the top of the stairs just as Nick was about to come down.

"Hey." He'd wet and combed his hair, the vainglorious ass, but he was still bare-chested and flushed in the face.

"Hey." Now that I wasn't so distracted, I could better admire all the new ink he'd gotten. His entire right shoulder and arm were covered; the other arm had tattoos on the bicep and forearm; he had my name on the left side of his chest and something on the right side of his rib cage. Most of it was plain black ink except for a few spots of color on the right arm. My heartbeat quickened. "I like all the new tattoos."

"Thanks. I carried your suitcase up. You can sleep up here tonight. The sheets are clean. I'll sleep on the bean bag downstairs."

I rolled my eyes. "Nick, please. Now that we've broken the sex rule, I think it's OK to sleep in the same bed."

His eyes lit up. "Does that mean we can break it again?"

I eyeballed him through half-mast lids. "I haven't decided yet. Don't push your luck. Unzip me please?" Turning around, I lifted my hair off my neck.

"Sure." He pulled the zipper down slowly, all the way to my tailbone. Then he traced a line with one finger from the base of my neck to my bra strap, sending gooseflesh up my arms. When he stopped there without taking his hand off me, I smiled.

"You can undo it."

With a deft one-handed motion, he unhooked the strap and I inhaled deeply, my chest expanding. "Thanks."

His hands slid inside my dress, spreading it open to reveal my shoulder blades. "You covered it."

"What?"

"My name. Our wedding date."

"Oh." Dropping my hair, I turned around to see him looking sadder than he had a right to be. I swallowed. "Yes."

"Can I see?"

I hesitated. "I guess so. Sure." Turning around, I gathered my hair over one shoulder and stood still. He opened the back of the dress again, gently pushing the sleeves and the bra straps down my arms. I felt naked, which was silly, since he'd seen me naked for real probably hundreds of times, maybe a thousand. Actually, it wasn't that I felt naked. I felt judged—and the verdict was guilty.

Nick's fingers brushed over the two matching swallows, one on each shoulder blade. "They're beautiful."

"Thanks."

He was silent, and for some reason I felt like apologizing. *I'm sorry* was on the tip of my tongue, as though I owed him permanent real estate on my body. *I don't,* I thought, biting my lip. *I didn't then and I don't now and this moment needs to be over.*

"Mind if I slip into something more comfortable?" I shot him a coy look over my shoulder, dismayed to find him looking pensive and a little heartbroken.

"Huh? Oh, no, of course not." He replaced his forlorn expression with an impish smile. "You can walk around naked if you want to."

"I was thinking more along the lines of pajamas."

"Pajamas?" He looked pained. "That is definitely a distant second to naked, but make yourself at home. I'm gonna start cleaning up the kitchen so we can get that cake made while Noni still has a pulse."

"I'll be down in a minute to help."

Nick headed down the stairs and I opened up my suitcase, dropping onto the bed to pull off my sandals. I had the first one off and the second one dangling from my hand when I heard Johnny Cash and June Carter's "Jackson" start to blare from speakers somewhere downstairs. *We got married in a fever, hotter than a pepper sprout...*

Laughing at Nick's sense of humor, I changed into my pajamas, fitted boy shorts and a tank in blush pink trimmed with black lace. I debated putting a bra back on, since the material of the top was pretty thin, but it felt so good to breathe without underwire I left it off. In Nick's walk-through closet I found a spare hanger and hung up my dress, ignoring the impulse to rifle through his clothes and sniff his collars, or snoop in the upstairs bathroom beyond it for girly items. I didn't need to care if he entertained girls here, right? I was no longer his girlfriend and had no plans to be.

Pulling an elastic from my makeup bag, I wandered into the bathroom to put my hair in a pony tail. The walls were brick, the sink and subway tiles white, and the fixtures chrome. I checked my reflection in the mirror, my insides tightening a little at the thought of Nick wet and naked in the shower behind me. Is that where he jerked off thinking about me?

For fuck's sake, Coco. Knock it off and get out of here, you pervert.

At the last second, I couldn't resist a quick peak in the vanity drawers, which made me laugh. No pink razors or girly deodorant, but he had enough hair and grooming products to sink a ship. They were all manly, though, as manly as ginger and citrus hair wax can be, anyway.

Nick was cleaning the island countertop, but he looked up as I came into the kitchen. He'd put his white tank and blue plaid shirt back on, which was probably a good thing. His bare chest was way too tempting.

"Oh, good. I like a girl who bakes in lingerie."

I wrinkled my nose. "I'm not much of a baker. Maybe I'll just watch."

"No way. You're here in my kitchen, I'm putting you to work."

"Slave driver," I teased. "Got a broom? Or a vacuum?" Nick had picked up the things he'd swiped onto the floor, but the wood felt gritty with spilled sugar and looked dusty with flour. "Did we break the glasses of scotch?"

"No, actually. The broom's in the pantry over there." Nick glanced at my bare feet. "I wiped up the scotch but the floor might be sticky."

"I can handle it." I found the broom and dustpan and swept the floor while Nick scrubbed and dried the bowls and measuring utensils. "That was some good scotch sacrificed here."

"Totally fucking worth it."

I smiled. "I think so too." When I'd emptied the dustpan into the garbage, I wet a paper towel, got down on my knees, and began wiping the floor.

"Now there's something I never thought I'd see. Coco Thomas on her hands and knees washing the kitchen floor."

I stopped working and looked up at him. "What's that supposed to mean?"

He shrugged as he cracked an egg into the bowl. "Just that you've probably had a maid to do that stuff your whole life."

Sitting back on my heels, I scowled at him. Yes, my parents had always had a housekeeper, something I'd never thought twice about until I met Nick. Everybody I knew had one. Later I learned that Nick's mom had cleaned houses to supplement the money their family restaurant made when times were tough. But even then, I'd never understood why that should make him uncomfortable around my family. "Really, Nick? Right now you're going to start that shit again?"

"Start what shit?"

"You know what shit. The whole *I'm just a poor boy nobody loves me* routine."

"I never said you didn't love me."

"You know what I mean. Implying that I think I'm too good for you, or that you're not good enough for me because I grew up…" I struggled with how to put it. "Advantaged."

Nick laughed and cracked a second egg. "You grew up rich. And you *were* too good for me."

"Whatever, Nick. It was *you* that had the money hang-up when it came to us, not me. I never even thought about it."

"Because you never had to." He didn't sound angry or bitter, but this whole tired conversation bothered me. Irritated that he'd spoil our fun with it, I got to my feet. Why the hell would he even bring it up? I tossed the paper towel in the garbage and tried to slam the cabinet door shut, but it had one of those slow-close mechanisms that prevented it from making any noise. How fucking annoying.

"Fine. I never had to think about money," I snapped. "Yes, my college education was paid for. Yes, my parents bought me a car."

"A BMW," he clarified, beating the eggs with a fork.

"A BMW." I watched him for a few seconds, wishing I could take a turn. I felt like beating something right now. "Why are you doing this?"

His arm stopped, and he looked at me. "Doing what?"

"Starting a fight."

"I'm not starting a fight, Coco. I was just commenting that I've never seen you wash a kitchen floor."

"Or mow a lawn or pound in a nail or use a goddamn drill." My hands curled into fists.

"No, now that you mention it." Nick had the nerve to look amused. "What's this about, cupcake?"

His nickname for me, which I'd always loved, now sounded childish and silly. Like I was pretty and sweet, a pink-frosted birthday confection. *He thinks of me as a helpless girl, just like my parents do.* "You think I'm just a princess. You think I can't do anything on my own just because I've never done it before. You think I don't know how to work with my hands."

"Now that's just not true." He set down the fork and bowl. "I've seen you work magic on me with your hands many times. Come here."

"No."

"Come *here*, stubborn." He pulled me in for a hug, and I didn't resist for long, allowing his arms to twine around my waist, my forehead to rest on his solid shoulder. "I'm sorry I upset you. I shouldn't have said anything."

"I'm sorry too." My voice was muffled in his shirt. I took a deep breath, inhaling his scent, which was now mingling with my perfume on his skin. "It's not really all about what you said. It's this house thing—I'd be taking on a huge amount of work on my own, and I'm scared that my family will tell me I'm crazy, like Mia did. Not only because it's a lot of money, but because of all the work it needs."

"I think that's great." He squeezed me tighter. "And you can do anything you set your mind to. I know you can."

I sighed. "You haven't seen this house. Part of the reason I'm scared to ask my parents for help buying it is that Mia could be right. But I just love it so much."

"Show it to me."

"Show it to you? When?"

Nick released me and reached for the sour cream. "Tomorrow morning maybe? We can drive through Indian Village before we get on the road."

"Really?" I clasped my hands together under my chin.

Nick spooned some sour cream into a bowl and added a teaspoon of baking soda. "Yeah. Do you think we can see the inside? If I'm going to give you an honest opinion about the investment in terms of time and money, I'd like to see the entire thing."

"Maybe. Let me text my agent." Hurrying toward the door where I'd dropped my purse, I pulled out my phone and saw that I had four messages, one from Erin wanting to know how things were going (which made me smile), one from Mia apologizing for being harsh with me today (which made me feel guilty), one from a vendor assuring me I could get all the outdoor furniture I wanted (which made me thank God) and one from Angelina, asking if we could change the whole party to a luau theme (which made me frown in confusion because she spelled it loo-ow. Took me a minute). She wanted me to call her immediately, no matter the time.

I groaned.

"Problem?" Nicked called over Johnny Cash's rough-hewn twang.

"No. But give me a minute, OK? Can we turn the music down slightly?"

"Sure." He picked up a remote and the volume decreased.

I wandered over by the windows, my phone to my ear. Angelina picked up after one ring.

"You got my message?"

"Yes, but Angelina, I really think your first idea was the best for your event."

"But it doesn't have a theme. I want a theme."

I thought fast. "Sure it does—Italian luxe. We're going to make your parents' front yard look like Donatella Versace's living room!"

"Hmm. I do like Versace."

"Trust me. It's perfect, just the way we discussed."

"But Jodi Mannino's party had a theme, and everyone's still talking about it."

"What was her theme?"

"Game of Thrones."

Oh dear God. She probably wanted dragons now. "Angelina."

"So maybe I should do a TV theme too. How about The Walking Dead? That could be crazy cool, like zombies and stuff walking around? But not me, of course. I want to be hot. So maybe not Walking Dead. Another show. Or a movie."

"Angelina."

"Or—oh! Oh! I know what theme it should be—Fifty Shades of Gray! We can have like whips and chains and things. I can dress like a dominatrix. That'd be hot."

My head was starting to pound, and I touched two fingertips to my temple. "Angelina!"

"Yeah?"

"I really think what we already have planned is the best. You hired me because you liked the Wedding of the Year, remember? That's what I do best—beautiful, luxurious events that are glamorous and sparkly, just like you are."

Behind me, Nick started to laugh.

"I guess. But it doesn't seem very fun." I could just imagine Angelina's frosty pink pout.

"It will be. I promise. And everyone will be talking about it for months to come—until your wedding, which will be an even bigger, more beautiful, more outrageously over-the-top bash. Girls will be telling their planners they want everything you had, but they won't even come close."

"I like that."

"Good. By the way, I got Nick Lupo for you."

The squeal that she emitted was so ear-piercing I had to hold my phone away from my head.

"Oh my God," Nick said, laughing again.

I turned around and saw him with the electric mixer in his hand, waiting for me to hang up before he turned it on. "So really, it's all coming together just the way you planned. Let's stick with it, OK?"

"OK. For now," she said, causing me to glare at my phone. "And you really got Nick Lupo?"

"I really did."

"What did he say? Was it hard?"

Hell yes, it was. Smiling now, I sauntered back toward the kitchen. "He was a little bit difficult to deal with. You know TV stars, they're temperamental and all."

Nick snarled, reaching out as if to choke me.

"And his ego is pretty massive." Moving around the island, he put his hands around my throat, gently throttling me. "Like Eiffel Tower massive. But we made a deal."

"I can't wait to meet him. Who cares if he's temperamental? He's so fucking hot."

"He's all right."

Suddenly Nick turned me into a headlock and tickled my ribcage with the other hand, right underneath my left breast where he *knows* I'm insanely ticklish. I shrieked into the phone and squirmed in his grip.

"Will you stop? No, not you, Angelina. But I have to go, I'll call you tomorrow. Bye." I ended the call and tugged on the elbow around my neck. "Stop it! You just made me yell at my client!"

He growled in my ear, then let me go. "Good. She was cutting into my Coco time. Which is very limited."

"Your Coco time." I rolled my eyes and scrolled through my contacts to find my agent's number. "OK, give me two seconds to text my real estate lady and then you can have me back."

"Can I really? Have you back?"

My stomach cartwheeled as I looked at him. He was giving me the Elvis grin, but I couldn't tell if he was joking or not. Best to play safe. "Yep. For two whole days." I dropped my eyes to the screen again.

But my phone was shaking.

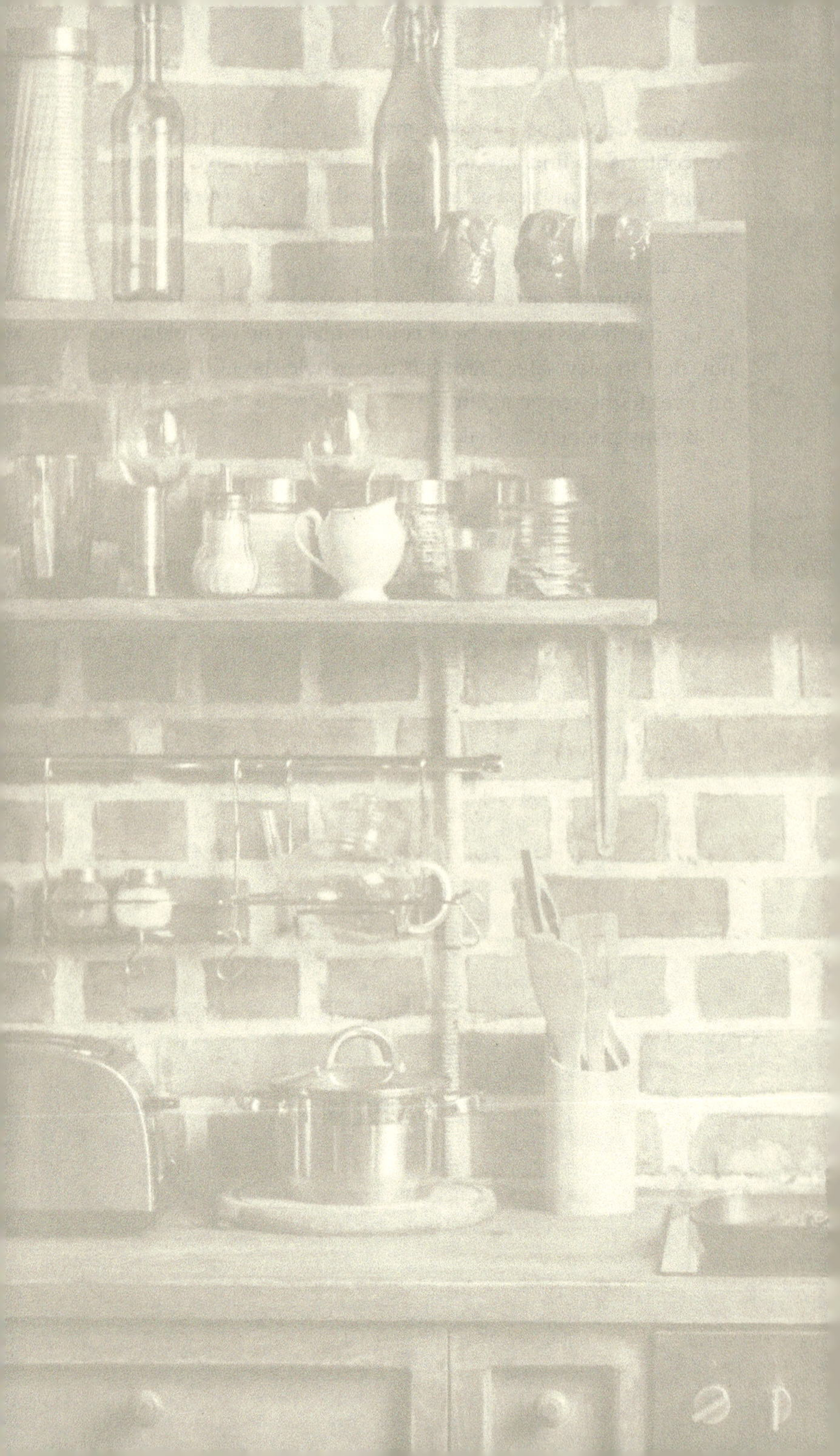

Chapter Eleven

While Nick creamed the butter and sugar—was there anything that tasted better than butter and sugar? Or maybe it was just that he let me lick it off his finger—I sifted together the flour, baking powder, and salt. After adding the eggs, he had me mix a half-cup of cocoa with an equal amount of hot water, rolling his eyes when I tried to use the dry measuring cup. Then he had me alternate adding the dry ingredients and sour cream while he kept the mixer going.

"Now the vanilla. One teaspoon please," he said, checking the recipe. "And then the cocoa mixture." I added the ingredients, and he laughed. "Now it says to beat vigorously."

I cocked my head. "Is there any other way?"

When the batter was prepared, Nick dipped the spatula in the bowl and held it out to me. "Want to taste?"

I closed my lips around it, and when he went to pull it out, I held onto it with my teeth. Then I reached up to take it from him, licking every last drop of rich, chocolaty goodness off the blue rubber tip, sucking it like a popsicle, running my tongue along every inch of its surface.

All while looking him in the eye and moaning appreciatively, of course.

"You're killing me." His expression was tragic.

"Mmmm, good. Can I have some more please?"

"You can lick the whole damn bowl that way if you want to, but let me get the cakes in first."

Smiling gleefully, I hopped up on the counter while he filled two cake pans with batter, tucked them into the oven, and set the timer. "Twenty-five minutes." Grabbing the mixing bowl, he set it next to me. "And I know exactly how I want to spend them."

Peering into the bowl, I was delighted to see it still had plenty of batter left in it. He took the spatula, scooped some off the side of the bowl, and I thought he was going to feed it to me, but he didn't. He smeared it on my thigh.

And licked it off.

S l o w l y.

At the feel of his hot tongue on my leg, my stomach tightened, and I held my breath.

Next, he pulled down a black lace strap of my tank, fully exposing one breast, smearing it with batter. My nipple was already hard and tingling, and when his lips closed around it, sucking off the chocolate, I gasped and arched, my fingers curling around the edge of the counter. He circled the stiff peak with his tongue, taking it between his teeth and biting gently before dragging his mouth up to my neck.

"Get down," he breathed softly in my ear, one hand curling around my waist.

I let him pull me off the counter, my bare feet landing between his. Our mouths opened wide to one another in a long, deep, chocolate-flavored kiss. I slid one hand up the back of his neck and one down the front of his jeans, finding him hard and thick beneath my palm. If I hadn't been sure before about doing it again, I was now.

He lifted his mouth from mine. "Turn around and spread your legs."

I turned around and he slid my boy shorts to my ankles. I wore nothing under them. Leaning forward, I braced myself against the counter and opened my feet wider, rising up on tiptoe. Expecting to feel his cock between my thighs, I was surprised by cool batter against my hot skin. He spread it on my ass and licked it off, making me giggle and moan in delicious agony. He rubbed it along the backs of my legs and knelt between them to eat it off, his fingers and mouth and tongue teasing and tantalizing me, inside and out.

Closing my eyes, I moved against him, torn between wanting to come just like this and wanting to feel him pounding into me from behind.

My body decided for me, growing hotter and tighter as I spiraled higher. "Nick," I gasped, collapsing forward onto my elbows as colors danced behind my eyelids. He moaned, pushing his fingers deeper, and I came so hard I felt it in every muscle, every inch of my body reverberating with pleasure. My legs weakened, and it felt like he was holding me up with one hand and his tongue.

"God, you're so wet. And I love your ass." His breath was hot between my legs, his fingers gliding in and out of me. "I want to fuck you like this."

"Do it," I begged.

He got to his feet and I heard the glorious sounds of a belt coming undone, jeans being unzipped. Then he stopped.

"Fuck, I don't have a— "

"I don't care. I'm on the pill. Just do it." I arched my back and looked back over my shoulder, hoping my body looked irresistible. "Please."

He placed the tip of his cock at my entrance, sliding it in just enough to torture me. "Please what?"

"Please fuck me." I tried to push back against him, make him give me more.

But he held me steady, using his hands on my hips to hold me where he wanted me. "I love the way that sounds coming out of your mouth," he said, pushing deeper. "I don't think I've ever heard you say it before."

I smiled, exhaling with relief as he glided in and out. "I guess I was too shy to tell you what I wanted back then. Or maybe I didn't know yet."

"So tell me now."

I looked back. "Fuck me. And don't be gentle."

He began to move my hips, his fingers digging into my flesh as he jerked me back onto his cock. "I was always so scared to be rough with you," he said, the strain in his voice telling me how he struggled to keep control. "I never wanted to hurt you."

"You won't." But each time he hit the deepest spot within me, I felt a sharp little twinge, and once or twice it was enough to make me gasp.

"Good. Because ever since I saw you today, I've been thinking about fucking you just like this." He reached up and tore the elastic from my hair before fisting a hand in it and pulling so hard I cried out. "Tell me if you want me to stop," he said through clenched teeth, his hips driving forward now in powerful thrusts that made my teeth clatter, "otherwise I can't promise not to tear you apart."

"I want you to," I managed between hard, short breaths. "I want you to tear me apart. I want it to hurt."

And as he cursed and groaned and fucked me so hard against his kitchen counter my skin would bruise, I was shocked to realize it was true—I wanted him to hurt me. Beyond enjoying rough sex, I wanted *pain* at his hands, wanted it bone-deep and razor-sharp. Wanted him to inflict damage on my body and make me feel unsafe, unsteady, unloved.

Safer that way.

Yes, I thought, gleefully, deliriously, maniacally, as he

wrenched my head back. *Yes*, as he squeezed my breast too hard, pinched my nipple too tight. *Yes*, as he dropped my hair and clutched my neck, gripping hard. Yes, as his climax seized him and he groaned, pushing my hips painfully against the granite, his hand a collar around my throat. *Yes, just like that. Make it hurt.*

But as his breathing calmed, he released his hold on me. Bracing his arms on the outsides of mine, he kissed my spine between my shoulder blades and laid his forehead against it.

"Coco."

I was hot and sweaty, but my arms prickled with gooseflesh. His voice was too soft, too tender. *If you tell me you love me right now, I will fucking kill you.* "Yes?"

"I need to tell you something."

Oh, God. No. Please.

"Wait, Nick. Don't."

"Don't what?"

"Don't say anything that...you might regret. This weekend will be fun, but it's just this weekend, remember? I don't want us to get carried away and think it means more than it does. I don't want to confuse things by saying—or hearing—anything too serious."

He picked up his head. "Jesus, Coco. I was just gonna say that my dick is so fucking happy right now. That too serious for you?"

My mouth hung open, and my face burned even hotter. *I just made a total fool of myself.*

Nick burst out laughing as he slid out of me and zipped up his pants. "Let me get you a towel, OK? Hold on." Chuckling, he opened a drawer, pulled out a hand towel, and wet it at the sink.

Pulling the lace strap onto my shoulder, I straightened up and turned around, hoping that my facial hue was at least one shade paler than Russian Red. Nick went down on one knee in front of me, running the towel up the inside of one leg.

"No, I can do that." I took the towel from him. "Please. Just let me."

"Are you sure?" He looked up. "I don't mind."

"I'm sure. And I'm..." I sighed, squeezing my eyes shut for a second. "Really sorry for lecturing you just now. I thought you were—never mind." Shaking my head, I quickly swiped the towel up my other leg, scooped up my pajama bottoms, and headed for the downstairs bath. "Be right back."

Inside the bathroom, I used the towel to clean up, shaking my head. How dumb was I? And how conceited? Thinking that a few random fucks meant that he was in love with me again. He wasn't in love—he was just having a good time, like he always did. And honestly, I was too. It had been so long since I'd had sex, especially good and rough like that. Nick and I'd had plenty of sex when we were together, but I knew myself and my body much better now. I had sexual preferences I'd never have been able to voice back then, either because I didn't know them or was too self-conscious to do it.

My body shivered involuntarily as I recalled Nick's reaction to my request. It was fucking perfect. You couldn't tell just any guy you liked rough sex—I'd tried it a few times. One guy thought it was a free pass to be selfish, and I ended up feeling like a piece of gym equipment—overworked and dripping with someone else's sweat. Another guy, one with Mommy Issues, didn't get what I meant at all. "Like, you want me to hit you? I don't think I can do that. I've got some childhood trauma." And then there was the one who ran to his closet and came back with a leash and collar and asked if he could take me for a walk around the house on all fours before he fucked me. And would I mind barking?

Um...no. No judgies, but no thanks.

After rinsing out the towel, I pulled my bottoms back on, washed my hands, and opened the door in time to hear the oven's buzzer going off. The heavenly scent of chocolate cake hung in the air—chocolate cake and sex.

Not a bad combination on a Friday night.

"Are they done?" I asked as I reached the kitchen. Earlier I'd seen a stacked washer and dryer in the pantry, so I ducked in there and set the towel on the washing machine.

"I think so." Nick set the pans on the counter. "Now we let them cool, and then frost them. Up for some Scrabble while we wait?"

"Sounds like a plan."

Nick poured us some more scotch, retrieved Scrabble from the top of his coat closet, and turned the cakes out onto cooling racks before sitting down next to me at the island.

I opened the box. "Now, no cheating, Lupo. I've got my eye on you."

"I'd like your ass on me. Want to sit on my lap?"

"Tempting, but no. You stay in your chair, I'll stay in mine."

We played one game, drank too much scotch, and laughed so much my sides hurt. At one point, Nick tried to use *panky* and I told him it wasn't a word.

"Yes, it is," he insisted. "I can use it in a sentence. 'The panky in the kitchen tonight was delightful.'"

"Still not a word."

"Did you know what I meant?"

"Yes, but—"

"It has a definition, so it's a word!" He pulled me off my chair and onto his lap. "Or perhaps you need a demonstration of the word." He slid his hand down the front of my shorts.

"Nick, come on. Again already? I thought you had to frost the cake." But his fingers were already working their magic, making my knees open wider and my spine go slack against his chest.

We never did frost the cake that night. Or finish the game. Or empty our glasses. Instead, Nick decided to prove to me how much better the beanbag was than a couch.

And after two hours of panky on it, I had to agree.

Eventually, we made it upstairs, although my leg muscles were so fatigued that I desperately wished for a banister to hold on to. We collapsed onto the bed, both of us on our bellies.

"This is insane," I said. "I haven't had this much sex in one day since…" *Our wedding day.* "Since college."

Nick laughed. "Me neither."

"Stop it. Really?"

"Really. But I like it. Maybe we should get married."

"Haha, very funny." *And yet so not funny.* I went to get off the bed but he dragged me back down. "Relax, Coco. I'm kidding."

"I know," I lied. "I'm just getting up to brush my teeth."

"Oh. Yeah, I guess I should go put the cakes away. Hope they're not all dried out tomorrow."

"If they are, we can start over." I ruffled his hair, and he let me. "I like baking with you."

I brushed my teeth, turned out the light, and got under the covers, barely able to keep my eyes open. It had to be one in the morning, I'd been up since six, and I was not a night owl by any means. Nick's bed was amazingly comfortable, and I fell asleep even before he got back upstairs, waking only when he slid between the sheets, smelling like chocolate and toothpaste.

"You smell like mint chocolate chip ice cream," I told him sleepily. I opened my eyes to see him turn onto his side, one elbow beneath his head, facing me.

"Still your favorite kind?"

"Yes."

"Red still your favorite color?"

"Yes."

"Fall still your favorite season?"

I smiled. "You really do remember a lot of things about me."

"Told you."

We lay in the dark, silent for a moment. I wondered if he would sling an arm over me, or what he'd say if I flung a leg over him. It didn't have to mean anything; I just felt close to him and liked that he would sleep near me tonight. He felt reassuring somehow. Like a forgotten lullaby you hear again years later, the melody taking you back to a time when you felt safe and loved.

He moved his pillow a little closer to mine. "This is nice."

"Mmhmm." My eyes drifted shut.

"Poor baby. You're tired."

"Mmhmm." I was already half-asleep when I felt his hand brushing the hair back from my face. A second later his lips rested briefly on mine.

"Night, Coco."

"Night."

His hand kept stroking my hair, and a moment later, he spoke again. "Do you ever think about what would have happened if I hadn't left Vegas?"

"No." I was so tired, I answered him honestly. I didn't have the energy to make up a lie. "I don't let myself."

"Why not?"

"No point," I murmured drowsily. "And it makes me sad."

"Me too." He exhaled, his hand still moving slowly over my hair. "Although I think about it all the time."

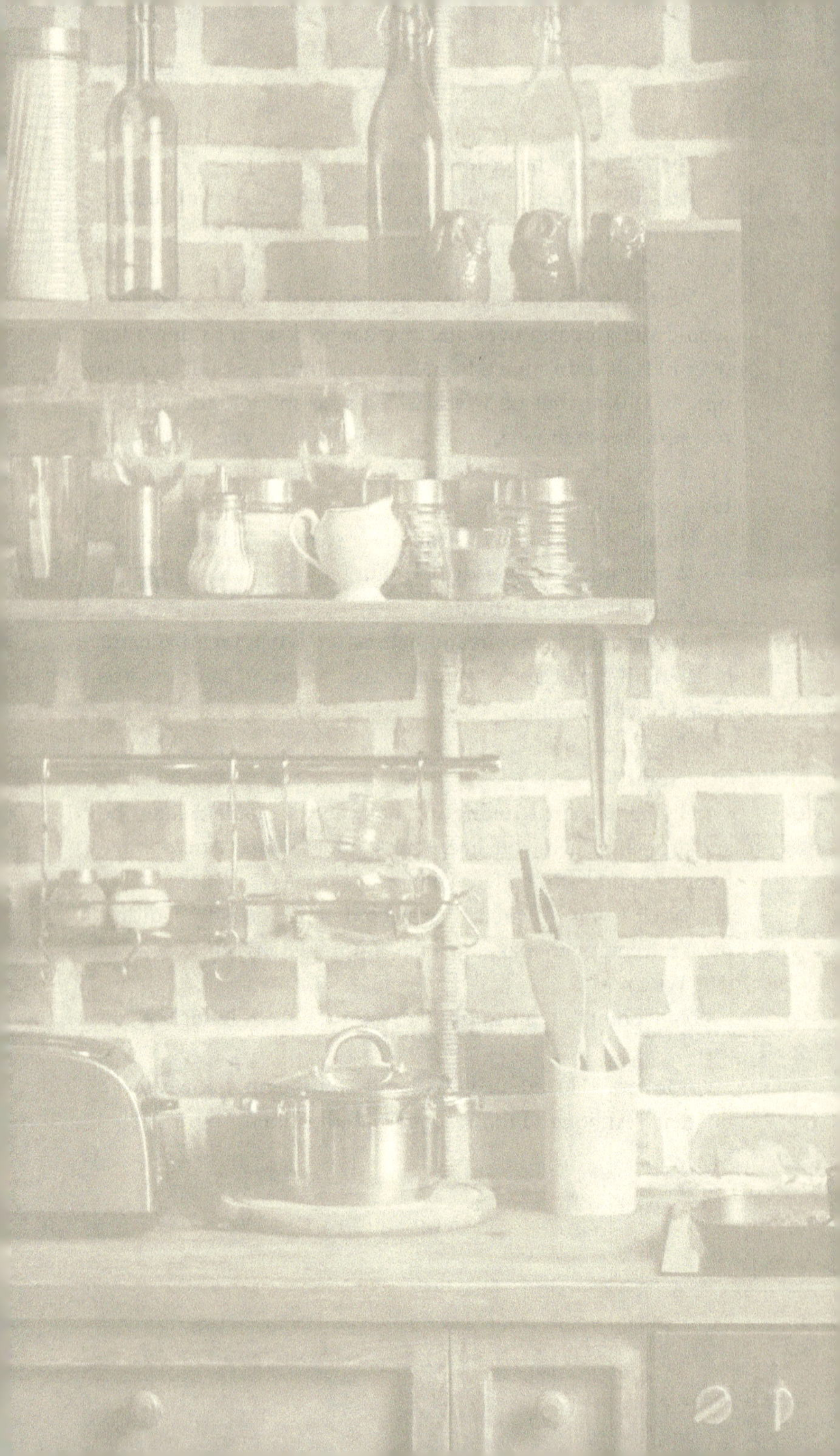

Chapter Twelve

I woke up slowly, feeling content and happy, although it took me a minute to think of why. When I opened my eyes, the room was light but not bright, and the bed was unfamiliar but not strange.

Oh, right. It's Nick's bed.

Smiling and stretching, I turned over, expecting to find him sleeping beside me, but he wasn't there. My face fell—actually my heart dropped too. It was kind of irritating how crushed I was that he wasn't there. *You should be glad he's not here...spontaneous sex in the kitchen is one thing but sex in a bed, in his bed, might be too personal.*

His side of the bed was neat, as if he'd pulled the covers up to keep me warm, and I swung a leg into the space where he'd slept—the sheets were cool. He'd been up for a little while.

Nick didn't have a clock up here, and I'd left my phone downstairs, so I had no idea what time it was. Judging from the light coming in through the huge windows downstairs, it was probably mid-morning.

I used the bathroom and wandered downstairs, feeling oddly nervous when I rounded the corner into the kitchen.

Last night had been crazy, but I didn't regret a moment of it. Did he? Should I be prepared to blow it off? Laugh it off? Or would it be awkward—what if he apologized?

Four words went through my head.

This was a mistake.

I walked into the kitchen on wobbly legs.

"Good morning, cupcake." Nick, electric mixer in hand, walked over and kissed my head. Barefoot, he wore jeans and a plain, clean white t-shirt. His hair was neat and damp. "I'm glad you're up. I have to finish the frosting and I didn't want the noise to wake you. There's coffee there. Cups are in the cupboard above."

"OK. Thank you." I smiled at him, grateful there didn't seem to be any weirdness between us. On the contrary, this felt easy and natural...was that any less worrisome? Tugging my bottom lip between my teeth, I poured myself a cup of coffee and glanced at the clock on the oven. Not quite eight. "I'm surprised you're up so early."

"Me? I'm always up early. All those mornings I had to be at work at five AM, I guess."

I sipped my coffee as he plugged the mixer in near the stove. "That's right. I'd forgotten about your days as a short order cook."

"Not very glamorous, but I had to pay for college somehow. Not all of us could send the bills home to Mom and Dad."

Stiffening, I debated a sharp-tongued defense of myself, but decided against it. Instead I brought my coffee cup to my lips and vowed to be the bigger person. I patted his shoulder blade. "You made it look good, darling." The mixer came on with a whir and I peeked around him at the white mixture he was beating in some kind of two-layered pot.

"What is that thing?"

"It's a double boiler. You have to mix this frosting over heat."

"Jeez, that cake is a lot of work."

"It is. But it's worth it."

"Good things always are." Setting my coffee cup on the island, I picked up my phone and noticed I had a text from my real estate agent. "Ooh, we can see the house at ten forty-five," I told him, raising my voice to be heard over the noise at the stove.

"Perfect. That will give me time to frost the cake and cook you breakfast before we go. Still like bacon and eggs?"

"I like bacon and anything. But don't feel like you have to make a big meal. We might be a little rushed, and I still need to take a shower."

"I do too."

"Really? You look like you already took one. OK, well what about if I get in now, you finish the frosting, then you can shower, and we can just grab a bagel somewhere on our way to the house?"

"I've got a better idea. I'll finish this, and while it cools, I'll make breakfast. We can shower together, saving time *and* conserving water, and I'll frost the cake while you dry your hair." He flashed me a grin over his shoulder. "How does that sound?"

I laughed, my stomach turning somersaults at the idea of a shower together. *So it's still on for today.* "Resourceful and environmentally conscious. Very impressive."

He nodded, turning off the heat under the pan. "Babe, I'm a fucking model of efficiency."

Despite all the sex we'd had last night, I still hadn't seen Nick completely naked, a fact I realized when I stood staring at him through the glass door of his shower. The sight of him in there wetting his hair, eyes closed, the water running down his long, lean body, cascading over all his tattoos, dripping off his firm, round muscles, nearly brought me to my knees. Immediately I felt self-conscious of my soft curves, especially since I'd just eaten Nick's equivalent of the Grand Slam at Denny's. God, why did I have to eat that last slice of bacon? I knew I'd had enough but it was just sitting there in the pan, all lonely and crunchy and delicious. I couldn't walk away.

Nine days out of ten, I was perfectly happy with my body—I was healthy and shapely and felt beautiful in my skin. But on that tenth day, I suffered self-criticism just like all women do, no matter their size. Even Mia, who never struggled with weight, had things she disliked about her body.

"What are you doing?" Nick pushed open the glass door. "Get in here."

Flustered at being caught staring, I twisted my hands together in front of my stomach. "I'm being nervous."

He gave me an incredulous look. "About what?"

"About my body."

"For fuck's sake, Coco. You can't be serious. You have the most knockout body I've ever seen."

"But you've been around all those Hollywood types. Those girls are so skinny and—"

"Fake. Most of them are nothing but fake and I like real. I like curvy. I like you." He reached for my arm and pulled me into the shower. "Now come here." He moved so I could stand under the hot water and watched as I wet my hair. While my eyes were closed and my arms over my head, he lowered his mouth to one breast and brought his hand to the other. "I can't believe," he said between kisses that made my nipples stand at attention, "that you think I'd prefer any body in the world to yours." He lifted both breasts in his hands, sucking on one pebbled tip and then the other while I stretched languorously, reaching high above me, feeling lithe and desired.

He straightened, kissing his way up my neck and finding my mouth with his. As his wet body pressed close to mine, I felt his cock growing hard between us. Sheathing it in my hand, I let it slip through my fingers, nice and slow. His hands traveled down my sides, one coming to rest on my ass, the other reaching between my legs. I moaned as his fingers rubbed slow, wet circles on my clit, rising up on tiptoe and tightening my grip on his erection.

"God, that feels good," I said. "But I think we're supposed to be in here getting clean, not getting dirty."

"Mmm. First one. Then the other." He slipped a finger inside of me. "Dirty first."

I took his other hand and brought it to my mouth, slipping a finger between my lips and slowly dragging it out. "But it's my turn." I kissed his collarbone before moving down his chest, running my mouth over ink and muscle, brushing my lips down the ridges of his stomach and the trail of hair beneath his navel, kissing the points of his hip bones. Sinking to my knees on the tiles, I slid my tongue along the V lines on his lower abdomen—up one side, and down the other, my heart beating hard and fast in my chest.

"Oh my God." Nick's voice was deep and rusty. I smiled up at him, and he brushed some wet strands of hair off my face. He looked so good standing above me, dripping and hungry-eyed and breathing hard. "You're so fucking beautiful."

"You just like me on my knees." I vaguely remembered the fumbling blow jobs I used to give Nick in college, but they were usually over *really* quickly (Nick said that was his fault, not mine), and I was always a little tentative. Scared of hurting him with my teeth, of choking myself, of not doing it right. And it wasn't as if I thought myself an expert now, but I had learned a thing or two in the last few years, and I was eager to demonstrate my progress.

"I like you every way. But this is… Oh fuck." He put a

hand on the wall as I teased his cock with my tongue, making it dance in front of me. I ran my hands up the back of his legs, over his muscular calves and tight thighs. I squeezed his ass before dragging my nails around his hips and taking his solid flesh in both hands.

"Fuuuuuck." Nick swore again softly as I swirled my tongue over the tip, then licked around the sides. Murmuring softly, I ran my tongue up one long, hard side of his shaft and down the other, then from the thick-veined bottom all the way up to the velvety top, smiling when his cock jumped, as if it couldn't wait to get inside my mouth. "Coco," he pleaded.

Yes, beg me.

I eased the first couple inches between my lips, continuing to whirl my tongue around the tip before sucking gently.

"Yes. Jesus." Nick cupped my head with his other hand as I sucked him harder. "You're fucking amazing."

I slipped his cock from my mouth and grinned up at him. "I'm just getting started."

"Oh my God," he moaned when I slid him in deep, all the way to the back of my throat. Keeping him there, I used my hands. Firm, rhythmic pulls that had him pounding on the shower wall, his groans echoing off the tiles.

I looked up again, saw his eyes going even darker as he watched me rub my lips back and forth over the tip, then brush it across my cheek, down my throat, over my chin. "I like it when you hold my head," I said, my voice soft.

He threaded both hands into my wet hair, and I slid him to the back of my throat once more, hugging his hard length with my lips and tongue, sucking him hungrily. At first he just held my head steady, but as I took him deep again and again, he began to get rougher, thrusting into my mouth and pulling my head toward his body.

I moaned to let him know I liked it, and he cursed again and again, the words lashing from his lips between strangled breaths. His cock grew even harder in my mouth, and I could taste the salty sweetness dripping from it. He was close, but I still had a couple tricks left.

I reached between his legs, exploring, teasing, boldly stroking and sliding my fingers anywhere he'd let me. Nick's groans grew louder, his fists tightening in my hair. His legs trembled. "Fuck, Coco...I'm gonna come...so if you...where do you...*fuck*!"

I'd grabbed his ass with the other hand, letting him know I didn't want him to pull out like I used to in college. Back then he'd warn me and I'd finish him off with my hands, letting him come on my breasts or stomach or legs, and even though I'd love to watch him do that again for old time's sake, this time I wanted him to come with my mouth on him, the way he made me come with his mouth on me.

With one final thrust, Nick's hips stopped moving and he went rigid, but I kept my lips and tongue sliding over him, bringing my hand from his ass to his cock and jerking him into my mouth. Liquid warmth streamed to the back of my throat. I waited for his fingers to relax in my hair before taking my lips from him and swallowing. *There. See what you missed by leaving me?*

The thought came out of nowhere, surprising me with its cool resentment. Had it been in the back of my mind all along? That this was an opportunity to make him even sorrier for what he'd done?

Stop analyzing, Coco. It was a blow job, not a Great American Novel. You enjoyed it, he enjoyed it. The end.

Nick tipped my chin up. "You can't leave. I'm never letting you leave my shower."

I laughed, and he helped me to my feet. "You have to. In fact, we better hurry or we'll miss the appointment to see the house. This is a one-time deal, remember?"

He groaned. "You mean I will never experience this nirvana again? You *vixen*. I want to revisit the rules."

I shook my head. "Uh uh. No way. We are allowed to have our fun this weekend, but that's that. Got any shampoo?"

"Wait a minute." He caught me around the waist as I tried to reach past him to the bench where his arsenal of hair products was lined up. "You're not even going to let me return the favor? Like a good friend would?"

"You can wash my hair. How's that?"

His face fell. "It's not licking your pussy but I guess it will have to do. For *now*." Shooting me a look that said *later* would be another story, he picked up a bottle of shampoo. "OK. Turn around."

I loved getting my hair washed. Sometimes I made blowout appointments at the salon just for the mesmerizing, swoony feeling I got when someone else massaged my scalp, rubbed the suds through my hair, rinsed it with warm water, and then cool. I was half in love with the gay stylists' assistant at my salon just for the way he made me feel during the shampoo. As Nick's fingers on my head sent chills down my spine, I closed my eyes and moaned softly.

Behind me, Nick laughed. "That good, huh?"

"Yes. I'm pretty much in heaven right now."

"Me too. OK rinse." I turned and rinsed, and when I opened my eyes, Nick was ready with the conditioner.

"Wow, the full treatment."

He cocked a brow at me. "You want the full treatment? Because I'll give you the full treatment."

I rolled my eyes. "Nick. Focus."

But when his hands started lathering my limbs with shower gel that smelled herbal and clean, the scent that I'd caught on his skin last night, my body responded sexually to the sensory overload. It was too much—Nick's nakedness, his hands on me, the smell of summer and sex, the water streaming down our bodies, the taste of his kiss, the stroke of his tongue on mine...Before I knew it, I was sitting on the bench with my knees open, Nick's tongue dancing over my clit, his fingers pinching my taut nipples.

"Oh my God!" I leaned back against the tile wall. "It feels so good—you're just so good—you're spoiling me."

"I'm just trying to convince you never to leave my shower. And my strategy involves an orgasm." Nick dropped soft kisses onto my inner thighs and the soft, wet warmth at my center before taking the swollen little bud in his mouth. Sucking softly at first, and then harder, making my toes point, and my fingers curl beneath my palms

"You're doing…a good job…Fuck…Yes!" My head dropped back as the orgasm bloomed at my center and unfurled in rippling waves throughout my body. As my breathing slowed, Nick's hands slid to my waist and he kissed one knee. "Was that a yes, you'll be my shower prisoner?"

"Oh my God." Sighing, I ran my hands through his hair. My fingers were totally pruning up. "It's tempting, but I'd miss your cooking."

He nodded. "I'd miss food too. OK, how about if you just stayed in my apartment all the time?" Helping me to my feet, he turned off the water before opening the door and reaching for a stack of huge, fluffy white towels on the sink.

I pretended to consider it as he handed me the first towel and reached for a second. "I don't think so. I have to go to a wedding in two weeks. Mia would probably be angry if I skipped it in favor of sex."

"Hmmm. That *is* a problem." He dried himself off, stepped from the shower, and slung the towel low around his hips. Gah, that was hot—why was that so hot? Was it the way the towel hugged his ass? The way I could see the top of the V lines in front? The naked chest and arms? Whatever it was, I almost wavered in my resolve not to consider giving him another chance.

Almost.

"Sorry, babe. You asked for two days, I'm giving you two days." Stepping onto the rug, I dried my arms and legs before wrapping the towel around my midsection. "I said no talking about the past, and no talking about the future, and I meant it."

"You said no sex, too." Nick gave me a meaningful look in the mirror.

I struggled to think up an answer that would absolve me of breaking my own rule. "I know, but…sex is different."

"Different how?"

I bit my lip. How could I explain that somehow having sex was safer than talking? That offering myself emotionally would be far riskier than offering myself physically? That this whole arrangement was becoming problematic, because the more fun we had together, the more tempted I was to forgive him and try again? But I couldn't tell if he was just playing me with all the sweet gestures and stay-with-me stuff. The last time I trusted him, he'd crushed me.

When I spoke, my tone was harsher than I intended. "It just is. I'm sure you're used to getting exactly what you want from people these days, but I can't offer you anything more than this. Take it or leave it."

I went to walk out of the bathroom, but he grabbed my arm. "Hey. Don't get mad. I'll take it, OK?" Then the asshole lifted my hand to his lips and kissed the back of it. "I'll take it."

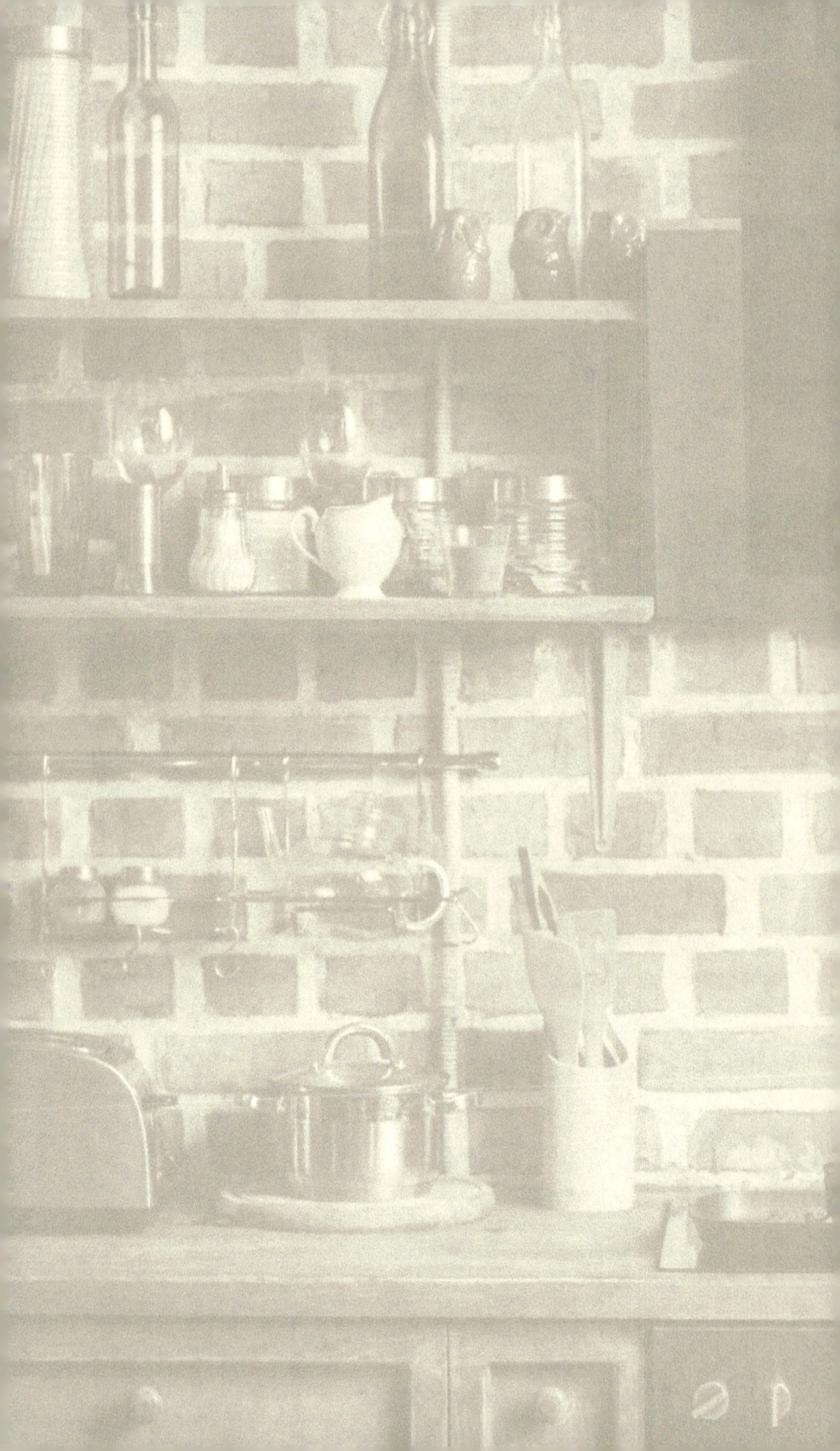

Chapter Thirteen

We dressed in silence. I chose one of my sundresses, gray cotton eyelet with a full skirt and camisole straps, while Nick put on jeans and a red t-shirt. While he frosted the cake downstairs, I blew out my hair and put it up into a ponytail since I wanted to take my convertible. I went light on the makeup and repacked everything I'd taken out of my suitcase. Sinking down on the bed to buckle my red sandals, I looked around, wondering if it was the last time I'd ever see this bedroom. It seemed likely, unless I reconsidered my position, which I wasn't prepared to do. Running my hand over the spread, I wondered who the next girl would be to sleep in this bed. The thought hit me like a jab to the gut.

I felt nauseated for a minute, until I reminded myself that in less than an hour I'd be walking through the front door of my dream house—I didn't need to get sad about not being in this room again. Soon I'd have more rooms than I'd know what to do with, and they'd all need my time and attention. There would be no sitting around moping about Nick, his bedroom, or his bedmates.

The house, the house, the house.

I'd think about that. I'd be happy about that.

Bounding down the steps, I resolved to be in a better mood. I crossed the room, set my suitcase by the door, and smiled at Nick, who was just putting the white-frosted cake into a small cooler. "That looks good."

"Thanks. Hope it travels OK." He snapped the lid in place and looked at me. "You look pretty."

"Thank you. Ready to go?"

"Yes. Let me throw a couple things in a bag, and we're off."

While he was upstairs, I put away the Scrabble game, rinsed the breakfast dishes and utensils he'd used frosting the cake, and put them all in the dishwasher. I was just turning it on when he came down, a small duffel bag over one shoulder.

He took the cooler from the island, tucking it under one arm. "You don't have to do that."

"I don't mind. It's the least I can do, since you cooked breakfast for me."

He switched off all the lights and dug his keys from his pocket. "That was my pleasure, as is seeing you in my kitchen. I love how domestic you are now. Shall we go?"

I nodded, walking briskly, picking up my suitcase and vowing not to look back at Nick's apartment before the door slammed behind me.

"Hey, this is fun, going on a little trip like this," Nick said, following me down the hall. "It's like we're married or something."

I shot him a murderous look over one shoulder, wishing he didn't look so hot in those aviator sunglasses.

"Can I carry your suitcase for you, honey?"

"No. I've got it, thanks." Eyes ahead, I strode toward the elevators.

An older woman got on the elevator at the tenth floor and smiled at us. "What a beautiful couple you are."

"Thanks," Nick said at the exact same time I said, "We're not a couple."

We glared at each other, and the woman remained silent the rest of the way down.

"I thought it might be fun to take my car," I suggested as we entered the parking garage.

"Why?"

"Well, it's a convertible. Don't you think that would be fun?"

He looked at me. "My truck wouldn't be fun?"

"Your what?" I squawked. "I mean…what do you drive now, another truck?" I tried not to sound snotty about it. Lots of trucks were perfectly nice.

"You know. My pickup. Still got plenty of good years left."

I stumbled slightly. "You still have that same truck?"

"Not good enough for you?" He was testing me. "You always hated it, didn't you?"

"I didn't hate it—I just…" I sighed heavily. "It's fine. The truck will be fine."

"Good."

I followed him up a row of cars and looked around for the big honking heap he called a truck, but I didn't see it. I was about to ask where it was when Nick went over to a car that was covered with a giant beige cloth.

"What is this?" There was no way his old pickup truck was under that cover.

Nick put down his bag, setting the cooler alongside it. Then he began pulling the cover off, revealing a shiny red vintage car with a soft top.

I gasped. "*That's* your car?"

Nick laughed. "It's not the one I drive every day, but I thought it would be fun to take it to Noni's. You like it?"

"Yes!" I ran one hand along its curvy side, admiring the whitewall tires. "It's beautiful. What is it?"

Nick opened the trunk. "A 1954 Mercury Monterey."

"It's a convertible too?" I swept my fingers along the cloth top.

"Yep." He put the beige cover in the trunk and reached for my suitcase. "Is it nice enough for you?"

I handed it over and smacked his shoulder. "You told me you still had your truck!"

He grinned, adding his bag to the trunk before closing it. "And you believed me."

"Well, my God, you adored that stupid thing. Did you actually get rid of it?"

"Sadly, yes." Nick came around and opened the passenger door for me before opening the driver's side and setting the cooler on the floor in the back seat. I slid in across the fabric-and-leather front seat, marveling at how roomy it was, how big the steering wheel, how shiny the dash.

I felt like a kid riding the ferris wheel for the first time—my insides were jumping with excitement. Nick got in and started the engine, then unhooked the lever connecting the top to the windshield on his side. "I've got this one," I told him, unlatching the lever on my side.

Nick put the top down, which folded behind the back seat much like it did on my VW, and got out to fasten the cover over it. A few minutes later, we were on our way.

It was hard to keep a smile off my face as we pulled out into the July morning sunshine. I tipped my head back and listened to the staticky sound of AM radio and the loud thrum of the engine as we drove toward Indian Village, delighted with all the stares we got from people on the street or in other cars. Some waved at us, some just smiled, but it was easy to see that the sight of a beautifully restored classic car cruising down Jefferson made people happy.

I was happy too.

About fifteen minutes later we turned onto Iroquois, and nerves mingled with my exhilaration. I twisted my hands together, glancing at Nick. Would he think I was nuts? What if he reacted just like I thought my parents would? What if he told me there was no way in hell a girl like me should buy such a big old thing that needed so much work? Maybe I shouldn't have brought him here.

Immediately I was annoyed with myself—why did I care so much what he thought?

"Is it that one?" he asked as we neared it. "The one with the sign?"

"Yes." My agent's black Audi was parked on the street. "You can pull in the driveway. No one lives here."

Nick pulled into the drive, and we got out. Linda, my agent, glided over to us. She was tall and thin with dark skin and wide-set brown eyes, and always dressed in impeccable suits with matching heels. "Coco." She offered her hand. "Good morning."

"Morning, Linda. This is my friend, Nick Lupo." She took his hand too, tilting her head thoughtfully.

"Are you the Burger Bar Nick Lupo?"

He nodded.

"I love that place!" She shook his hand enthusiastically. "This is so exciting." Her eyes traveled from Nick to me and back again. "And how do you know Coco?"

Nick and I exchanged glances. "From college," I said. "We met at Michigan State. Shall we go in?"

Linda unlocked the box on the side door but insisted we go in through the front. "I'll meet you there. It's a much more impressive entrance." I was glad, since the side door led into the kitchen, which was probably the area in the worst shape.

"What year was this built?" Nick asked as we approached

the front door. He tipped his head back to take in the peeling gray-blue paint on the shingles, the flaking white trim. I hoped he'd see the possibilities and not just the disrepair.

"Nineteen-oh-two, I think? Linda mentioned that Albert Kahn might have designed it. And look—it's on a double lot. It has a nice, deep yard too. It was on the Home and Garden Tour a few years back." I chirped away, nervous on many levels.

But when Linda pulled the front door open, Nick took my hand and squeezed it briefly before going in. "It's beautiful. I'm excited to see the inside."

It sounds insane, but walking through the house with Nick at my side, I was reminded of the time I took a pregnancy test in college. We discovered that the condom broke one night, and two weeks later, my period was late. After I peed on the stick and brought it out, Nick and I stared at the stupid thing for the longest minute of our life, his hand gently rubbing my back. I remember how I kept glancing over at him to try to figure out what he was thinking. He said no matter what the outcome was, we'd be fine, but I wanted to know how he *felt*. Was he scared? Was he mad at himself? Was he thinking that we'd ruined our lives? Just like then, his expression today gave nothing away, and he moved through the rooms with a maddeningly calm demeanor.

(The test was negative, although Nick eventually admitted he was nervous as hell but didn't want me to know it. When I asked if he thought we'd come close to ruining our lives, he gave me a strange look and said, "Of course not." However, I noticed he bought a different brand of condoms after that.)

But underneath my anxiety, that *feeling* that I got the first time I walked through the house was back. In fact, it was even stronger. I could actually see myself here...hanging new wallpaper in the dining room, painting the master bedroom walls, ripping out linoleum in the kitchen.

And I saw Nick too.

Tearing off the old kitchen cabinets, laying new tile for the backsplash, advising me on the layout of my sink, fridge, and stove. But I imagined him not only in the kitchen—I saw him laying new bricks in the patio out back, carrying heavy furniture up the stairs, cracking open a beer and wiping the sweat from his forehead with the top of his wrist.

Catching me behind the waist on the staircase.

Setting me on the counter in the butler's pantry.

Crawling up my body, my hands threading through his hair, in a king-size bed in the master bedroom, moonlight streaming through the windows.

I saw it so vividly it was as if the wind was knocked out of me, and I paused in the doorway to the bedroom, unable to move.

"You OK, Coco?" Nick put a hand on my shoulder.

"What? I'm fine."

"Oh, well, you're sort of frozen there, and I'd like to see the master bedroom."

"Right. Sorry." I stepped aside so he could enter the room, flustered and hot in the face.

And in the pants.

When we'd gone into every room, peeked in the dank basement and admired the deep, wide backyard with its overgrown grapevines and a huge weeping willow, I thanked Linda and told her I'd be in touch.

"All right, sounds good, honey. Like I said, I heard from another agent that his clients—she's a bigwig at GM, just transferred, been living in corporate housing with four kids—are planning to make an offer this week, so just let me know."

"OK. I will." We got into the Mercury, and I looked up at the house, a dose of reality sinking in. This week? Was I nuts? That meant I had to ask my parents for money within a day or so…was I up for that, considering I'd be dealing with Angelina too?

And why was Nick so quiet?

"You think I'm crazy," I said as he turned on the engine.

"Not at all. It's a beautiful house."

"Then what? You're too quiet."

He looked at the house. "I'm just...taking it all in, that's all. I'm thinking."

"Could you think out loud, please? I need some advice. Mia thinks it's ludicrous."

He shrugged. "It's not her decision."

"I know, but I don't want to make a huge mistake. I'm trying to be responsible...ish."

"Why do you want such a big place? Are you planning on having a family?"

The question took me by surprise, and annoyed me a little. What did that have to do with anything? "I don't know. No, not right now. Can't a single woman buy her own big house?"

"Sure she can. I was just curious. Because I'm positive you could find a historical fixer-upper that's not so demanding of your bank account or your time."

I sighed, toying with my ponytail. "What else do I have to do with my time? I mean, I'm busy with work, but I need something outside of that, you know? And I have my friends, but even that's changing."

Nick looked at me. "How so?"

"Mia's getting married, and she and Lucas have a new house. I bet they have kids soon too."

"That doesn't mean she won't be your friend, Coco."

"I know that, but she'll be busy with her grown up life. And Erin quit her teaching job to open a dance studio like she always wanted to. She'll be busy fixing up the space and launching a business—that's *her* grown up life." I threw my hands up. "And I've got nothing grown up! I live with my parents, for fuck's sake!"

He patted my leg. "That's temporary."

"Doesn't feel that way."

"You know what? You are grown up. Because the Coco I

used to know would have already asked her parents for the money. Honestly, that's what shocks me the most about all this."

I was half-pissed, half-flattered at the half-compliment. Sighing, I looked away from the house. "Let's go. This is stupid. I can't afford that house. I can't even afford the down payment."

"How much do you need?"

"About thirty grand."

Nick whistled. "That's a good chunk of change."

"Tell me about it. That's why I needed you to do Angelina's party so badly. I think I'll get at least ten grand out of it, and then I was thinking I could ask my parents for the rest." I took a deep breath and blew it out. "But I think they'll be a harder sell than you were."

Nick smiled as he put the car in reverse and backed out of the driveway. "I didn't give you enough trouble, did I?"

I eyed him sideways. "Making me spend the weekend with you isn't trouble?"

"Is it troubling you?"

"No. Not at all." I shifted my gaze to his lap, and he laughed.

"You're such a bad liar, Coco. Some things never change."

I slapped his shoulder. "Fine! You want the truth? Yes, it's troubling me," I admitted. "It's troubling me because I'm having fun with you and it makes me think about things I shouldn't."

Nick braked at a stop sign and looked at me. "What kind of things?"

I stared straight ahead. *Shut up shut up shut up.* "I don't want to talk about it."

"Why not?"

"Because that's not what this weekend is for."

We sat in silence a moment. "I'll give you the money, Coco."

"What?" I snapped my head toward him so fast, something popped in my neck.

"I'll give you the other twenty grand."

"I don't want your money!"

"You need it. That's why you came to me, isn't it? Because you need money?"

"No! You're twisting the whole thing into something it isn't! I came to you because a client requested you, not because I need your money, Nick. I told you—I want to do this on my own."

He shrugged. "Think of it as a loan, then."

"A loan?"

"Yes. That way you don't have to ask your parents for anything. I'll even charge you interest if you want."

Could I? Could I, *really*? It was one of those moments in life where I wanted a pause button so I could powwow with Mia and Erin before giving an answer. I had that feeling in my gut, the dessert tray feeling, like what I wanted was right there in front of me, and all I had to do was take it. But the thing was, I knew what Erin and Mia would say.

Erin: This is a Very Bad Idea.

Mia: Five Reasons Why You Should Not Take His Money…

They'd never tell me not to order dessert, but taking money from an ex seemed like a clear-cut no.

"I don't know, Nick. It doesn't seem right."

He put a hand on my leg. "I'm investing in a friend. And in a historic home. In a neighborhood and a city I love."

Damn. He was hot *and* he knew how to spin things. I chewed on my lower lip.

Putting the car in park, he shifted on the seat to face me, checking behind us to make sure there wasn't a car waiting for us to move forward. "Listen. You think I wanted to be on Lick My Plate? I didn't. It's a ridiculous show with very little to do with real cooking, and I knew my credibility would take a hit. But I couldn't get backing from investors to open a space in Detroit without putting my name out there a little. So I gritted my teeth and did it, and it paid off."

"That's different," I argued.

"No, it isn't. You don't want to borrow money from me because of your pride. I get it. But unless you want your dream house to go to someone else, or you want to ask Mom and Dad for the money and deal with all their opinions, you should just grit your teeth and do it. Take it."

"It's a lot of money," I said quietly. Was he doing this because he felt guilty about what he'd done to me seven years ago? Or did he really want to invest in me?

"I can afford it. Look, I'm not a millionaire or anything, but I won some prize money and have several endorsements. And you'll pay it back—we'll work out a payment schedule. We can even involve my lawyer if it makes you feel better. Then it's totally official."

I swallowed, gulping back the yes that was dying to escape my throat. For once in my life, I was not going to jump too soon and do the wrong thing. "No. Thank you, but no…I really want to do this on my own if I can."

"OK. I won't pressure you about it. The offer's on the table."

"Thanks."

"You're welcome." He put the car in drive. "And for what it's worth, I don't think you're crazy. The house does need some renovating, and I think they should come down in price, but it's a beautiful old place. I totally see you in it."

Smiling, I slipped my sunglasses on as we pulled onto Jefferson, wondering if he saw himself in it, too.

Fucking me in the butler's pantry, perhaps.

But I thought it best not to ask.

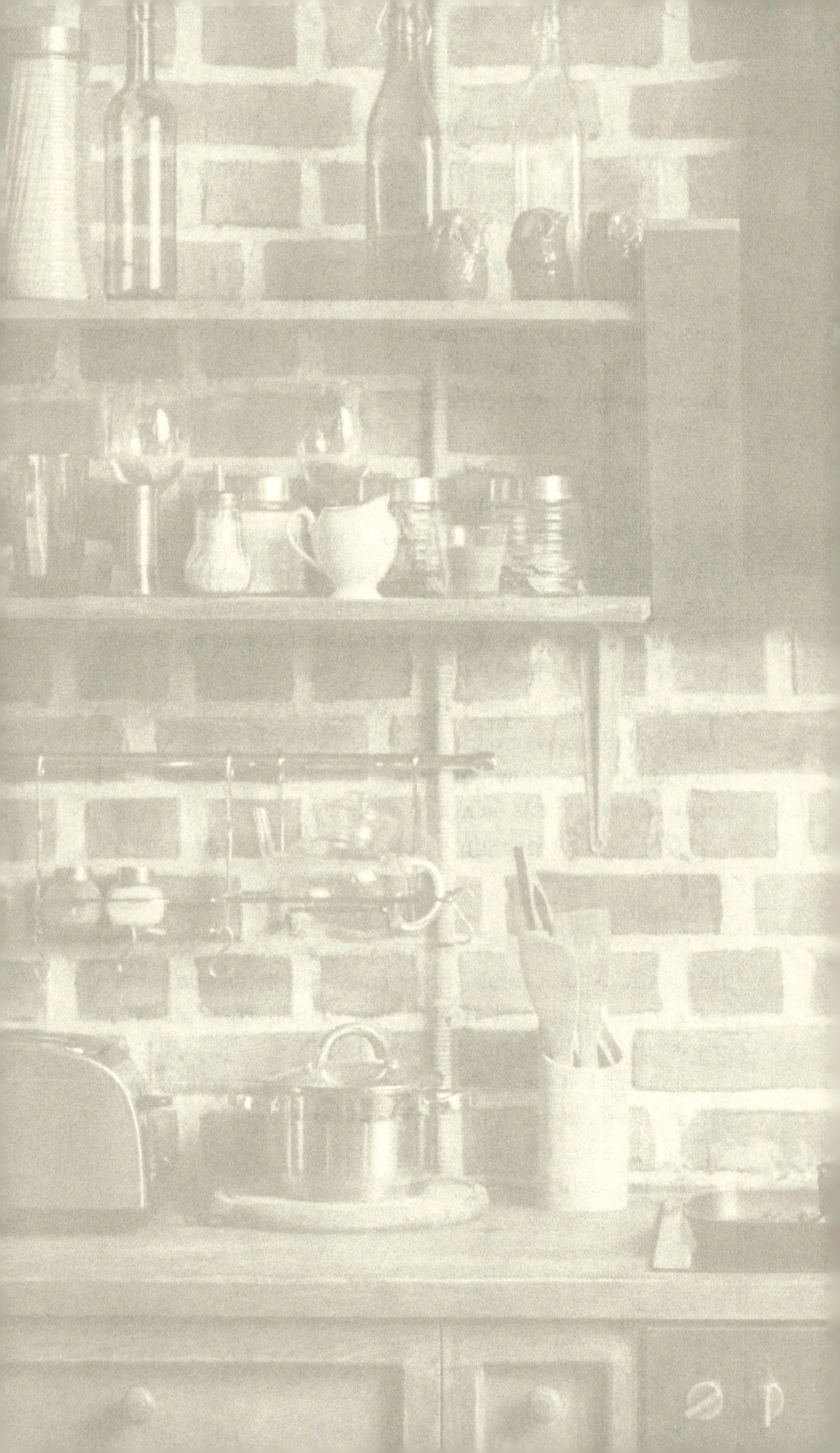

Chapter Fourteen

We didn't talk at all on the ride to the farm, mostly because once we got on the interstate, it was too noisy with the top down. But once we exited I-75 and got on smaller highways and then country roads, the ride was quieter.

It had been so long since I'd driven through a rural area—I lived in the suburbs, worked in the city, and when I traveled, I usually flew somewhere urban and outside of Michigan, like Chicago or New York. I'd forgotten how pretty and restful the Midwestern countryside was on a clear summer day, everything warm and golden. I loved the old red barns, the solid little brick farmhouses, the Victorians with their lacy trim and old-fashioned front porches. The neat green rows of beans and cabbage, thick fields of sweet corn and sugar beets, huge cylinders of hay dotting the flat, still landscape. Horses and cows grazed in paddocks fenced with railroad ties, and occasionally I'd see children on swings hanging from big old trees or jumping on trampolines in their yards.

And of course, there were orchards. Would I ever be able to pass an apple orchard without feeling like my panties might melt? Tipping my head back against the seat, I closed my eyes and let the sun warm my face as memories warmed by body. Beside me, Nick cleared his throat. Was he thinking about it, too?

"I'm hungry," he announced.

I almost laughed. He was thinking about food, not sex. I picked up my head. "Are you?"

"Yes. Want to have a picnic?"

"Sure. Sounds like fun."

"OK. There's a little country store up here. We'll buy some picnic food, and then I know the perfect spot to go eat."

Of course he did. He knew the perfect way to do everything. I couldn't stop thinking about his offer. The way he'd described it, sort of like a business loan, appealed to me, but was I just rationalizing it because I wanted the house so badly? What if repairs ate up all my money and I couldn't pay him back? Wouldn't it be easier to say to my parents, *Hey I'm a little short this month*, than it would be to face Nick—or God forbid, his lawyer—and have to say the same?

I knew he would offer a low interest rate and give me a fair payment schedule, but still...this kept him in my life. I'd be tied to him until I paid off the debt. Could I handle that? Clearly he didn't have a problem doing business with his ex-wife, and maybe he saw this as a way to make amends for what he'd done. Atonement.

Was I prepared to offer that?

Or maybe he got a kick out of being in the position to lend me money after all the time he spent feeling bad about himself because I grew up wealthy and he hadn't. Maybe it was an ego boost. That was possible.

I fretted about it as he turned off the road into the dirt parking lot of a store housed in a little old barn. I wanted the money, but I didn't want to feel icky about it. At least, I didn't want to feel ickier than if I took my parents' money.

Ugh, there was no good way to go about this. Bottom line was, I couldn't afford the house. I should just let it go.

"Want to come in?" Nick turned off the car and opened his door.

"No. I'll wait here. I have to check my messages anyway. Go on, you can choose lunch. I trust you."

"Dangerous words, cupcake."

I returned his smile, but I felt a little like crying.

God, why couldn't I have fallen in love with something else, something small and reasonable? Something new, perhaps, that didn't need so much work? Why did I have to want something old and broken down...something I couldn't have?

While Nick was in the store, I checked my text and messages. Erin had texted, wanting to know how things were going, and Mia had sent me a long list of things she was freaking out about. I messaged Erin back that I was fine and told Mia to relax, for the millionth time. Her wedding would be perfect. I said I was out shopping for the day but if she wanted help, I'd be around tomorrow and Monday. Secretly I hoped she wouldn't, though. One look at me and she'd *know* something was up.

My mother had left a voicemail, letting me know she and my father had decided to go up to their place in Harbor Springs for the week and could I please remember it was trash day on Thursday and not to leave the air conditioning lower than 73 when I went to work in the morning and Sitty had an eye doctor appointment on Tuesday afternoon, would I be available to take her?

The woman exhausted me without even being in the room. I texted back that I'd follow all instructions and yes, I could take Sitty to the appointment.

I had one more voicemail—from Angelina.

"Coco, could you please call me back right away? Thanks."

Steeling myself for another conversation with her, I returned her call.

"Hello?"

"Hi Angelina. It's Coco."

"Oh, hey. I keep thinking about the whole theme thing."

"I thought we settled this. It's going to be beautiful as planned, I promise."

"I know, but it seems a little tame, you know? I came up with some ideas and narrowed it down to two—The Great Gatsby or True Blood."

My stomach dropped. "Um—"

"I think I'm leaning toward Gatsby though, because of the fun costumes. I'm like eighty, forty on it."

My head throbbed. "That doesn't even add up to one hundred percent."

"I'm not a hundred percent on anything," she said, like it was obvious.

Oh my God. "Angelina, I'm away for the weekend. Let's talk again Monday, OK?"

"OK. I'll keep thinking about it."

"You do that. Bye." I ended the call before she could say anything else and turned my phone off.

A moment later Nick came out of the store with a brown paper bag tucked under one arm and a quilt hanging over the other one. "Here's our lunch," he said, handing me the bag, "and our four hundred dollar picnic blanket." He tossed the quilt in the back seat and slid behind the wheel.

My jaw dropped. "Four hundred dollars!"

He nodded happily. "It's Amish."

I glanced back at the brightly colored patchwork quilt. "I don't think you're supposed to use those as picnic blankets."

"Hey, listen." He tapped me on the nose. "I only have so

many hours left to impress you. Show you how far I've come in life." He started the car and the engine roared loudly.

About twenty minutes later, he turned onto an old gravel road sandwiched between a cornfield on the left and a forest on the right. A clearing appeared in the trees about two hundred feet down. At first glance it looked like a grassy yard, surrounded by forest on three sides, like maybe a house had once stood there. But when Nick pulled over to the side of the road to park, I saw a little cemetery in one corner of the clearing.

"What is this place?" I glanced around. Not a house or barn or car in sight. Quiet but for the chirp of crickets and the wind in the trees.

"Noni thinks at one time there may have been a little church here. My grandparents' farm is just up the road and we used to go exploring through the woods sometimes. One day my brothers and I wandered farther than usual and came across this place."

I got out of the car, carrying the grocery bag in my arm, leaving my purse and phone in the car. It was so serene and pretty here, and it felt so removed from the noise and hustle of my usual life, I didn't want any distractions from what was right in front of me. Nick reached into the back for the quilt and followed me to a shady spot near the corner where perhaps only twenty old headstones rose from the ground, some tilted and toppling, weeds and wildflowers growing up around them.

I stopped and turned around. "This OK?"

"Sure." He spread the quilt on the ground and reached for the grocery bag.

After handing it over, I walked among the markers, curious about whose forgotten graves were here. *Not a bad place to rest*, I mused, taking in the picturesque setting, but it was clear no one had tended to this place in quite some time. While Nick unpacked our picnic, I examined the stones, trying to read names and dates etched into limestone and marble that had eroded over time. Most were small and rectangular, but there were a few larger monuments marked with crosses at the top. From what I could tell, the majority of people here had died between the eighteen forties and the early twentieth century. The names were German for the most part, but there were a few French and Irish surnames as well.

"Anyone you know?" called Nick.

Leaning over, I ran my fingers across the face of a stone marking the grave of a young woman, just twenty-one when she died. A cool breeze fluttered along the back of my neck. "No. Just curious about them, that's all. I'm a history nerd, can't help it."

"I don't mind. But lunch looks pretty good here."

Straightening, I walked back to the quilt and dropped to my knees. "It does look good." Nick had bought two sandwiches made with thick slices of rustic country bread and layered with turkey and cheese and vegetables, a jar of pickles, a container of blackberries, a bag of potato chips, and two bottles of water.

We ate in companionable silence, broken only by the crunch of a pickle or chip, the song of birds in the trees, and the occasional buzz of a fly interested in our lunch.

When I was done, I lay on my back on the blanket, full and warm. A little sunlight filtered through the branches of the birch tree overhead, turning its leaves from green to silver as they fluttered in the breeze. Closing my eyes, I thought about how different life would have been for a woman my age living around here a hundred years ago. At twenty-eight, I'd probably have been married with a whole bunch of kids—if I survived the birth of them all. I wondered about the young woman whose stone I'd seen and hoped she'd had at least some happiness in life.

"You sleeping?"

I propped myself up on my elbows. "No. Just trying to imagine life as a farm wife a hundred years ago."

He smiled. "Why?"

"There's a grave over there of a woman who was only twenty-one when she died." I glanced over my shoulder toward her headstone. "Made me think about her life. What did she get the chance to do? What were her greatest joys? Her biggest regrets?"

Nick nodded and popped a blackberry in his mouth. "What do you think she died of?"

"Probably childbirth."

"Right." A breeze ruffled my dress up around my hips. Nick reached over and smoothed it down over my thighs, leaving his hand there. "You want kids someday?"

"Maybe. What about you?"

"Definitely."

His certainty surprised me. In college, neither of us had been sure. "Oh?"

"Yeah. I loved growing up in a full house. We didn't have a lot of money, but we had a lot of fun." He smiled. "Drove my mother crazy. She used to yell herself hoarse. God, we were so bad. She used to chase us around with a broom and whack our butts with it if she caught us."

I laughed. "Really? I never knew that."

"Oh yeah. Why do you think I'm such a fast runner? Years of practice saving my ass from her damn broom." He stretched out on his side, head in his hand. "I can still see her with that thing. It was one of those old-fashioned ones with a wooden handle and red stitching and the straw stuff all different lengths."

"And these memories make you want children?" I asked dubiously.

"Sure. It was a noisy life, but we were never bored." He was quiet a moment, during which I lay back and closed my eyes again. "Do you think," he went on, "if we'd stayed together, we'd have kids by now?"

I had to smile. "Are you picturing me going at them with a broom?"

"Honestly, yeah." He laughed.

"Are they boys or girls?"

"Hmm. One of each. No—two of each."

My eyes popped open and I propped myself up again. "*Four* kids? I'm only twenty-eight!"

"But we've been married seven years already. And maybe we have twins."

"Lord have mercy. There goes my girlish figure."

"No, no, your body is still perfect. I can't keep my hands off you, which is why we have so many kids." Slowly he trailed a hand up my leg, over my hip, between my breasts. My nipples puckered as his fingers traced the neckline of my dress, brushing the tops of my breasts. Involuntarily, my lungs filled with fresh air, my chest rising toward his touch. He covered one full breast with his palm, kneading gently, watching his hand on me. Then he reached under my chin, tilting my face toward him. "I'm still crazy about you."

"Nick." This was dangerous territory.

Leaning over, he kissed me gently, sweetly, his lips as soft as the summer wind across my skin. "I'm still crazy about you," he repeated, whispering against my mouth.

"No more talking." I rolled over, pushing him onto his back so that I was lying on top of him. His hands moved over my ass, squeezing and pulling me tighter to him. I felt the hardness beneath his jeans and brought my knees astride his hips, freeing my dress so it wasn't caught between us. Opening my lips, I braced myself on my hands above his shoulders and sought his tongue with mine while my hips rocked in a slow, sensual rhythm.

He moaned, and I felt him swelling further beneath me. I moved a little faster, grinding hard against the bulge in his pants, wondering if it was against God or nature to have sex in a cemetery where there may or may not have been a church, especially with a man you'd divorced. But he felt so good between my legs—my lower body ached to slide down onto his cock, take control, watch him come undone beneath me.

"You think it's wrong to do it right here?" I rubbed my lips back and forth on his before kissing my way to that spot beneath his ear that drove him crazy. I licked it before pressing my mouth to his warm wet skin, smiling when I felt his body shiver.

"No, I don't think it's wrong. I think it's the rightest thing we could possibly do right now. It's all kinds of right." His hands slid under my dress and pulled at my underwear. "But let's hurry—this road isn't busy, but it isn't always this deserted either."

No argument here.

I slipped one leg from my panties, leaving them looped around the other thigh. Glancing over my shoulder at the road—no sign of anyone—I undid his jeans and took his cock in my hand. Rising up on my knees, I positioned the tip between my legs before sinking down on him, inch by mind-blowing inch. Nick watched me with a look of pure rapture on his face.

"Jesus," he breathed, grabbing my hips. "You're so beautiful."

"And so wet." I smiled, circling my hips a few times, arching my back to feel pressure where I wanted it. I knew we couldn't take our time, but I wanted to savor this moment a little—the sweet summer air, Nick's hot, hard body between my thighs; his thick fullness within me; even the secret thrill of getting caught. I'd never had sex outside in the daylight. It was delightfully liberating. I slid my palms beneath his shirt, flattened them on his torso. Fuck, he was just so gorgeous—I could look at that mouth all day. And those arms—my eyes skimmed over his muscular, tattooed forearms to the strong wrists at my hips. Guided by Nick's hands, I moved my body over his, faster and faster, the tension pulling tight between us.

"Yes," he growled, his eyes closing, his head dropping back. "Fuck yes. I'm gonna come...so hard..."

But I came first, my insides clenching his cock like a vise before the tension eased in beautiful, flowing contractions that had me sighing one long, drawn-out note. Just as my orgasm finished, Nick's began, and I felt his body stiffen and shudder, heard his low moan of blissful relief. *My God, we're so good together. Why does it have to be so good?*

Collapsing on his chest, I buried my face in his neck, my chest rising and falling in time with his.

His hands slid up my back. "Oh my God. I can't even think. What are we doing?"

I giggled. "Being friends?"

"Oh, right. Friends."

I knew I should get up, clean up, wise up. But it was just so peaceful and comfortable, lying there on his chest, our bodies still connected, Nick's hands rubbing my back.

"Coco. I have to tell you something."

I sat up and smiled at him, squeezed his cock with my core muscles. "Let me guess. Your dick is really fucking happy right now."

"No." He shook his head, his expression serious. "I just realized something."

"What?"

"I'm still in love with you."

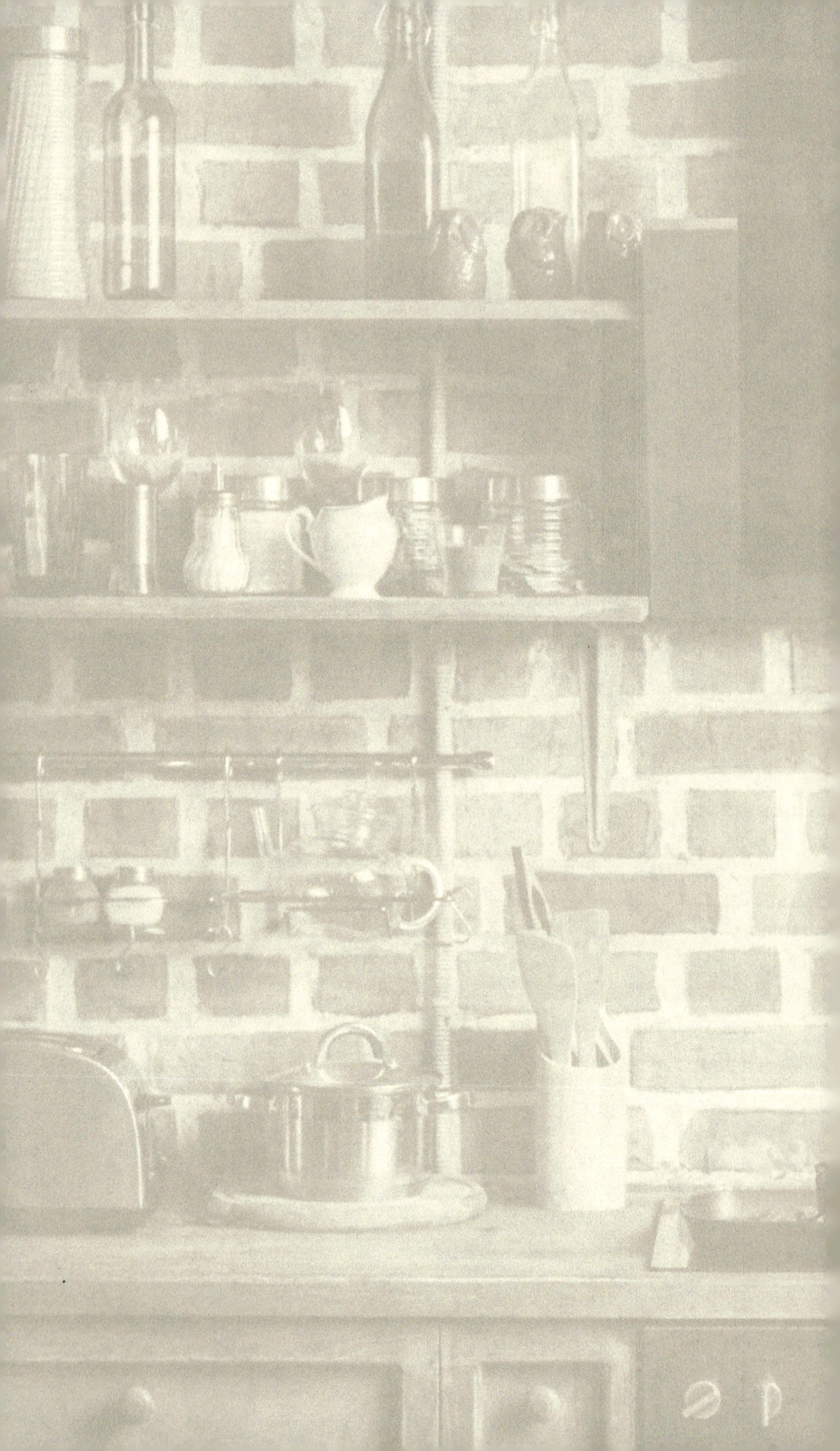

Chapter Fifteen

"Let me up." I tried to get off him, but his hands pinned me to his body.

"No. I want to talk about this. About us."

"Well, I don't. And if you can't separate sex from love, then we're eliminating sex from the equation. We should have done that already."

"These are my feelings, not a math problem."

"Fine." I looked around, threw up a hand. "I like how you bring me all the way out here to the country where I can't escape to break the rules."

"You never said I couldn't talk about my feelings."

Again I tried to get off him, and this time he let me. Warmth trickled down my leg, and I hunted around for a napkin. If it got on my dress, I'd have to change. "Do we not have napkins?" I asked, agitated.

"I think I forgot to buy them. Use the blanket."

"The four hundred dollar Amish quilt?"

"OK, here." Grabbing his t-shirt behind his neck, he whipped it off and handed it to me. "Use this. I'll grab another shirt from the car."

I took the shirt and cleaned up with it, turning away from

him a little, and Nick packed up the trash and extra food. When I was done, I folded up the shirt and tugged my underwear back in place. I was sticky and still a bit wet, but it was better than nothing. "Are you ready to go?"

"No. I want to talk."

"Nick, I said *no*." I started to stand, but he grabbed my arm, his grip firm.

"Then let me talk. You can just listen."

"I don't want to listen."

"Are you shutting me out to punish me? Is that what this is about?" he demanded.

"No!" Wait, it wasn't, was it?

"Then what? Why won't you even listen to me? What are you so afraid of?"

I looked at him, fighting the urge to tell him the truth. I might have beaten it if he wasn't shirtless and I couldn't see the sheen of sweat on his chest or my name near his heart. Maybe I'd have won if his hair wasn't a little messy, or if I hadn't looked down at his wrists, that Shinola watch glinting in the sunlight. "It's a list a mile long."

He let go of my arm. "Starting with…"

"Starting with being afraid to hear your excuse for leaving me."

"It's not an excuse—nothing excuses what I did. It's just an explanation."

"Well, I don't want to hear it. It will only make me feel worse."

"Why would that be?"

"Because no matter what you say, the fact remains that you didn't love me enough to stay, Nick. You didn't even love me enough to say goodbye."

Nick closed his eyes and exhaled. "Go on. What else are you afraid of?"

"I don't trust you."

He met my eye. "I understand that. I hurt you deeply."

"You did. Many times, but especially the final time. So you can tell me you love me all you want, but it won't mean a thing to me. You said it then, too. You still broke my heart."

He set his lips in a grim line. "Is that everything?"

"I'm afraid of being hurt again, obviously. I don't want you to have that power over me. If I don't believe what you say, if I don't tell you how I'm feeling, if I don't even admit it to myself, then I can keep you from breaking my heart again."

"That's ridiculous, Coco. Just because you don't admit to a feeling doesn't make it vanish. Look, we said last night we were just going to be friends, I get it. But things are different now."

"It's been less than twenty-four hours!"

He put a hand on my leg. "But we have history. That has weight. It has meaning. And you of all people know that just because something is in the past doesn't mean it's dead and buried."

Oh, how I knew. I closed my eyes, feeling just how *alive* our feelings for each other were. But the fear was there, too. Would it ever go away? Would I ever kiss him goodbye in the morning and be absolutely certain that he'd be there in the evening? What if every time he walked out the door, I had that uneasy feeling he was leaving forever?

Then again, what if I never felt for anyone the things I felt for him now? What if my first love *was* supposed to be my last?

Give me a sign, I begged the universe. *Anything*. But the universe remained silent.

"What do you want from me?" My voice was small, retreating, just like my defenses.

"Right now, I just want you to say that we can talk about...things. Maybe the past, maybe the future, but I want to hear that you're at least open to the idea."

You will regret this, said common sense, but I heard my

voice say, "Fine. We can talk. But not right now, OK? I need some time to think things through."

"No problem. I'm ready when you are." He stood and reached down to help me up. "I mussed you," he said, smoothing a few stray hairs away from my face.

"It's OK. I think it was more the convertible than you. I'll redo it when we get to Noni's." We gathered up our things and folded the quilt. "You want to know something else that scares me?" I asked as we walked back to the car.

"What?"

"I liked your daydream about our alternate present a little too much."

He looked at me sideways, a smile hooking up one corner of his mouth. "Yeah? The one with the broom and four kids?"

"Yeah." I shook my head, as if I could rid it of such insanity. I didn't want his kids...did I? "What the hell is that?"

Nick pulled on a clean shirt from his bag and I discreetly traded my damp panties for a new pair before we left. On the short drive to the farm, we listened to the radio instead of talking to each other, and even though I was addled, I found myself humming along to a scratchy old Ella Fitzgerald tune. Everything about this day was telling me to relax and enjoy life, but I couldn't shake the nagging feeling that things weren't as perfect as they seemed. Was I just paranoid?

We turned off the road onto the winding drive leading to the big old white farmhouse. I hadn't been here in years, but little details about the place had memories swarming my mind like honeybees—the tire swing hanging from a huge old maple tree, the long front porch with its Adirondack chairs in need of a fresh coat of paint, the second floor window of the room I used to stay in, not far from the window of the room Nick used to sneak out of and come visit me in the night. My room had the creakiest bed on the planet. Nick said Noni couldn't hear a thing so we should just do it anyway, but I never could bring myself to have sex on that bed. (We did it on the floor instead.)

Beyond the house were barns and other outbuildings, and beyond those stretched fields of corn and the orchards. Somewhere out there was a small lake we used to swim in after a run. I wondered if Nick felt like running this afternoon—after the way I'd been eating, I sure could use one. Nick put the top up, and I latched the lever on my side before getting out.

"How about a run this afternoon?" I asked as we pulled our bags from the trunk.

"Did you bring your running stuff?" He looked at me, surprised, before leaning into the backseat to retrieve the cooler.

"Yeah, and my bathing suit. I remembered how we used to run here and then swim afterward. That was a lot of fun."

"It was." He shut the trunk. "I have my running stuff too. Let's say hi to Noni and then we'll go. Although," he added as we walked up the steps to the porch, "I didn't bring a bathing suit." He moved ahead of me to open the screen door and grinned over his shoulder. "Guess I'll have to swim naked."

"Swim *naked*! Who's that?"

I smiled at hearing Noni's voice again for the first time in years.

"Fuck, her new hearing aid. I forgot," Nick whispered as we stepped into the entrance hall. Time flowed backward as I breathed in the fresh-baked-pie meets dusty-antique-furniture smell of Noni's house and heard the squeak and slap of the wooden screen door closing behind me. I was nineteen again. Young, bursting with feelings for Nick, up for anything.

And fearless. Utterly fearless.

To the left of the stairs in front of us was the dining room, and to the right was the room Noni called her parlor. She sat in a rocker near the front window, a book on her lap.

"Hi, Noni. I brought you a birthday present. Remember Coco?"

She winked at me. "Coco? The lesbian girlfriend?"

"That's the one. Although she's not quite as lesbian as I'd like her to be. At least occasionally."

I slapped Nick on the shoulder. "Nick, for heaven's sake. Happy Birthday, Noni. I hope it's all right that Nick invited me along. I've missed visiting here."

Noni reached out one hand. "Give me a hand standing up, will you, honey?" I took her hand and helped her to her feet before kissing her on the cheek. Except for a bit less silver hair on her head, she looked exactly the same. Little old lady glasses. Sky blue tracksuit with orthopedic shoes. Slightly hunched posture, which made her seem even shorter than she was. "Look at you, just as pretty as you were years ago. How did this no-good bum get you back?"

"I haven't yet, Noni. You have to help me. This is all part of my scheme to win back her affections." Nick put the cooler down and kissed his grandmother's cheek while I shot him a dirty look. He was enlisting Noni in this effort? No fair.

"Oh, she's too smart for schemes, honey." Noni squeezed my hand and held my gaze. "You'll have to make an honest effort. She's no fool." Then, in a move that reminded me of Sitty, she slid her keen eyes over to him. "*Capisce?*"

Nick nodded, and they exchanged a look that made me wonder what his grandmother knew.

"Are you kids hungry? I got some ham. Come on, let me fix you a plate." She moved between us, walking slowly with a slight limp. Nick and I exchanged a secret smile at her familiar desire to feed every mouth that walked through her door within five minutes, and my heart ka-whumped unexpectedly.

"No thanks, Noni. We just ate. How's your new hip these days?" Nick picked up the cooler and followed her from the room, dropping his bag near the stairs. I did the same, glancing briefly up the stairs and wondering if Nick expected us to share a bedroom here.

"Oh, fine." She thumped her hip twice as she walked through the dining room. "Practically good as new." Pushing open an old swinging door, she shuffled into the spacious farmhouse kitchen. It had probably been remodeled several times in the last hundred years, but I doubted much had changed in the last twenty-five. Even though I was full, my mouth watered at the sight of two pies on the counter, one lattice-topped and one with tiny teardrop shapes cut into its golden crust.

"I brought a cake, Noni. Do you want it in the fridge?" Nick set the cooler on the old round table for eight and opened it up. Carefully he lifted the cake plate from it and set it on the counter.

"There is fine." Noni opened a low cupboard and pulled out a blue plastic cake plate cover, which had cracked in several places and was held together by brown tape. As she placed it over the cake, Nick and I looked at each other and shook our heads. Noni never threw anything away with a day's use left in it.

"Now I know what to buy you for a present," Nick said. "A new cake plate cover."

"Nonsense, that one's fine. Want some pizzelle? Marie made them yesterday." She opened up a large margarine container that actually had cookies in it. Old lady Tupperware. "We could have a snack out on the porch since the heat's not so bad today."

Marie was Nick's mother. I'd always liked her, but I experienced a strange twist in my gut, realizing that I'd have to face all of Nick's family tonight at the birthday dinner. What did they know? What would our story be? I'd have to ask

Nick what he'd told them seven years ago, which meant opening the door to a conversation about our past.

But maybe it was time.

The last thing I needed was more food, but it was homemade pizzelle. I couldn't say no. Nick and I each took one and followed Noni out onto the porch. She chose a rocker at one end, and Nick and I dropped into two chairs side by side. The first bite of my cookie—sweet and light and delicious—made me smile, remembering how Angelina had said *anus* when she meant *anise*.

"What's funny?" Nick asked.

Giggling, I told them the story, cringing slightly when I had to utter the word *anus* in front of Noni. But Nick laughed out loud, shaking his head. "I can't wait to meet this girl."

"She's quite a character." I munched the last of my cookie and contemplated having another one.

"Hey, these chairs need a little paint, Noni." Nick ran a hand along the peeling surface of one arm. "Do you have any? I can do them before I go tomorrow."

"I think so. In the shed. You can ask your uncle Bill, he'd know."

If I remembered right, Bill was the uncle that ran the farm, and his family lived in a home somewhere on the extensive property. But Nick had a lot of aunts and uncles and cousins—I never could keep them straight. "Hey, Nick," I said, remembering our conversation about family history from last night, "let's ask Noni about that picture."

"What picture?" Noni asked.

"It's a wedding photograph of Papa Joe and Tiny Lupo. My mother gave me a copy to put in the restaurant."

"It's a beautiful picture, and I was curious about when it was taken, and about the bride." I nudged Nick's foot with the toe of my sandal. "Nick didn't know much about her, not even her name."

Noni laughed, her cloudy blue eyes lighting up the way an old person's do when talking about the distant past. "No one ever called her anything but Tiny, that's why. Even I was taller than she was, and I was barely five foot two at my best. But her name was Frances. Frances O'Mara. She was Irish, a real hellcat."

"Lupo men like hellcats." Nick nudged me back.

"They sure do," Noni agreed, giving me a decisive nod, the grandmother equivalent of a high five. "But Tiny was a sweetheart too. She knew how hard it was to come into this big Italian family and try to fit in. She was so kind to me all her life."

"I was telling Coco that Papa Joe was a bootlegger during Prohibition," Nick said.

She nodded. "That's right, he was. Used to bring whiskey from Canada and run with gangsters. The stories they told... Like a movie or something." She recounted tales of speakeasies and rum running and mob kidnappings. Each detail she recalled unlocked a dozen more from dusty corners of her mind, and Nick and I sat listening for close to an hour, slack-jawed and wide-eyed.

"This is amazing," I said. "Did all that really happen?"

Noni shrugged. "They said it did. It's a good story, anyway. Although the love story of Tiny and Papa Joe is wonderful too. I'll have to tell you that one sometime."

"Love at first sight?" I rhapsodized.

"Well, *he* said it was. *She* said she couldn't stand him, not for years. But he wore her down."

"We're good at that." Nick poked my shoulder.

Ignoring him, I leaned forward in my chair. "You should

write all this down, Noni. I could help you," I offered. "I could type as you talk about what you remember."

"That's a great idea," Nick said.

"OK, sure." Noni tilted her head. "You know, I think I have an old photo album of the Lupo family around here somewhere. Maybe in a trunk in the attic. I can't get up there anymore but you kids could look."

"We'll definitely do that." Nick stood and stretched. "Coco and I are going to take a run before dinner. Maybe a swim. Is that OK? Or do you need me to do anything for you now?"

"No, no. You two go on. I'm going to stay out here a little bit. Dinner won't be until around seven."

"OK. I'm cooking tonight, Noni, so don't even try to make dinner without me," he threatened, offering me a hand getting out of the chair.

"I might let you in my kitchen, Nick Lupo, but not if I catch you swimming naked in my lake. You tell that boy to keep his trunks on, Coco."

I grinned as he helped me to my feet. "I will, Noni. You can count on it."

Nick held the screen door open and followed me into the house. I snagged my suitcase and headed up the stairs, whispering over my shoulder, "You keep your trunks on, boy. You hear me?" Then I squealed as he lassoed me with an arm around my waist, pulling me tight to his body and carrying me the rest of the way up.

"You watch who you're ordering around, little girl. I've got gangster blood, and it runs hot."

Gangster blood.

Damn.

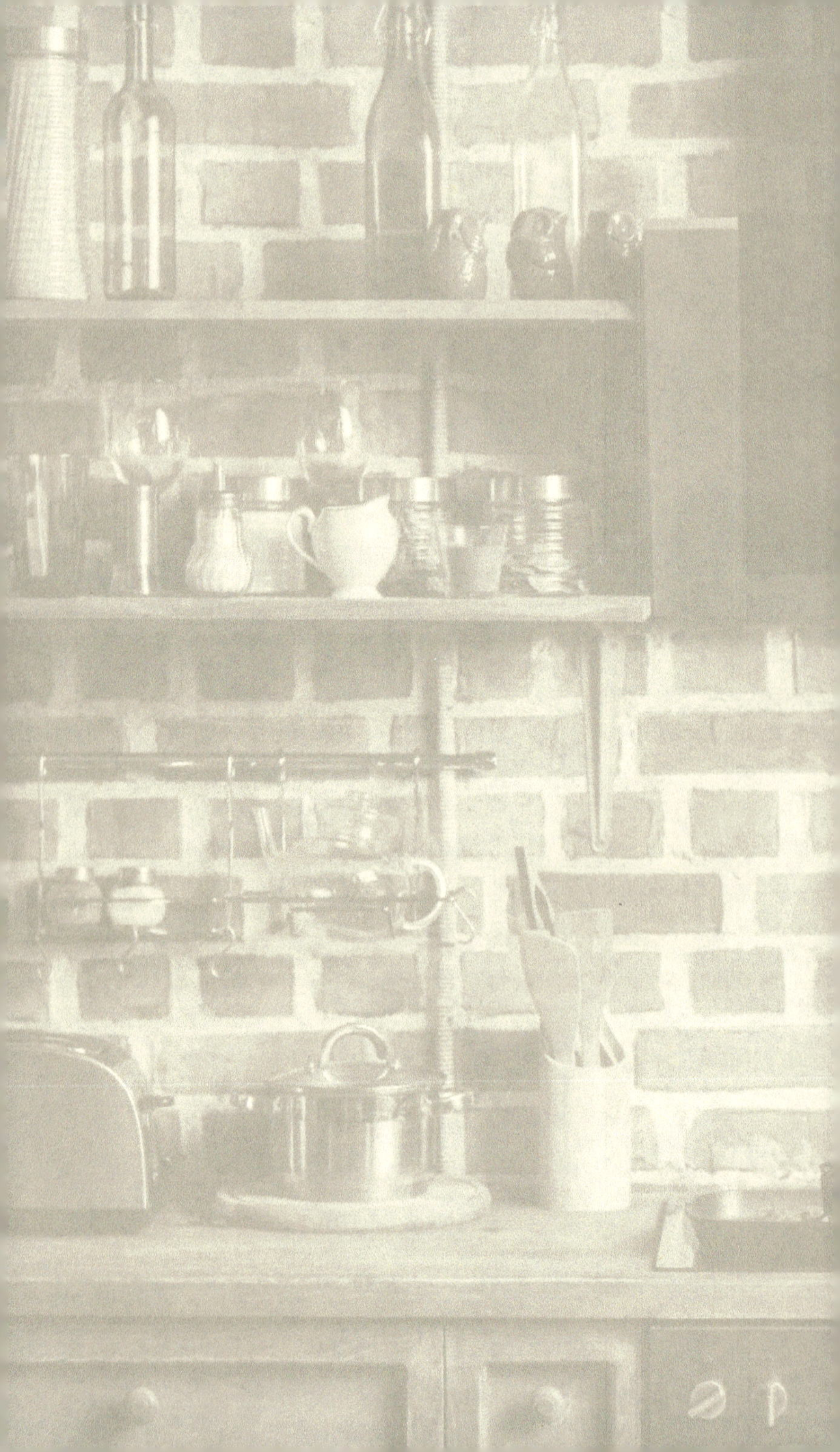

Chapter Sixteen

I ran hard, the soles of my Nikes stirring up dust on the dirt road. My body was bursting with trapped energy, fueled by frustration and adrenaline, which only seemed to replenish itself the harder I pushed.

"Jesus, Coco, pace yourself." Nick easily kept up with me, although I was glad to hear he was breathing heavy. "You're going to wear yourself out on the first mile."

"Can't keep up?" I teased, stretching my legs to lengthen each stride.

Instead of answering he took off at a speed I'd never attain in this lifetime, moving about a hundred feet ahead of me and then jogging backward as I caught up. "Hey, cupcake. What took you so long?"

I punched his shoulder and he turned around, running alongside me again. "No fair," I panted. "You have much longer legs than I do."

He glanced down at my blue running shorts. "I don't know, your legs look pretty long to me. Long and luscious and begging to wrap themselves around my neck. What do you say we stop up here for a breather?"

"No. Do you know how many calories I've consumed in

the last twenty-four hours? I'm getting a run in if it kills me." Ignoring a stitch behind my left rib cage, I pumped my arms harder and sped up again.

"It might, the way you're going at it. Why don't you save some of that aggression for later? It's turning me on."

"Everything turns you on."

"True. At least where you're concerned."

We ran in silence for a few minutes, following the dirt road as it curved around a bend. On our left was a field of greens; on our right, land thick with trees.

"How far do you want to go?" he asked.

"Three miles," I panted. "Same as always."

"Perfect. We'll go to that silo up there, turn around, and then head east through the trees when we get back here." He gestured to our right. "The reservoir is that way."

"Great." I slowed down a little, breathing deeply in an effort to relieve the ache in my side. Eventually it dissipated, and my mind strayed from my body to my heart, which ached in a different way. I needed to ask myself some hard questions.

What was I really doing here with Nick? Yes, I needed him to do me a favor by catering for Angelina, but he and I both knew he owed me a favor without this *weekend together* business. I could have argued harder that being friends and getting to know each other again did not have to involve sleeping under one roof. And I should have. But the truth was, I'd wanted to say yes. I wanted to spend time with him under one roof. Alone. With others. Clothed. Naked. Cooking. Talking. Drinking. Laughing.

Kissing.

Showering.

Fucking.

Christ. My shorts felt wet with something other than sweat, and my breasts tingled in my sports bra. It didn't help that he was right here next to me, sweaty and shirtless and breathing hard, muscles flexing. Before thinking about sex could derail my introspection, I put it aside and tried to examine how I really felt about Nick.

When I looked at him, I had all the stomach-flipping, panty-melting, heart-fluttery feelings I had all those years ago. When I thought about his success and saw how hard he'd worked to get where he was, I felt proud and happy. When I thought about being here at the farm, talking to Noni about family history, I felt like I belonged somehow. And when I thought about never being back here again, about saying goodbye to Nick tomorrow when the weekend was over, about going back to my regularly scheduled days of work, living with my parents, and no sex, I felt empty. No, worse than empty. Sad. Lonely. Depressed. Doomed to spend countless nights alone with my vibrator, getting myself off by thinking about Nick—and that's only when I knew the house would be empty.

But. When I thought about what he'd done, I got *so mad*. I felt bitter and humiliated and betrayed. Served him right if he still loved me—here was my chance to make him feel a little of what I felt back then.

Only trouble was, I still loved him too.

Looking skyward as we turned around at the silo, I waited for lightning bolts to streak the sky or thunderclouds to burst. But there were just birds and trees and puffy white clouds. Did that mean the universe was in favor of a second chance? The lake came into view, and I made up my mind. I'd listen to what he had to say, and I'd tell him how I felt. If he could somehow convince me to give him another chance, I'd try again—barring any signs from the cosmos telling me to run for the hills.

Because this felt real. Familiar. Right. As if we were picking up our story where we left off, but now we had a chance to give it a better ending.

In order to do that, we had to go back to where we went wrong...we had to talk about it.

The thought was scary as hell. But it was the right thing to do, and the decision to face it freed me somehow. I felt like a weight was lifted off my shoulders. With a fresh burst of energy, I surged ahead. "Race you to the lake!"

He laughed and shot past me through the trees within five seconds. I caught up just as he was ripping off his socks.

"First one in wins!" I yelled, barely slowing down to yank my Nikes from my feet and run right off the end of the rickety old wooden dock into the water, fully clothed, Nick at my heels.

Heart pounding, I went all the way under, the water blessedly cool against my hot skin. I rested for just a couple seconds under the water, my toes digging into the mucky sand bottom. The world around me rumbled when Nick jumped in beside me, and we surfaced at the same time.

"Cheater!" He shook his head to clear the dripping hair from his eyes and reached for me.

"Look who's calling who a cheater." I tried to swim away from him, but his hand closed around my right ankle.

He pulled me back toward him, reaching for my waist when I was close enough. "What's that supposed to mean?"

"Only that one of us has a history of cheating, and it isn't me." But I let him turn me into his arms, running my hands up his shoulders and wrapping my legs around his torso. The water came up to his chest, just below the tattoo of my name. Every time I looked at it, I felt a surge of desire for him.

"Aren't you ever going to let the cheating thing go? It was so long ago, Coco." His hands slid beneath my ass.

I shrugged. *Would* I ever be able to let it go? Not a bad place to start. "Maybe we should talk about it."

He groaned. "Now? I *do* want to talk to you, like I said before, but now I can't concentrate. It was bad enough when you put on your little running outfit but now that you're all wet too..." He kissed me, and his cock stirred between us. "Now I have other ideas."

"Mmmmm." I squeezed him with my thighs, pulled him closer with my heels. "Tempting. Except remember what happened that last time we did it in this lake?"

His face fell. "Oh yeah. It gave you an infection."

"Right." I'd never had a UTI before, so I was terrified by the symptoms. Nick had gone with me to the campus clinic and held my hand in the waiting room. It cleared up after a round of antibiotics, but I didn't feel like repeating the experience. Shuddering, I shook my head. "Sorry, no sex in the lake."

"No. I agree." He spun around, making my stomach go weightless. "I'll just look at you, then. I could do that all day."

I smiled. "Liar."

"You're right. That's a lie." He spun around the other way. "I wouldn't last all day."

I hugged him close, chest to chest, and rested my chin on his shoulder. Cool water swirled between us, the sun warming my arms and glinting off the surface of the lake. "It's OK. I wouldn't last all day either."

We stayed like that for a couple minutes, so peaceful that I was loath to disturb the mood with a painful conversation, but I wasn't one to wait around when I had something to say. And the sooner we dealt with the past, the sooner we could try to bury it and move forward.

At that moment, I honestly believed it was possible.

I opened my mouth, but Nick spoke first.

"Coco."

"Yes?"

He swallowed. "I lied to you. That night we broke up."

Gooseflesh broke out on my skin. The night we broke up? What the hell was he talking about? "About what?"

"About cheating on you. The last time."

I pulled back from him. Looked him in the eye. "What do you mean, you lied?"

"I didn't do it. I never slept with anyone else that spring."

The water, which had been pleasantly chilly before, suddenly felt icy. "What? Why did you tell me you did?"

"So that you'd break up with me. But I'm tired of being called a cheater. Being thought of that way. I didn't do it."

I unwrapped my legs from around his waist, and my feet floated down to the bottom. "I don't understand. Why did you want me to break up with you?"

"After Mia told me you'd been accepted to that program in Paris, I thought about it a lot. I didn't want you to leave, but I realized how important it was for you to go."

I took my arms from around his neck and stared at him, waiting for him to go on.

He ran a hand over his hair. "I went to your apartment to tell you to go, but you refused. So I made up the lie about sleeping with someone else so you'd do it."

My heart was thundering so hard it sounded like canons in my head. "I don't believe it."

"It's true," he said, his expression sincere. "And it worked. You threw me out. You threw everything out."

"Because I was fucking mad!" I yelled, smacking the water. "You deserved it! And I'm not even sorry, because that was a shitty thing to do to me, even if it was a lie. You destroyed me that night. You watched me fall apart."

"I'm sorry."

I shook my head, tiny little movements that mimicked the drill of my pulse. "No. No. I don't believe you. You fucked some random girl just like you told me you did. You did it because you were mad that I lied to you. You'd done it before, and you did it again."

"I was mad that you lied, but I hadn't cheated on you in over a year, Coco, I swear." He held up his palms. "And I'm only telling you now because I want to move forward with a clean slate. And I thought it would help you to know that I wasn't unfaithful to you that year."

"Help me?" I stared at him, my stomach churning. "My God, do you know what I went through that night? The agony of thinking you betrayed me after we'd been so close that year? Of thinking you fucked someone else?" I put my hands to my head. The world was spinning.

"I went through it too. I hated hurting you. It killed me, knowing it was all a lie."

I ducked under the water, exhaling so I'd sink to the bottom. I couldn't hear another word. Was he telling the truth? He hadn't slept with someone else? That lie had changed *everything*. It set things in motion that brought us to the end. The morning after we broke up I'd called my mother to say I'd changed my mind and had decided to go to Paris after all. She'd been so thrilled, she'd booked a flight and paid my deposit within hours, probably because she was scared I'd try to back out. But I'd assured her things between Nick and me had ended, and I couldn't wait to get away from everything that would remind me of him. Now he was telling me my decision had been based on a lie? Goddamn him!

With my lungs about to burst, I surfaced again.

"Jesus Christ, Nick," I said, gulping air. "I can't wrap my brain around this. I don't know whether to be glad you didn't cheat or furious you told me you did. That lie was the start of everything."

"I know, but I thought I was doing the right thing, especially when Mia told me you'd decided to go. You had a ticket by the next day."

"Well, you weren't doing the right thing, manipulating me that way. That wasn't your decision to make. And damn Mia for telling you that."

He reached for my arm, but I wrenched it away. "Don't blame her. I called her and begged her to tell me if you were going. I didn't want to think I'd wrecked everything for no reason. And she didn't know I'd lied about cheating."

I gave him a cold stare. "She couldn't have. She would have told me the truth long before now, because she knew what it did to me, thinking you'd been unfaithful. Christ, Nick. What a shit thing to do."

Nick pressed his lips together for a second. "I was twenty-two, Coco. I didn't reason through it the right way. I just knew your family wanted you to go and knew they'd blame me if you didn't. No matter what you say," he went on, holding up his hand when I opened my mouth to argue, "they never thought I was right for you, good enough for you."

"They didn't think anybody was good enough for me! I'm the youngest and the only girl, Nick. For fuck's sake, I wasn't even allowed to date until I was sixteen. And they never liked anyone I brought home—they still don't!" I couldn't believe we were back to this again. Was he really trying to pin our problems on my family? *He* was the asshole here!

"They wanted someone with money," he said, his jaw set. "Just admit it. Someone who drove a nice car like yours and majored in poli sci and took his junior year abroad and played tennis at the club and owned his own golf shoes."

"Are you crazy?" I stared at him. "Where are you getting all this?"

He closed his eyes and took a breath. "Maybe it's crazy now, but it's how I felt at the time. My truck wasn't good enough for you, my clothes weren't expensive, I couldn't take you out to nice places—and if I did, you always insisted on paying the bill."

"Because I knew how much you worked and struggled! I knew you had loans to pay off. And I was the one who wanted to go to the nice places, so I felt guilty when you'd try to pay."

"I'm not saying you made me feel bad on purpose. And

looking back, I can see that it was probably in my head. But I never felt like I fit in with what your family wanted for you. I had nothing to offer you—until then. When I heard you were accepted, then there was something I *could* do for you in their eyes. Let you go."

In *their* eyes? Suspicion snaked up my spine. "Did my parents contact you or something?"

He looked away.

"Did they?" I yelled, my nostrils flaring.

He didn't answer for a full ten seconds, during which I clutched at the hem of my tank instead of throttling him. He was the one who wanted to talk, so he'd better fucking come clean about everything! "Your mom wrote me a letter on behalf of both of them. She was perfectly nice, so you don't have to get incensed about it. She just wanted me to know what a wonderful opportunity this was for you, and how all the women in her family had done it for three generations, and how she hoped I would do everything I could to encourage you to go. She said she could see we cared very much for each other but we were very young. She didn't want you to throw it away for me, although she never said that outright."

"Goddamn it," I said softly, putting the heels of my hands to my eyes. "Why did she have to do that?"

Nick took me by the shoulders. "Because she loves you. And she was right. It was a wonderful opportunity and part of your history and your legacy...she was *right*, Coco. You had to go, I could see that."

"But it wasn't their decision to make," I went on angrily, pushing his hands off me. "And it wasn't yours, either. It was mine, and you all took it away from me."

"I know. And I'm sorry. So many things could have gone differently if I'd just been honest from the start. I hated myself that night I lied to you."

We looked at each other a moment, each of us remembering what came next. "You came back the next night. Why didn't you tell me the truth then?"

"I was going to, I swear to God, because I couldn't let you go to Paris thinking that I'd betrayed you that way. Not when I'd worked so hard to earn your trust after those other times. All I'd planned to do was tell you the truth and say I was glad you were going."

I sniffed. "You didn't stick to that plan too long."

He shook his head. "One look at you and I fell apart. Begged you to take me back."

That detail brought a mite of satisfaction. "You did beg, didn't you?"

"On my knees."

I sighed, closing my eyes. "We drank a lot of whiskey that night."

"Still, I meant every word I said."

My eyelids opened a sliver. "You *proposed* that night."

"Guess I liked being on my knees."

I splashed water at him. "Don't joke. This is serious."

He swiped at his eyes. "Sorry. Yes, I proposed. It was spur-of-the-moment, but I meant it—I wanted to marry you. I wanted forever with you. In my mind, this was the perfect solution. I'd marry you, you could go to France but you'd go as my wife, even if no one knew it, and we'd stay together. We'd have this amazing secret. I'd know you would come back to me and not run off with some jackass with a title and a trust fund."

"I wouldn't have done that," I said sullenly. "I never wanted anyone else."

"Maybe, but I was young and stupid and scared and crazy about you. So I proposed."

"Oh God," I said, touching my fingertips to my forehead. "What a fucking mess…we flew to Vegas, got married, and then of course I refused to go. Because I was your *wife*."

Nick nodded slowly. "We fought so hard about it that night. Remember?"

I looked at him helplessly. "How could I forget my wedding night?"

"I'm sorry," he said, his voice cracking. "You deserved a better wedding night."

I turned away from him, chilled to the bone now, but not ready to end the conversation. "Parts of it were good." Closing my eyes, I saw him above me in the darkened hotel room, his body centered between my thighs, his skin warm and soft, just like his voice. *My wife,* he'd said, burying himself deep inside me. *My wife.*

He cleared his throat. "Yes. Parts of it were amazing. You fell asleep first, you know. And I watched you sleeping. You were so beautiful."

I swallowed hard. "So then why did you leave me?" My voice shook. It was the question I had to ask. I'd been afraid of the answer for seven years, but I steadied my nerves and turned to face him. "Tell me now. How could you leave me that way?"

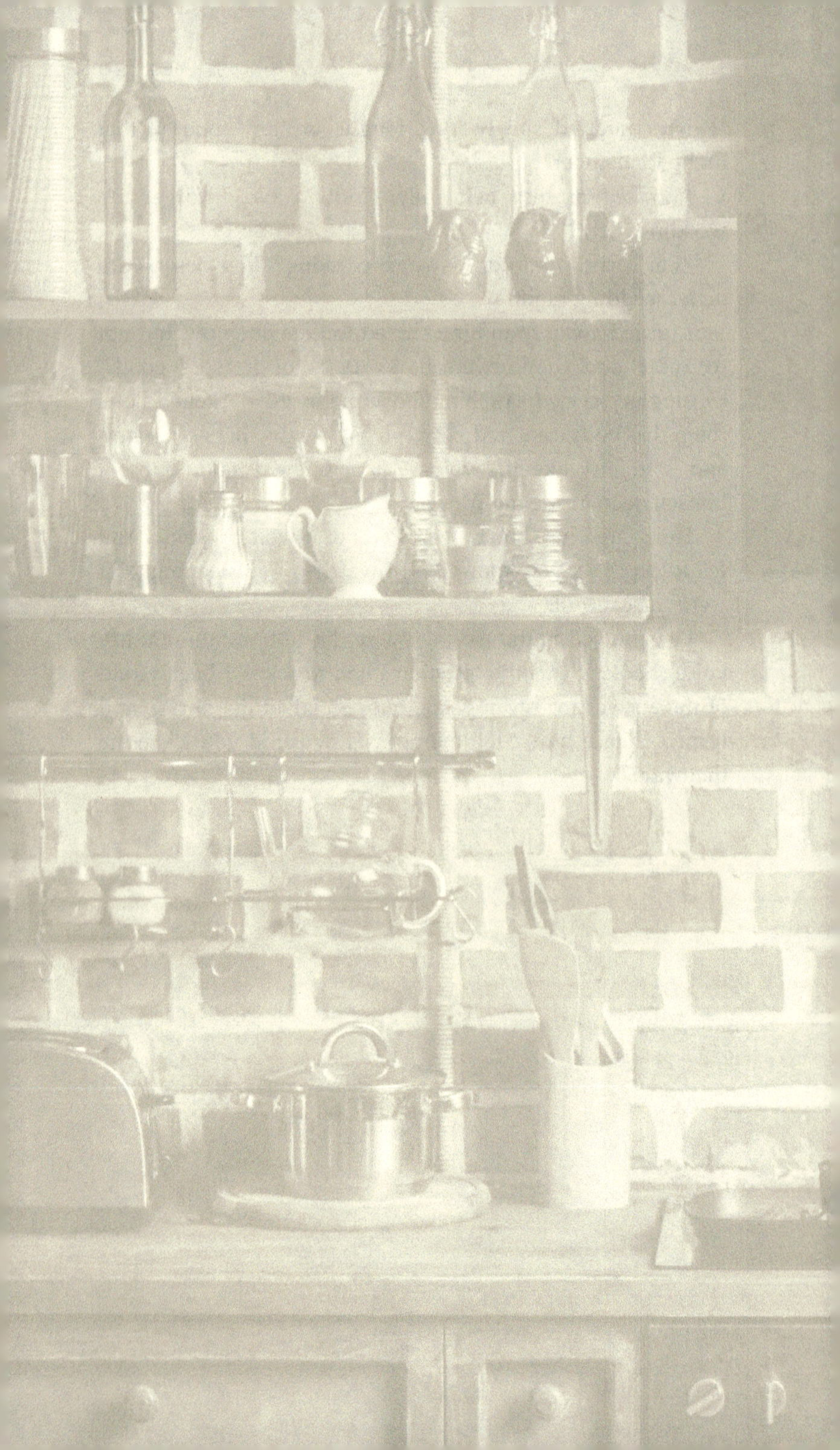

Chapter Seventeen

Nick held up both hands. "Before I tell you, let me say that I know now that *no* reason was good enough. But at the time, it made sense to me."

"Just tell me."

"OK. I was watching you sleep and I started thinking about everything I wanted to do for you. Everything you deserved in life. And what you deserved far outweighed what I could offer. I'd just maxed out my one credit card on the ring and the room. I was up to my ears in debt."

"I cared about you, not your bank account," I said through my teeth. He wasn't really going to blame money, was he? What an insult.

"You would have. You had no idea what it's like to live without money. You still don't."

I threw my hands in the air. "How dare you say to me! I *married* you, didn't I? And I'm not the one who changed my mind! You did." I poked his chest. "So don't pretend I didn't think you were rich enough for me or whatever. That was all in your head."

"It wasn't only the money, Coco. I was lying there thinking about that program, and how much I wanted it for you. About how, if you were my daughter, or if we had a daughter some day, I'd want her to have things like that." He put a hand to his chest. "I understood what your parents felt. When you love someone, you want what's best for them, even if it means sacrifice."

I glared at him. "So it was because of my parents? You dumped me because you understood them, all of a sudden? Well, I hope they fucking appreciate it," I said bitterly. "No wonder they were so helpful with our divorce."

Nick shook his head. "It wasn't just them—it was me. I started to think that you'd wake up one day and regret that you hadn't gone. And it would be my fault. And even if you said you didn't resent me, you should—because I had done a selfish thing. I had robbed you of this incredible opportunity. Deep down, I knew if you married me you wouldn't go. Somehow leaving seemed the unselfish move."

Mouth agape, I looked at him for five full seconds. "You asshole!" I was tempted to slap his face, but I settled for shoving a wall of water at him. *"Leaving seemed the unselfish move,* are you fucking kidding me?" My eyes felt as if they would bug out of my head. "You broke me! You shattered me! I was..." I shook my head, unable to come up with a word that adequately captured my emotional state. "Devastated!"

Nick wiped the water from his face. "I'm sorry. It was the wrong move, I see that now. But I panicked, Coco. And then when I tried to apologize, you wouldn't speak to me. Wouldn't return my texts, take my calls, wouldn't stop the divorce proceedings."

"I was hurt, Nick. I loved you, and you *left me*." This couldn't be real. He'd abandoned me for my own good? No. No. He was not the hero here. He was not the good guy. For years I'd nursed this anger, and he wasn't going to evade it now just because he'd had good fucking intentions. "Do you know what it felt like, waking up that next morning and finding you gone? Seeing that goddamn note on the nightstand? Your wedding band beside it?" The hurt and humiliation of that morning returned to me tenfold, stabbing me repeatedly in the gut. "It didn't click right away, you know, what you'd done. There was no light bulb that went on, no immediate understanding of what the note really meant. I even thought it might be a joke."

Nick looked miserable, but he nodded. "Go on. I deserve this."

"You do, but I don't even know what words to use to describe what that day was like."

How could I convey the slow, sickening dread that started with a few erratic heartbeats as I checked the bathroom? How could I make him feel the way it dropped into my stomach like a bowling ball when I saw that his suitcase was gone? How could I tell him what I felt when I turned on my phone and saw those two words from him, like two bullets to the heart?

I'm sorry.

"Do you know how long I lay in that bed, sobbing? Hoping you'd change your mind? Hours went by, and the longer I lay there, the clearer it became—you weren't coming back. You weren't sorry you'd done it; you were just sorry I got hurt. And yet I stayed there. All day. All night. Desperately praying for you to return. Smelling the sheets where you'd slept. Crying so hard I made myself sick. Finally I had to face it—you were gone. And you didn't love me enough to come back." The violent anger I'd felt moments ago was replaced with a sadness that threatened to pull me under. My vision went silver at the edges, and I swayed in the water. Nick gripped my shoulders.

"Believe me, Coco, I did. I loved you more than I thought it was possible to love someone, and leaving was the hardest thing I've ever done. I was sick too. Physically ill. I forced myself to get on that plane. I didn't talk to anyone for two days. I couldn't eat. I couldn't sleep."

I narrowed my eyes. "Am I supposed to feel sorry for you? Because I don't."

Nick dropped his hands into the water and exhaled. "No. I don't deserve your sympathy. I don't even know why I'm even telling you this—I know it doesn't make up for what I did."

"No, it doesn't."

"Hit me," he said suddenly.

"What? Are you nuts?"

"No. I'm serious. Hit me. I deserve it." He closed his eyes and put his hands behind his back. "As hard as you want. As many times as you want."

He looked ridiculous. "Shut up."

"Come on, do it. You know you want to. You've wanted to do it for years. Now's your chance. Come on, hit me."

I stared at him in disbelief. In all honesty, part of me did want to hit him. How dare he lay all this out for me now, years later, when he'd had so many chances to be honest before but kept lying and manipulating me and fucking everything up? And what about his seven-year silence after the divorce? Another part of me wanted to kiss him, tell him it would be OK, we would be OK. (But that was a very, very small part. Mostly I wanted to hit him.)

He opened one eye. "Are you gonna do it?"

I glared at him. "No, asshole. I'm not going to do it. I hit you once and it didn't make me feel better."

"The night we broke up."

"Yes." I looked at the palm of my right hand. "It probably hurt my hand more than your face."

"Probably. Remind me to teach you how to throw a punch."

I curled my fingers into a fist. "I'm ready for a lesson."

He couldn't keep the smile off his face, the bastard. "That's your fist? Coco, you can't throw a punch with your hand like that. You'll break your thumb." He unfurled my fist and tucked my thumb alongside my fingers, leaving his big hands wrapped around my smaller one. "There. Like that."

"Thanks." I stared at our hands. "I guess if an unsatisfied bride ever comes at me, I'll be better prepared."

Nick smiled slightly and took his hands off mine. "Can I ask you a question?"

I shrugged, miserable and cold.

"Did you even come back to campus after Vegas?"

"Just to pack up my clothes. Exams were done, and I had no reason to be there. Plus everything reminded me of you. It was too painful."

"I know. I left too."

That surprised me. "You did?"

He nodded. "I applied to the Culinary Institute and got in. I went in the fall. But Coco, you have to believe I wanted you back. I called, I wrote. I even drove to your parents house, but you were gone."

"My mother and I took a vacation."

"Did your grandmother tell you I came?"

"Yes. She did." And I'd gone into the bathroom of our hotel room in Rome and cried my eyes out in the shower. If my mother noticed my puffy eyes that night, she didn't mention it. "Sitty always liked you because you were Catholic. And because you cooked and were interested in her recipes. But it wasn't enough to change my mind. I still didn't want to hear your damn apologies."

"I know. It was clear the divorce was what you really wanted. Eventually I figured I should just leave you in peace."

My eyes went wide. "Peace? I didn't have any peace where you were concerned. Not for years! Maybe not ever!" I put a hand to my chest. "I never got over it, Nick. I never got over you." Admitting it to him now was like cutting out my own heart. I burst into tears, and Nick gathered me into his arms. Maybe it was stupid but I went, crying into my hands against his shoulder. This was all so fucking sad. It wasn't that I was sorry I'd gone to Paris—it *was* a wonderful experience, one that I'd want my own children to have—Nick was right about that. But still…

"You gave up on me. You gave up," I wept. "You left, so I left. And you gave up. You could have fought harder, longer. I was back from Paris the following summer, and not once did I ever hear from you."

"I didn't give up on you, Coco, but I didn't know what else to do. I didn't have the guts to show up on your doorstep after everything that had happened. I thought about it a million times."

I took a few slow, calming breaths and backed away from him. "It's better you didn't. I don't think there was anything you could have said to make me listen. I was too angry to forgive you."

"And now?"

We stared at each other a long moment, during which we both realized that a second chance might be impossible. "I don't know."

Nick took a deep breath. "Coco, not a day goes by that I don't regret what happened between us. I thought I was doing the right thing, but I made a mistake. And it cost me the love of my life."

My lips fell open.

Argue with him. Say it didn't. Say what you planned to say before you jumped in the lake. Tell him you love him again and maybe you always have. Tell him you accept his apology. Admit that you made mistakes too, that you know what it's like to act on impulse, that, in fact, part of what thrilled you about his spur-of-the-moment proposal was that it was much more like you than like him. Say that you knew it was a bad idea, that you knew your parents and friends should be a part of your wedding day, that a Vegas quickie was not what you'd had in mind as a young girl dreaming of her wedding day. Own up to the fact that you booked those tickets to Nevada within minutes of accepting his proposal, putting them on your own credit card, because you were scared that he'd change his mind. Tell him that you saw getting married as a way to hold on to him, a way to ensure he'd never sleep with anyone else ever again. Tell him you saw it as a way to show your parents they couldn't control you.

Tell him your wedding bands are still in your jewelry box.

Tell him how you cried the day your tattoo was altered.

Tell him you'd put his name on your body again.

Tell him you might be crazy enough to run away with him again.

Tell him he makes you feel alive.

Tell him he makes you feel everything.

The words were all right there in my mind. But uttering them would've meant peeling back every layer of protection over my heart, an open wound.

I wanted to say them, but I didn't.

I was afraid of bleeding to death.

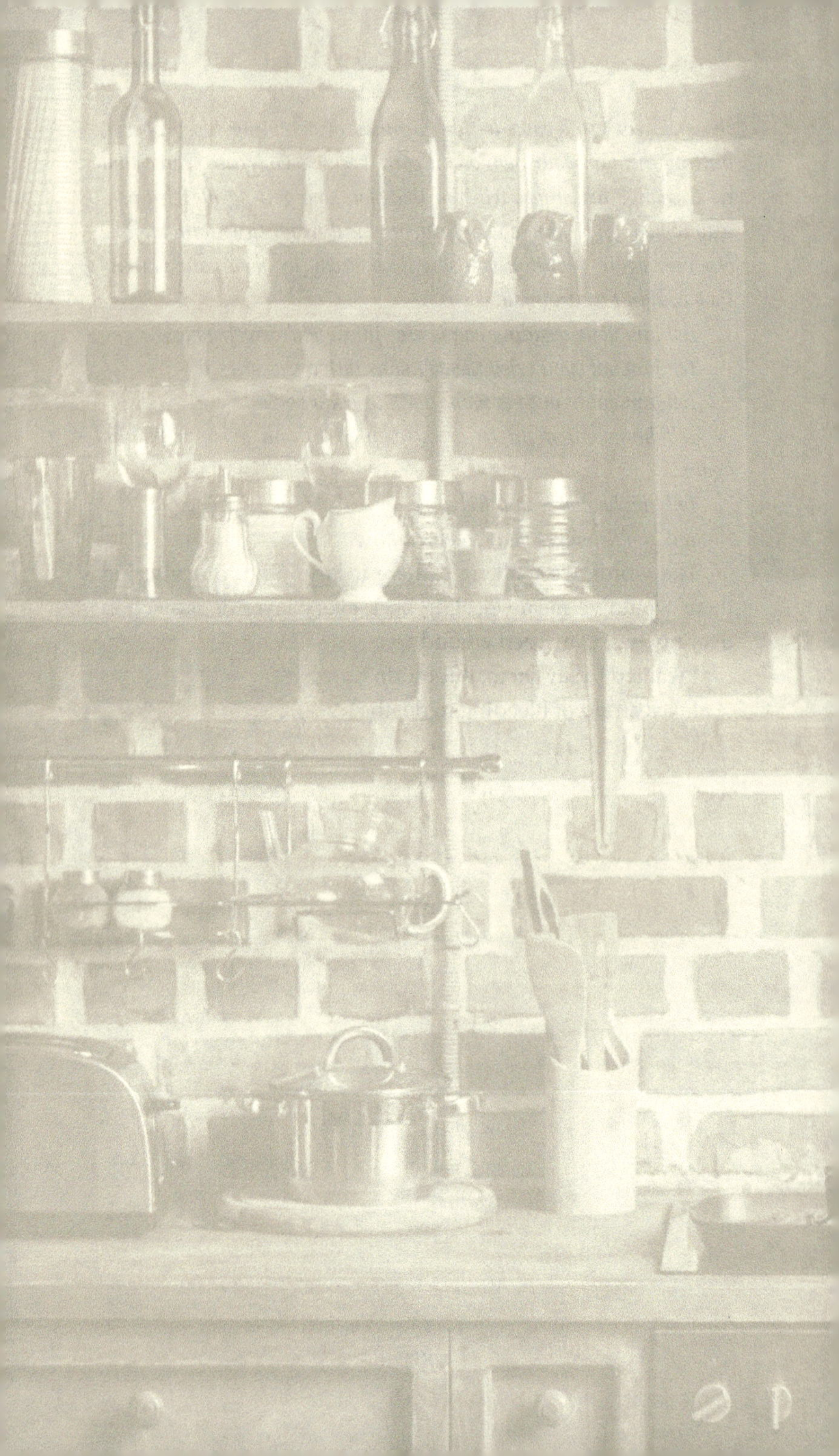

Chapter Eighteen

Nick sighed, rubbing his face with his hands. "Maybe you were right. This talking about the past stuff kind of sucks."

I nodded. Swallowed the lump in my throat.

"Ready to go back?" Nick asked. "I should get dinner started."

"Yes." But the thought of running back made my limbs feel heavy in the water. Rehashing the past had exhausted me. I dragged myself to the ladder on the dock, and Nick motioned for me to climb up first.

"I wish I had a big warm towel to wrap you in," he said as I emerged, my running clothes dripping. I was shivering, but it wasn't because of the water.

"I'm OK." Squeezing the water from my ponytail, I walked toward my shoes on the grass, my legs shaky and my footsteps squishy. "Guess I should have stopped to take my socks off too." I looked down at them, wrinkling my nose.

"Yeah, but then you wouldn't have beaten me into the lake."

"True." I pulled my shoes on and leaned over to lace them up, tempted to make a joke but not quite up for it.

Nick sat on the grass to tug his socks and running shoes on. "You up for running back? Or would you rather just walk?"

I straightened up, pulled out my ponytail elastic, and shook out my wet hair. "I think I'll walk, but you go ahead. I know you have to get dinner going."

He got to his feet. "No, that's OK. I can walk with you."

"Actually, Nick, I could use the alone time."

He nodded. "You know the way back?"

"Left when the path reaches the road, right?"

"Yes." He put his hands on his hips, glanced at the path through the trees and then back at me. "You sure you're all right?"

I took a deep breath, concentrated on slipping the ponytail elastic around my wrist. "I'll be fine, really. That conversation was hard on me. It brought back a lot of feelings I've done my best to forget. But I'm a big girl." Managing a shaky smile, I looked up and waved him off. "Go on. I'll see you back there."

"OK." He began jogging through the trees, looking back once over his shoulder. I waited until I couldn't see him anymore to start walking.

Wrinkling my nose at the first few waterlogged steps, I wrapped my arms around myself and started through the trees at a slow pace. I'd told Nick I wanted to be alone so I could think, but I was unable to draw any conclusions about what had just happened. There were so many feelings battling inside me. Was I more sad than anything? Hurt? Scared? Angry? And who was I most mad at? Nick? My parents? Myself?

I turned left at the dirt road, and admitted the truth. I still loved him. If I didn't, none of this would matter. Revisiting our history wouldn't hurt so much. But love hadn't been enough to make things work between us before. How could I know this time would be different? What if I never learned to trust him? What if he was the kind of person who felt lying was OK if you had good intentions? (Oh, God. I had to call Mia and come clean about Angelina, didn't I?) What if he was still as big a flirt as he'd always been...could I deal with that? Especially now that he was a celebrity? He'd be away from me a lot, traveling, working, celebrity schmoozing. I'd have to put up with all kinds of Internet gossip and selfies taken with pretty girls and paparazzi pics of him with women famous and beautiful and wealthy.

At least we wouldn't argue over money anymore. I'd happily let him pay the bill at dinner whenever he wanted to.

But what about this resentment I felt? Why couldn't I get past it? I wanted to believe I could, wanted to believe the day would come where I would look at him and not think about that fucking goodbye note. The ring on the nightstand. The text message. I wanted to forgive and forget and move forward. So why couldn't I do it? When he called me the love of his life, all those things I wanted to say to him were racing around in my brain, but I couldn't bring myself to say even one of them.

Oh God, that was a bad sign, right? What if the universe was trying to warn me against being taken in by him again? Nick had burned me once. Why should I give him the chance to do it again? What kind of fool takes a second bite of a bad apple?

Approaching the house, I vowed to stick to the original plan. No relationship, no promises, no more love-of-my-life conversations. No second bites. We were friends, nothing more.

Just at that moment, a monarch butterfly floated in front of me, and I nearly smiled. That was a good sign, wasn't it? A good sign that I'd made the right decision and the universe supported me.

It should have been, but right after that I looked up at

Nick's bedroom window just in time to see him toweling off after a shower.

Then I tripped over a tree root and went down on my hands and knees, cursing softly.

Fuck. Why did the bad apple have to *look so good?*

I managed to sneak up the stairs without being seen by anyone, although I heard voices coming from the kitchen, and more cars were parked in the driveway. Nick had originally put my suitcase in a bedroom with his bag, but I'd moved it to the room I used to stay in, still too embarrassed to share a bed with Nick at his grandmother's house. And maybe it was better that way. Plans were good and all, but I didn't entirely trust myself to behave, which was why I had to talk to Mia. I needed to hear someone tell me I was right in refusing to give Nick another chance. Mia couldn't stand Nick, so she was a safe bet.

Inside my room, I shut the door and pulled down the shade. After peeling off my wet running clothes, I draped them over a white wicker chair in the corner. Hopefully they'd dry before I had to pack them up again.

Someone, probably Nick, had thoughtfully placed two large sage green towels on the bed, and I wrapped one around me, dug my phone out of my purse, and lowered myself onto the bed.

Creak.

Noisy as ever. Good.

I had a few more text messages from Angelina, which I ignored, and one from Mia asking me to call her. Wrinkling my nose, I faced the fact that I had to tell her what I was doing if I wanted her advice.

"Hello?"

"Hi, it's me."

"Thank God. I've had the weirdest feeling all day that something is not right with you. Is everything OK?"

I sighed. Mia and I had such a great connection. I should have been honest with her from the start.

"Everything's fine. But I have to confess something."

"You took that party."

"I took that party."

She sighed. "I knew it. Look, I'm going to be very Zen about this. Lucas says I have to let this go because I'm leaving and you're here and I trust you. So I'm going to breathe and relax and say, you've got this, Coco. Because you better fucking have this."

"I do, I swear. It's going to be great. But I need to talk to you about something."

"Oh, God. What?"

"Relax, it's nothing bad." I shut my eyes and sighed. "Actually, it is bad. Or it could be. I don't know."

"Out with it already, you're killing me!"

"OK. It involves Nick Lupo."

Silence.

"Mia?"

"I knew this was coming. The moment he walked into The Green Hour, I knew it."

"He told me he saw you. He likes Lucas."

"Yeah, Lucas likes him too, much to my outraged dissatisfaction. He says we shouldn't judge people by their pasts."

"He's a good person. We're not."

"Ha. OK, so you ran into Nick Lupo."

"There's more to it than that…" I told her about Angelina's insistence on having Nick at her party, about seeing him again at the restaurant, about drinks at the bar, and the bargain that included spending the weekend together.

"Oh no. Oh God. Tell me you said no."

"Ummmm...I'm at his grandmother's farm right now."

"Coco!"

I touched my fingers to one temple. "Just let me get this out, OK? Because there's more to this than you think. More than you know. We didn't simply break up seven years ago... we actually got married."

Silence.

"Are you there?"

"I'm here. I'm just...in shock. You guys got married? For real?"

"Yes. But it was a mistake." I squeezed my eyes shut, took a deep breath, and told her the whole story, from the first drop of whiskey we drank the night he proposed to the last tears I cried in that hotel room.

"Oh my God, Coco! All these years, and you never told me! I can't believe it—you're *horrible* at keeping secrets!"

"This was more than a secret. It was a terrible, embarrassing, painful mistake. And I just wanted to bury it. I wanted to go to Paris, forget him, forget everything. And it kind of worked."

"No wonder he kept asking for your contact information —and no wonder you told me not to give it to him. Jesus, Coco. You poor thing! I'm so sorry you went through that alone. You should have told me! I would have been there for you!"

"I got over it, eventually. Being in Paris helped."

"Yes...Paris is magical."

I had to smile—Paris was where Mia and Lucas met. "I could use another spell. Turns out I wasn't as over him as I thought I was."

"Of course not. Like I said, I knew this would happen as soon as he came to town. You two cannot be within a fifty-mile radius of each other without feeling it. Like a magnetic field or something."

"We're definitely still attracted to each other, that's for

sure. And he told me this afternoon he's still in love with me. And I think…" I swallowed and forced the words out. "I think I might be falling for him again too. Actually, I know I am."

"Coco. Listen to me." Mia's tone was serious. "You cannot take him back. What he did was unforgivable!"

"But he apologized." I told her about the conversation in the lake. Her gasps and squeals of indignation told me she was as angry as I was about his lies and faulty logic.

"He said *what*?"

I got off the bed and wandered to the dresser, running my thumbnail along its varnished edge. "He said he did it for me. He said he thought he was doing the right thing, and that afterward he was sorry." I slammed my eyes shut. What the hell was I doing? Defending Nick? Hadn't I called Mia so she could reassure me I was doing the right thing by *not* getting back together with him?

"Sorry doesn't cut it," she said angrily. "Sorry is for 'oops, I stepped on your foot' or 'whoops, I forgot your birthday.' Sorry is not for leaving your wife on your wedding night."

"I know. And he knows." Turning around, I leaned back against the dresser. "He said not a day goes by that he doesn't think about me and regret what he did. He called me the love of his life."

"Tough!" she exploded. "You were the love of his life then, too. It's not like he just realized this. He told me you were the love of his life when he begged me for your address in Paris. He just didn't tell me you were his wife, too."

"He never said it to me before. About being the love of his life. And then I didn't give him the chance."

She was quiet for a moment. "Do you think he's the love of yours?"

"I don't know. What if he is? What if we're supposed to be together?"

"Oh God. Do you have *a feeling* about this or something?"

"I thought I did. But then we talked about the past and I got mad and hurt all over again."

"Have you forgiven him?"

"I told him I did."

"But do you?"

I closed my eyes, feeling heaviness in all my limbs. "No. I don't. But I still love him," I said helplessly. "Because he's sweet and funny and hot and he knows me so well. He understands me. And he's *so good* at sex."

"But he lies. And he's a flirt. And he left you." She sighed. "Your list was longer than mine."

"I know nobody's perfect," I said. "And he's not the same person he was back then. I'm not either."

"OK then…What would it take for you to forgive him?"

I lifted my shoulders. "I honestly don't know. But if I can't figure it out, there's no hope for happily ever after. I love him, but I don't want to be in a relationship that's poisoned from the start by resentment and distrust. How do I know he won't do something like that again?"

"I don't know," she said softly. "I guess you'll have to do a little soul searching and see if there's any way he can earn your trust again." She exhaled loudly. "Look, I haven't been Nick's biggest fan over the years, but I do believe that he loved you. Maybe he still does. And I also know that love involves taking risks without being able to know for sure how things turn out. But mostly, Coco, I know this—you deserve that happily ever after."

I smiled, closing my eyes against tears. "Thanks. I love you."

"I love you too. It's going to be all right."

"How do you know?"

"I don't, not for sure." She laughed gently. "But I've got a feeling."

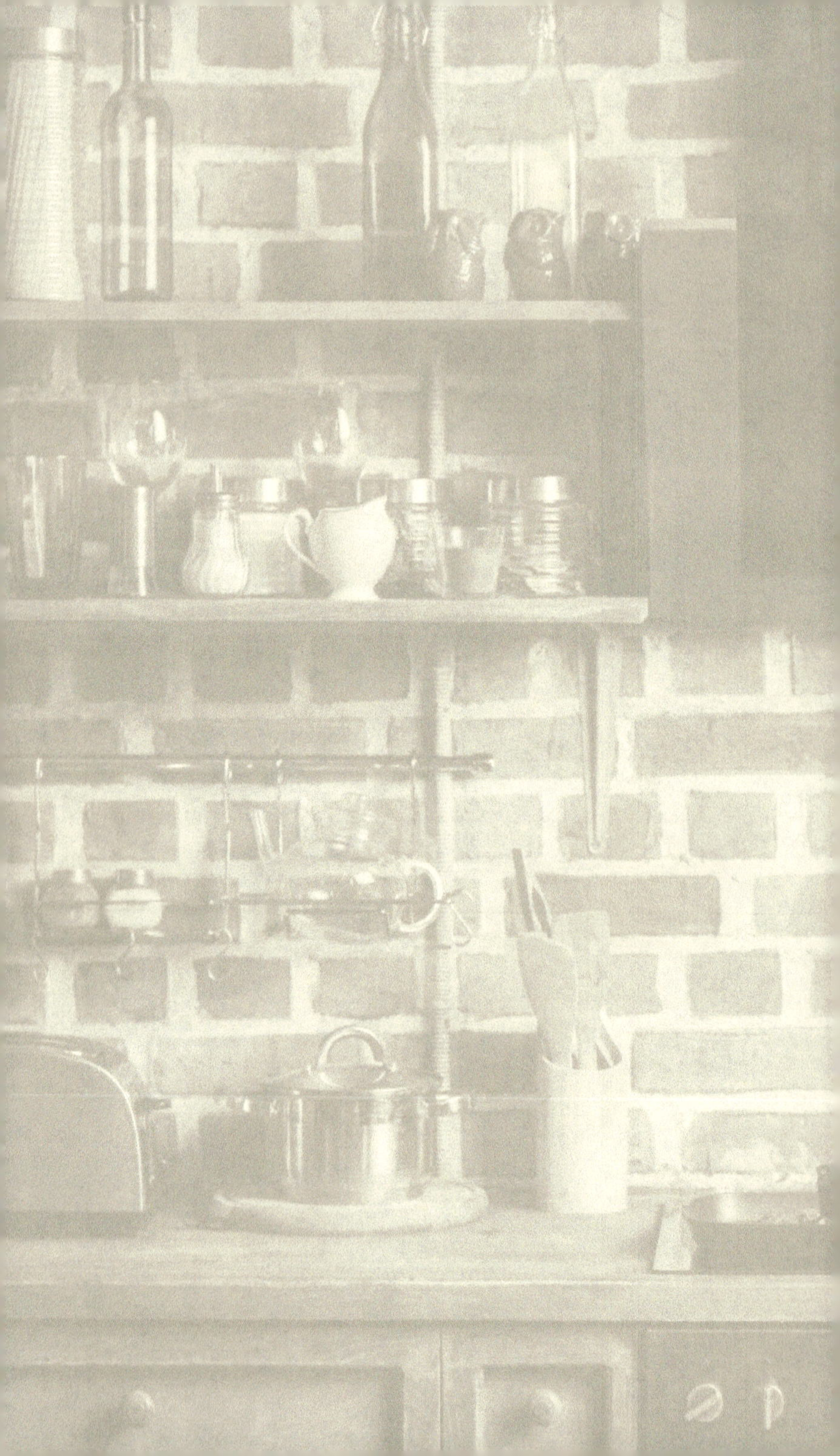

Chapter Nineteen

Nick was already down in the kitchen singing along to Frank Sinatra by the time I hung up with Mia and scurried down the hall to the guest bathroom. I took a shower, washed my hair, and put on the other sundress I'd brought, a navy and white chevron print with camisole straps. Since I wasn't sure who else might be staying in the guest rooms, I didn't want to monopolize the bathroom blow drying my hair in there, so I plugged my dryer in behind the dresser in my bedroom and used the mirror hanging above it.

There was a row of family pictures on top of the dresser—Noni and Nick's grandpa, who'd died before I met Nick, in a shot from maybe fifteen years ago; Nick and a whole gaggle of cousins sitting on the front porch steps eating popsicles; and a wedding photo from the nineteen forties. I could tell the era because of the Victory rolls in the women's hair, the cut of the bride's dress and the wide ties on the men. It was clearly a Lupo family photo, but I didn't recognize anyone in particular, not even a young Noni.

Although, wait a minute...I turned off the dryer and picked up the photo frame to study it more closely. Standing to the right of the bride and groom was a middle-aged couple that looked familiar, and the woman was so short I knew in a heartbeat who it was—Nick's great-grandparents, Papa Joe and Tiny.

I couldn't help smiling as I looked at them. I loved the way they held hands, the way his body was inclined slightly toward hers in a way that was both tender and protective. And her red lips—loved those red lips.

I set the photo down and picked up the dryer again. Although it was noisy, I could still hear Nick as well as some others singing down in the kitchen. I shook my head—they were such a loud, rambunctious bunch. I remembered feeling overwhelmed the first few times I attended Lupo family functions. Their boisterous Sunday dinners (which took all day) were so different from my family's sedate, relaxed meals, served promptly at six, done by seven, everyone on their way home by eight. I mean, Nick's family was relaxed too—they were just noisier about it. But they were more fun, too. I'd always loved his family.

Grinning at a particularly off-key rendition of "Fly Me to the Moon" (I'd bet money someone was dancing down there too), I thought how surprised they would be to see me again.

Coco, what are you doing here?

I'm fucking the cook. How've you been?

Marveling at the absurd turn my life had taken, I went over to my suitcase and unzipped the side pocket to look for my curling iron.

That's when I noticed my birth control pills.

My jaw dropped and I sucked in my breath—I'd forgotten to take one last night! Fingers fumbling, I hastily popped out the one for Friday, shoved it into my mouth and raced down the hall to the bathroom, sticking my head under the faucet and gulping noisily. When I'd swallowed it, I wiped my mouth with the back of my wrist and straightened slowly. In the mirror over the sink, I saw flushed cheeks, dilated pupils, scared doe eyes. My heart thundered in my chest.

I closed my eyes. God, how could I have been so stupid? We'd used a condom at Nick's place the first time, but after that, I'd assured him it was OK to go without one. Today at the house I'd thought about the one big pregnancy scare we'd had in college, and I *still* hadn't realized I'd forgotten a pill!

Damn you, Nick Lupo. You're making me crazy.

A sweat broke out on my back and I realized I'd forgotten to put on deodorant too. *Christ, Coco, anything else you overlooked?* I checked to make sure I was actually wearing clothes before darting back into my room and applying copious amounts of Secret Invisible Solid in Fresh Scent under each arm. Boy, this stuff would have to work overtime tonight—I was sweating like crazy.

In case it helped improve the strength or something, I took Saturday night's pill right then too—somehow doubling up seemed like a good idea. In my mind I saw Lupo family pictures with bazillions of kids and babies in them—the family was prolific, no doubt about that. Jesus, Nick probably had some kind of superpower sperm that would easily overtake my lame efforts at doubling up. My stomach churned as I imagined little tadpole-shaped things throwing a huge bash in my fallopian tubes right now, laughing at my attempts to thwart their objective and impede their mission.

With shaking hands and a queasy gut—wait, was that morning sickness? God help me—I finished my hair and makeup in a daze and slipped on my flats, trying to think where I was in my cycle. OK, the last week of pills, so that wasn't too dangerous, was it? Wasn't it the beginning or middle that was more critical? I was too scared to look it up.

Fuck, fuck, fuck. This was *so* my fault. And now I had to tell Nick. Not in the middle of Noni's dinner, though. That seemed like bad manners. I'd wait until tomorrow.

My legs were unsteady as I descended the stairs, and I held on tight to the railing. The voices from the kitchen and parlor got louder, and I admonished myself to put a smile on my face and act natural. *Pull yourself together! You've missed pills before, right?*

Yes, but never after having unprotected sex—or right before. I double whammied myself!

Nick double whammied me!

I reached the bottom of the steps and put a hand over my belly, praying—no, begging God—not to be pregnant. Then, plastering a smile on my face, I walked into the kitchen.

Nick's family was surprised to see me again, but they were gracious and kind and made me feel welcome, as always. His mother in particular hugged me hard and said how nice it was to see me again. At dinner, I sat between Nick and his sister Katie, who'd recently gotten engaged and had a million questions about weddings. I tried to answer them all, but mostly I fretted about pregnancy and stuffed my face. Some girls, like Mia, can't eat when they're anxious about something, but not me. I gobble my way through anxiety like a lawnmower, and I fuel it with booze.

Setting my fork down with a clank, I reached for my wine. No, wait, I shouldn't have alcohol, right? Fuck!

I picked up my fork again, hoping no one noticed that I took not only seconds but thirds. In addition to what Nick and Noni cooked, everyone had brought a dish, and the counter was loaded with platters heaped with food. There was antipasto and Caesar salad and stuffed shells and linguine with arrabiata and grilled lamb with rosemary and braciole and bread—homemade loaves of Italian bread, golden and flaky on the outside, soft and white on the inside. It didn't need butter but I slathered it on anyway, nearly moaning aloud at the first bite. Maybe I did, because while I was chewing Nick leaned over to whisper in my ear.

"Wow. You eating for two?" He poked me in the side.

I froze, swallowed, and reached for my water glass without commenting. Without even looking at him.

"I'm kidding, Coco. I love your appetite. It totally turns me on."

Not what I needed to do right now.

After dinner, we lit candles on the cake, sang to Noni, and I took a family picture with everyone standing around her. They had to squeeze in tight and I had to back way up to get all twenty-eight family members present into the frame, but I managed to get a decent one on Nick's phone. A funny feeling came over me as I scanned their faces—if things had gone differently years ago, maybe I'd have been *in* the picture instead of taking it. Maybe I'd have been happy about a potential pregnancy instead of terrified.

Nick reached for his phone and handed it to Katie. "Hey, will you take one of Coco and me?"

"Sure." She smiled at me. "How cute that you guys are back together again."

"Oh, we're not really tog— " I started to say, but Nick put an arm around my shoulders and clamped a hand over my mouth.

"Thanks. We are cute, aren't we?"

Katie snapped the shot just as I turned my head to glare at him, his hand still over my mouth. "Oops. Want another?"

Nick took the phone and burst out laughing. "No, actually. That's perfect."

Having to choose between a slice of Noni's pie or Nick's chocolate cake or his mother's cannolis or any of the other treats laid out for dessert was pure torture.

"Go for the cake," Nick whispered from behind me. "There's only one and everyone will want a piece."

I took a piece of cake, a napkin, and a fork and followed Nick into the parlor, where one of his aunts was pouring coffee. Balancing my cake plate on my knee, I nodded when she asked if I'd like a cup. Then I remembered.

"Oh, wait—is it decaf?"

She looked at me a little funny. "I think it is. Should I make sure?"

"Uh, no. That's OK. I'll pass."

She smiled and moved on to the next person, but she glanced back at me one more time. I pretended not to notice her gaze go to my middle, although it nearly made me want to cry. My throat squeezed shut.

Cake. Just eat the cake. Think about nothing but cake.

Actually, that was pretty easy to do, once I took the first bite. Nick's chocolate cake was the kind of delicious that would make even those annoying people who say *I'm not a dessert person* trample old ladies and small children to get the last piece. The frosting—what the hell was in it? I'd watched him make it, hadn't I? Was it vanilla? It tasted almost like a marshmallow but I hadn't seen any marshmallows on the counter. And how did he get it to stiffen into those delightful little peaks that gave the texture a hint of a crunch?

Then there was the actual cake. I'd tasted the batter and thought that was orgasmically good, so I wasn't surprised to discover it was even better baked and frosted. Plus every bite reminded me of Nick in the kitchen—and not just the sex. I loved sitting at the island and watching him work, loved how much he enjoyed it, how easy things had felt between us last night. Why did things have to be so complicated? Nick was like that miraculous pair of platform heels that somehow manages to be wickedly sexy and yet comfy too. Would I never have that sexy, comfortable feeling with anyone else? How cruel that it was our history giving our friendship that ease, and yet it was that very thing preventing me from trusting him.

But now there was a new wrinkle. If I was pregnant, Nick and I needed to have a pretty serious discussion about where to go from here. I wanted to know so badly, but it was too soon to take a test, wasn't it? I had to wait until I missed a period, right? Quickly I counted the days—I should get my period on Tuesday next week. Maybe there was a test I could take a couple days early.

"Coco?" Nick's voice came through a fog.

"I'm sorry, what?" I hadn't been paying attention to the conversation at all.

"Are you OK?" He spoke so quietly no one could hear, putting a hand on my shoulder. "You've gone really pale all of a sudden."

Oh God, was pallor a sign of pregnancy? It was, wasn't it?

"Nick." My anxiety trumped my manners. "I have to tell you something. In private."

Taking the empty plate from my lap, he stood and offered me a hand. I rose—crap, was the waist of my dress tight or was I imagining things?

Stop it. That's a braciole baby, not an actual baby.

Nick led the way into the kitchen, where he put our dishes in the sink, before taking my hand and tugging me out the back door. As soon as it shut behind us, he turned to me, his brow furrowed. "What's up?"

"I—I did something stupid." I swallowed, unable to get the rest of the words out, and twisted my fingers together.

"You did?" He planted his feet wide and crossed his arms. Even in the twilight, I could see the confusion in his face. "So tell me. It can't be that bad."

"Yes it can." I took a shaky breath, feeling a sob working its way up. "I forgot to take a pill last night."

His eyes went wide. "*That* pill?"

I nodded slowly. "*That* pill," I whispered, my eyes filling with tears. "And I'm scared."

"Oh, cupcake." Nick gathered me in his arms and held me tight to his chest. "It's OK. Come on. Let's go for a drive."

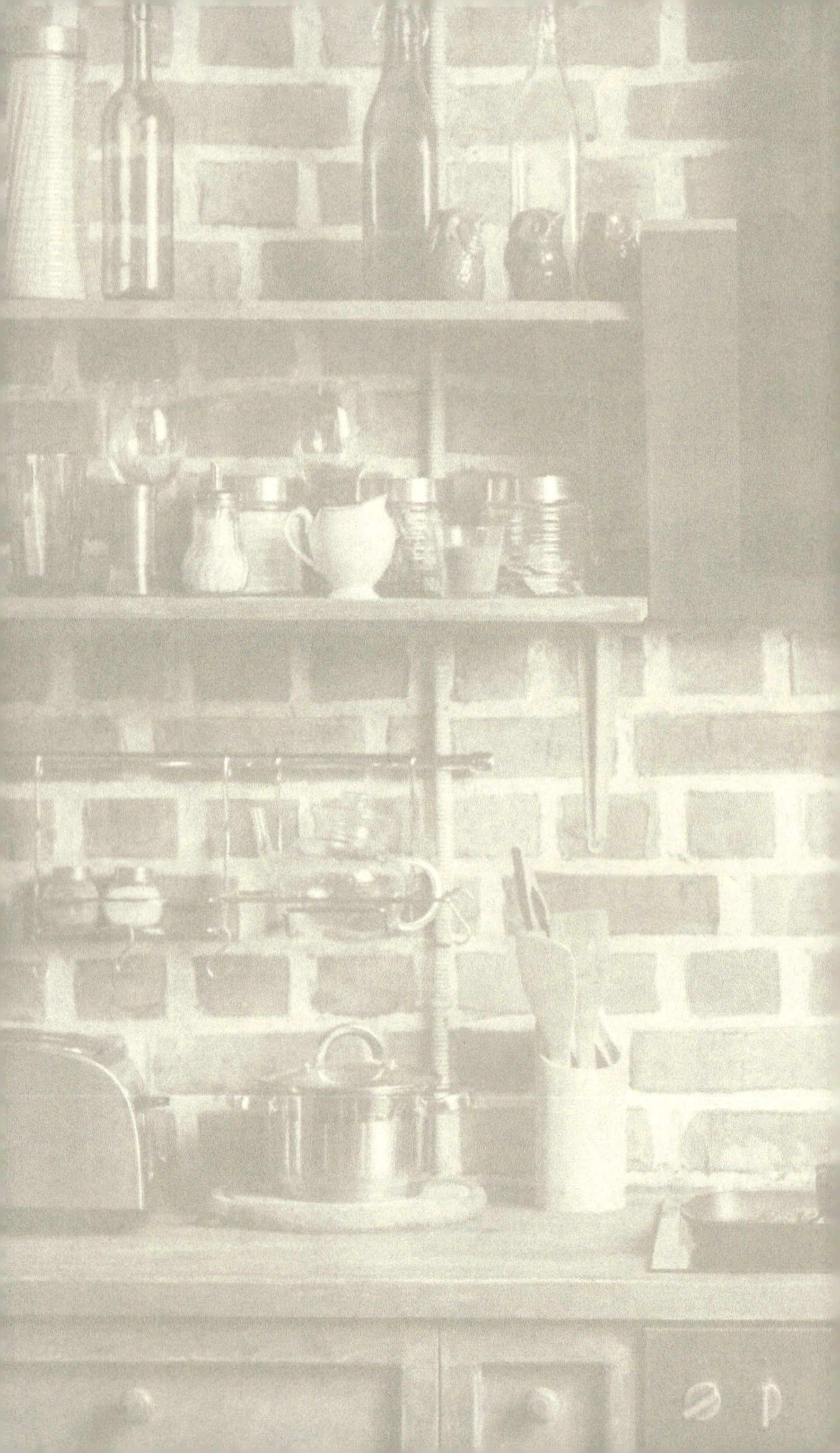

Chapter Twenty

Keeping an arm around my shoulder, he guided me around the house toward his car.

"Where you going?" called a female voice from the porch. Katie, maybe.

"Just out for a drive. We'll be back." He opened the door for me, and went around to the driver's side. Without bothering with the convertible top, he pulled away from the house and drove down the same dirt road that we'd run on. I rolled down the window, still desperate for fresh air. We kept going until we reached the road that cut through the orchard. Halfway to the end, Nick pulled over and shut off the engine.

I looked over to the right...somewhere out there was the place where I lost my virginity to the man next to me. On a fall night, when the air had a crisp chill to it. I remembered how the moonlight barely filtered through the branches to the ground, where we lay in the shadows.

I hadn't been scared. I remembered that vividly. I'd put up a little resistance—after all, I didn't want Nick to think I was easy—but the truth was, I couldn't wait to share my body with him that way, and have him share his with me. He would be *inside me*—what would that feel like? I wanted him there, wanted him to be the one to show me. I wanted to discover the thrill of it together.

Because of course, I'd thought he was a virgin too.

I remembered how he'd brought me to orgasm with his tongue first that night, leaving me drenched and swollen and ready for him. Then I'd pulled him up my body, reaching between us to free his cock from his jeans, my heart pounding. The details were so clear in my mind—the floral dress and red cardigan sweater I wore, the way the skirt bunched up around my waist, the crunch of the leaves under the blanket, the taste of apples and cinnamon in his kiss, his mouth wet. The look in his eyes as he pushed inside me for the first time, inch by inch, and the feel of his shirt in my tightly clenched hands. Willing my body to ease up, to take him in, I breathed deeply, my fists relaxing. *God, you're so tight*, he'd whispered. *So tight and wet and it feels so good.*

"I can still feel it, you know." I spoke without taking my eyes from the orchard. "That first time. You went slow for me." Between my legs an ache was building, and I squeezed my thighs together. The memory would have to be enough.

"Yes."

"You kept asking if I was OK."

"I was so nervous."

"More nervous than I was, I think."

"I didn't want to hurt you. And I didn't want it to be over too quickly, which was always a problem in those days."

I looked at him. "You knew what you were doing." A subtle reminder that he'd lied about his virginity.

"Didn't feel like it. In fact, *that* felt more like a first time than my actual first time, which was pretty fucking terrible, to tell you the truth. Terrible and very, very fast. Not that I really cared." He reached over and took my hand. "With you I cared. I wanted it so badly, but I wanted it to be perfect. I was so in love with you."

My throat felt like someone's hands had closed around it. "It was perfect."

"I never wanted it to end."

I managed a smile. "Not even you can last that long."

"I didn't mean sex. I meant us." He brought the back of my hand to his lips. "I never wanted us to end. I still don't."

I tried to pull my hand away, but he held it tight. "Nick, stop."

"Come here, please." He scooted over toward the passenger seat, reached beneath my arms, and hauled me onto his lap, my knees on either side of his hips. "Let's talk about this. What are you thinking?"

"I can't talk—I can barely think." I braced myself on his shoulders, keeping him at arm's length. "And being on your lap does not make that easier."

He tightened his grip on my hips, lifted his slightly. "I know, it makes it harder. So. Much. Harder."

I sighed, exasperated. "No jokes, Nick. We need to have a serious discussion. I messed up really badly! I've been stupid all weekend."

"No, you haven't. You've been enjoying yourself. So much that your regular routine slipped your mind. You're human."

"But that slip might have resulted in a pregnancy. Do you understand that? A baby. I'm totally unfit to be a parent!"

"You won't be alone, Coco. I'm here."

"You're totally unfit, too!"

"Hey, come on. I want kids, remember?"

"Not like this, you don't. With your ex-girlfriend who—"

"Ex-wife, actually. Hey, let's get remarried!" he said, as if it were the best idea he'd had in years.

"—ex-*wife* who hasn't forgiven you for what you did and probably never will. And could you please stop proposing to me out of the blue?"

"Sorry. I just got carried away when you said baby."

"I don't want a baby with you, Nick. And I don't want to marry you again."

He was silent a few seconds. "Ouch. I'm not sure which part of that hurts most."

I closed my eyes and tried to rethink what I'd said. "I'm sorry. I don't mean to hurt your feelings, and if I *am* pregnant, that may change things, but right now, Nick…I am not OK with this. I wish I were. I wish I could accept your apology and understand your excuses and forgive and forget and all that, but I can't. I just can't. Because I don't know how to trust you."

"Why not?" His hands locked behind my hips. "Tell me what to say and I'll say it. Tell me what to do to make you change your mind. I love you, and I don't want to give up on us."

"But you did! You already did!" It struck me then that maybe that's the part I couldn't get over. Even if I forgave him for leaving me in Vegas, I couldn't get beyond feeling that he didn't try hard enough to get me back, if that's what he really wanted. "If you were truly sorry for calling our marriage a mistake, you would have tried harder to find me, to keep me. Even after I got back from Paris."

"But I did try! You divorced me in sixty days!"

"I wanted to hurt you. Like you hurt me."

He exhaled, dropping his head back on the seat. "I left you in peace after the divorce because I thought that was what you wanted. If you love something, set it free and all that. I'd fucked everything up, and I thought for once I'd try to be a gentleman."

"I never wanted a gentleman. I wanted you."

He picked his head up. "Thanks."

I almost laughed at the offended look on his face, but every time I felt a moment of levity, reality sucked me down again. Groaning, I dropped my forehead to his shoulder.

"What the hell, Nick? What are we going to do? Why can't we ever get things right?"

He rubbed my back. "It's your body, Coco. And I will support you no matter what you decide. It's going to be OK no matter what."

Giving in to the feeling of being comforted, of being told it would all be OK, of feeling like I wasn't alone, I turned my face into his throat. Inhaled the scent of his skin, which would forever say sex-and-sugar to me. Except when it said sex-and-bacon.

I chuckled in the crook of his neck. I couldn't help it.

"What?" He sounded shocked that I was giggling.

"Nothing. I was thinking something dirty."

"What a coincidence."

I laughed again, lifting my head. "This would be so much easier if I didn't like you."

His mouth formed that crooked grin I couldn't resist. "I knew you still liked me."

"A little. Maybe." *What are you doing?* screamed a voice in my head as I leaned forward impulsively to kiss those lips. *What the actual fuck are you doing?* It was the anti-dessert tray voice, the one that remembers to count the steps it takes me to walk away.

Oh, now you show up, I thought, feeling Nick's hands move up my back. *Where were you in the kitchen when I told him to fuck me without a condom? Where were you in the cemetery this morning? Why didn't you sound the alarm then and remind me that I hadn't taken a pill?*

No answer.

I took that as a sign.

Our kiss grew frantic, and our hands began to wander. I freed my dress from between us and Nick's fingers crept beneath it. His palms slid up my thighs, settling on my ass and squeezing it tight. I took his face in my hands, meeting his tongue with mine, shivering with anticipation at the growing bulge in his jeans beneath me.

Reaching behind me, I unzipped my dress and let the straps fall off my shoulders, then slipped my arms from them. Nick's hands moved up my back, which arched instinctively, pressing my breasts closer to his mouth. He dragged his tongue around one nipple, teasing it into a stiff, tingling peak before sucking it hard into his mouth. "Oh God, that feels so good," I breathed, taking his head in my hands and holding it to my chest. My breath caught as he took the hardened tip between his teeth, biting down before sucking it again. His other hand slid down over my ass, this time inside my panties.

I grabbed onto the back of the seat and rocked my hips over his, widening my knees. He groaned, moving both hands to grip my ass, thrusting up beneath me as he pulled me against him, his mouth never leaving my breasts. *Remember this?* I almost asked. *Remember how we used to park your truck somewhere hidden and fuck each other through our clothes? I wanted the real thing. I want the real thing now.* But I was too scared to say anything—if I stopped to talk, stopped to remember, stopped to think at all, I might reconsider where this was headed, and right now I really wanted this to head somewhere that ended with my pussy hot and tight around his big hard cock.

"Coco." Nick's breath was cool on my wet skin. "Are you sure?"

"Shhhh." I kissed his cheek, his jaw, his neck, running my tongue over his favorite little spot. Between my legs, I was aching and wet, my panties soaked. *Fuck yes, I'm sure.*

But wait.

I picked my head up, breathing hard. "Do you have a condom?"

"Yes." Lifting his hips, which made my core muscles clench, he reached into his pocket and pulled one out.

"Give it to me." I ripped it from his hands and tore it open with my teeth while he reached beneath my dress and undid his jeans. My stomach jumping, I unrolled the condom over his dick and pressed up on my knees, freeing one leg from my panties. Nick closed his lips over my nipple again as I positioned him at my entrance and sank down slowly, reveling in the exquisite way he stretched and filled me, inch by rock solid inch. Pressing my hands to the car's soft roof, I stopped for a second to slide up and down a few times, exhilarated by the way it made him moan and suck harder. Finally I went all the way down, sighing as he reached the deepest place inside me.

"Coco," he said gruffly as I began to move. "I have to have you."

Arms overhead, I swiveled my hips in lovely little arcs and circles, each shape twisting me tighter, carrying me higher. "You have me." Trading swivels for thrusts, I set a hard, steady rhythm against him, my entire body humming. God, he was so deep inside me, hitting that spot that made everything rush to the no-stopping-this point. "I'm here. I'm right here." And then I couldn't speak or think or even move, every muscle in my body seizing up. Nick's fingers dug into my ass and he pulled me roughly against him, the base of his cock rubbing my clit. Tears came to my eyes, my mouth falling open as I teetered on the brink. *Take me over. Now. Fuck me, yes, yes, like that...* I exploded, his name on my lips.

He never stopped moving. "Fuck, I love watching you come. I love hearing you say my name. I love every fucking thing about you."

"I love you too." Taking his head in my hands, I rained kisses on his forehead, his cheeks, his lips. "I don't want to but I do." God, the world was tilting and spinning out of control. What the fuck was I saying? Was I delirious? The words wouldn't stop pouring out, as if a dam had burst. "And I hate you too. I hate you," I said, sliding up and down his hard, wet cock, my mouth pressed close to his. "I fucking hate you for what you did to me. I hate that I couldn't get over you. I hate that I can't say no to you. I hate that I still want you this way."

"Get on your back." Without waiting for me to move, Nick flipped me onto my back across the front seat. One leg ended up wrapped around him, the other dangling toward the floor. He pulled his shirt off before taking a wrist in each hand and pinning them against the door above my head. "Is this the way you want me?" He drove his cock inside me again and again, slamming into me with a force that knocked my head against the door. "You hate the way you want this?" His jaw was set hard, his tone hot with anger and desire.

"Yes, I hate it," I panted, lifting my hips to meet his, gasping at the violent way our bodies crashed together. "But I can't get enough."

"Jesus." Somehow he fucked me harder and deeper, causing stabs of pain to pierce the pleasure ballooning inside me. But I liked it that way—and he knew it. I turned my face to the side, trying not to cry out. "You're going to come again," he ordered. "I want that tight little pussy to come on my cock just like it was the first time. Remember?"

Hell yes, I remembered. I hadn't been expecting a second orgasm that night, but the way he moved and the things he said and the sound of his voice and the thought of him inside me...I'd climaxed again beneath him, my hand over my wide-open mouth, smothering a scream as my body pulsed around his for the first time. "Yes," I breathed, the past and the present converging within me.

"Good girl. I want you to scream this time, like you wouldn't then."

I thought about trying to stay quiet just to defy him, but then I made the mistake of glancing down at his bare torso, at my name on his chest, at the way his abs flexed as he rocked his body into mine. Unable to stop myself, I cried out, again and again.

My head banged against the side of the car but I didn't feel it—I felt nothing but his hot skin and hard cock, heard nothing but our gasps and cries in the falling darkness, imagined nothing but his body joined to mine until we came together and the world turned to liquid gold behind closed eyes.

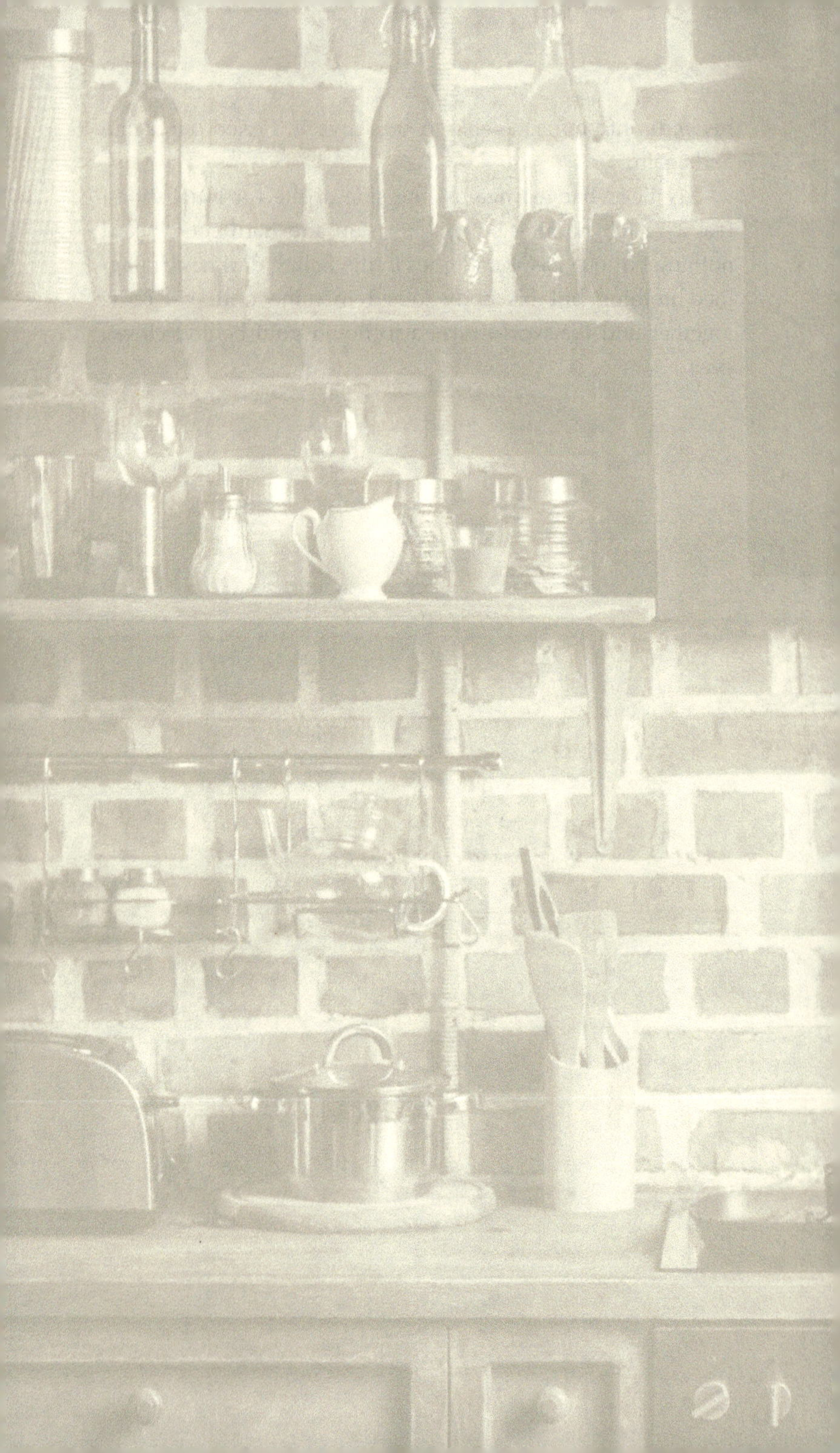

Chapter Twenty-One

Later we pulled the Amish quilt from the trunk and lay on our backs in a clearing near the orchard. Nick's hands were folded behind his head, and I rested my temple on his left bicep.

"What's that one?" I pointed high above us, where stars glittered in the cloudless country night sky. "The one that looks like a W." I tilted my head the other way. "Or maybe it's an M."

"That's Cassiopeia."

"Story, please?"

"She was beautiful, and a queen, so she had a pretty good thing going, but then she bragged that she and her daughter Andromeda were more beautiful than these other goddesses."

"Never a good idea. Which goddesses?"

"Some sea goddesses, I think. So they went to Poseidon, and he was pretty pissed, and said she had to sacrifice Andromeda to a sea monster to appease him."

I gasped. "Did she?"

"She would have, but Perseus came along and saved Andromeda."

"Perseus," I mused. "Remind me about him."

"He was this handsome chef with a big cock that—ow!"

I thumped him on the chest. "Come on, tell me."

Nick rubbed his ribcage and went on. "OK, fine, although I like my version better. Perseus comes along and sees the lovely Andromeda tied to a chair at the edge of the sea, and being the awesome hero that he is, he kills the sea monster and rescues her. Cassiopeia can't go unpunished, of course, so she gets placed in a throne in the sky, destined to spend all eternity circling the north celestial pole, half the time clinging to it so she doesn't fall off."

"Aha. Hard to look beautiful when you're upside down. So what happened to Perseus and Andromeda?"

"They got married."

I sighed. "Of course."

"And they had nine children."

"Yikes."

"But she gets her own constellation too, right next to her mother's. Right there, see?" With his right hand he drew a line across the sky.

"No." I frowned, holding up my right hand too. "Show me."

Taking my hand in his, he traced the outline of the stars with my finger. "See it now?"

"Yes." Truthfully, I wasn't sure I did, but it didn't really matter. I just liked being here with him again, hearing the stories, and forgetting about our own lives for the moment. "And what about that one over there?" I pointed to another cluster of stars and relaxed as Nick began to talk about them, recounting for me stories his father and grandfather had told to him. After a while, I moved my head to his chest and closed my eyes, but he kept talking in a low, soothing voice, smoothing my hair back from my face and pretending not to notice the tears soaking his shirt.

By the time we drove back to the house, most of the cars were gone from the driveway and the parlor windows were dark. "We stayed out there too long," I fretted. "You should have been at the party with your family."

"Nah, don't worry about it. Noni understands."

"What does she know?"

Nick turned the engine off. "About us?"

I nodded.

"Nothing. I mean, just that we broke up. She knows I screwed it up, though. She never let me forget it."

That made me smile. "I love Noni."

"She loves you too."

"Did she want us to get back together?"

He shook his head. "No. She pretty much said it was a good thing you'd moved on because you were too good for me anyway."

I laughed, in spite of everything. "Stop it. She adores you. Everyone does."

"I am kind of adorable."

I glanced at him and shrugged. "Kind of."

With a grunt of frustration, he grabbed the back of my head and pulled my lips to his, kissing me hard. "You drive me crazy. Tell me you'll do it forever."

His plea squeezed my heart. "I can't, Nick. I just don't know."

His hand loosened slightly, played in my hair. "What if… you know." His eyes swept to my stomach. "Should we take a test?"

"I appreciate the whole *we* thing, Nick, but I don't want you to feel like this traps us into anything, even if it's positive."

"I don't feel that at all." His eyes were steady on mine in the dark. "Not at all."

My mouth fell open as I realized something. "You hope it's positive, don't you?"

"Not necessarily." He dropped his hand from my hair to my shoulder. "But I wouldn't think my life was over if it was. Would you?"

"Hell yes, I would." I put my hand over my chest. "I'm not ready for it. We're not ready for it. We have a history of rushing into things, and now we're all fucked up, and no child deserves to be born to two people who've been divorced for seven years, made a sloppy mistake, and don't even know what they want."

"I know what I want." His thumb brushed my cheek.

"Well, I don't." I looked away from his crestfallen expression. "And until I figure it out, we have to cool off."

He took his hand off me. "OK. I understand."

"Thank you." I opened the car door and got out. Nick followed suit, putting a hand at the small of my back as we walked up the porch steps. I turned to him halfway up. "Nick, you have to stop touching me. Seriously. I can't think when you do."

He held up both hands. "OK, OK. Sorry." We continued up the stairs. "I guess that means we can't sleep together tonight, huh?"

"That's exactly what that means." It came out sharper than I intended and Nick stopped me before the screen door with a hand on my elbow.

"Are you still angry with me?" His face was solemn.

"About what?"

"Any of it. All of it."

I closed my eyes briefly, let the question ruminate. To my surprise, I wasn't. "No. You know what? I'm not angry anymore. And I'm sorry I snapped at you. I'm just sad and confused."

He sighed heavily as he opened the door. "I think I liked it better when you were angry with me."

Creak.

My eyes flew open as the unmistakable sound of the old springs beneath me groaned under added weight.

"Shhhh." Nick's scent filled my head as his warm body slid into the full-size bed behind me.

"Nick, what are you doing?" I whispered as he curled his body around mine.

"I love you," he whispered back. "And I'm not giving up this time. Now go back to sleep." He kissed the back of my head and tucked an arm around my stomach. "Night."

I swallowed hard.

See? He lies, said common sense. *He promised not to touch you. He said he'd let things cool off. He doesn't know how to play by the rules. He'd be a terrible husband and father.*

But his body was warm and cozy, his breathing deep and steady, lulling me back to sleep already.

I'd kick him out in the morning.

As it turned out, I didn't get the chance to boot Nick out of my bed, because he was up before me again. I sat up and stretched, breathing in the smell of fresh coffee and---oh God, that scent! Was it…I sniffed the air like a bloodhound…Noni's cinnamon buns?

I jumped out of bed and dressed in a navy blue romper,

brushed my hair with a few frantic strokes and headed downstairs, recalling the breakfast Nick and Noni always made when we were here in the past. Huge, doughy rolls, sticky sweet with cinnamon and sugar and dripping with icing. I might have to go on another run today, but I was having one of those buns.

The aroma grew stronger at the bottom of the steps and I nearly floated into the kitchen, where Nick sat at the counter with a cup of coffee and Noni putzed around, cleaning up.

"Good morning," she sang. "Did the noise wake you? I dropped a metal pan, and the whole house shook. My hands are a little unsteady these days."

"Nope. It was the smell." I inhaled, my knees twitching in excitement. "I have dreamed of this smell many times."

"Rolls are in the oven," Nick said. "Come sit. I went up to the attic this morning. Look what I found." He gestured to the counter in front of him, where an old black photo album rested. *Photographs*, it said on the front cover in curly script. The leather edges were soft and frayed, and the entire thing was coming apart at the binding, time doing its best to overpower the graying white ribbon holding the pages together.

I sat next to him and pulled it between us. "Is this the album you mentioned yesterday, Noni?"

"It is." She set a cup of coffee in front of me.

Nick opened the cover. Black and white photographs were fixed to black paper pages with tiny picture corners. Wedding photos, pictures of families, religious portraits of children. We turned the pages slowly, and sometimes we laughed at a particularly dour or mischievous expression on a child, but mostly we were reverently silent, going through more than a century of his family's history.

The first photos looked like maybe they'd been taken in the early twentieth century, but as time went on, the pages revealed less formal poses and more smiling faces. All the

Lupo men had the same full mouth and strong brow, the dark hair and eyes. Nick resembled them, although he must have gotten his leanness and height from his mother's side. Finally we came to the wedding picture of his great-grandparents, which we studied in silence for a moment.

"They're in love, you can just tell," I said.

"They must have been. They had eight kids."

"You don't have to be in love to have eight kids," I reminded him. "Or even one kid." Without thinking about it, my hand went to my stomach, and I glanced down at it.

Nick cleared his throat. "We found something interesting in the back. Look at this." From the back of the album he pulled a piece of material and spread it out in front of me. It was once white cotton but had yellowed with age. "It's a handkerchief," Nick said. "And look."

On the handkerchief, scrawled in what appeared to be red lipstick, were three words.

I love you.

At the bottom, in black ink, was printed, *Tiny and Joey, 29 July, 1923*.

I stared at it for a moment, gooseflesh rippling down my arms. "What's today's date?"

"July twenty-ninth," Nick answered. Then he leaned over and whispered in my ear. "Fucking weird, right?"

Weird?

No. Cheez Whiz was weird. Olive loaf. Haggis-and-cracked-pepper potato chips.

This was alarming as fuck.

What did it mean???

"Oh yes, that was a pretty famous family story." Noni picked up a coffee cup with a picture of a cat on it and took a sip. "Apparently, Tiny had turned Papa Joe down, and so he'd decided to go back to Chicago. Well, wouldn't you know, she realized she was in love with him as soon as he announced he was leaving. She shows up at his house to tell him, but he was right in the middle of cooking Sunday dinner for his family."

I smiled, although my heart was beating in a peculiar and uneven fashion. "Really?"

"Yes," she went on. "He was in the kitchen surrounded by his sisters. And she tried to get him to speak privately with her but he refused."

"As he should have," Nick put in, lifting his cup to his mouth. "Fickle women."

"So then what?" I asked. "She wrote him a note?"

Noni laughed. "Yes, in the bathroom, with her lipstick, on her handkerchief. Then she marched into the kitchen and handed it to him. And according to his sisters, they disappeared into the pantry downstairs for quite an inappropriate length of time.

I clapped my hands over my cheeks. "I love it! Nick, you should put the note in your restaurant too. Frame it or something. With the picture."

"Not a bad idea." He set his cup down. "Noni, do you think I could have it?"

Noni waved her hand. "Take the whole book. You know, I'm surprised it was just stuck in the photo album like that. It was so important to her. She must have forgotten it was there. They were married sixty-seven years, you know."

"It's a good thing Nick found it then. Otherwise it might have been lost to time forever." I couldn't get over the matching date. What did it mean?

Noni nodded, eyeing me thoughtfully. "Yes. Although, nothing is really lost forever. When a thing is meant to be found, the right person will find it. So I bet there's a reason why that note was discovered again after all this time."

"You mean…you think it was a sign?" I asked carefully.

Nick laughed. "You're getting to her, Noni. Coco believes in signs. Keep going with it, please."

I was too flustered to even hit him.

"Not a sign, necessarily. I just meant that I think it's right Nick came across the note. That he was meant to have it." She took another sip of coffee and winked at me over the rim of her cup.

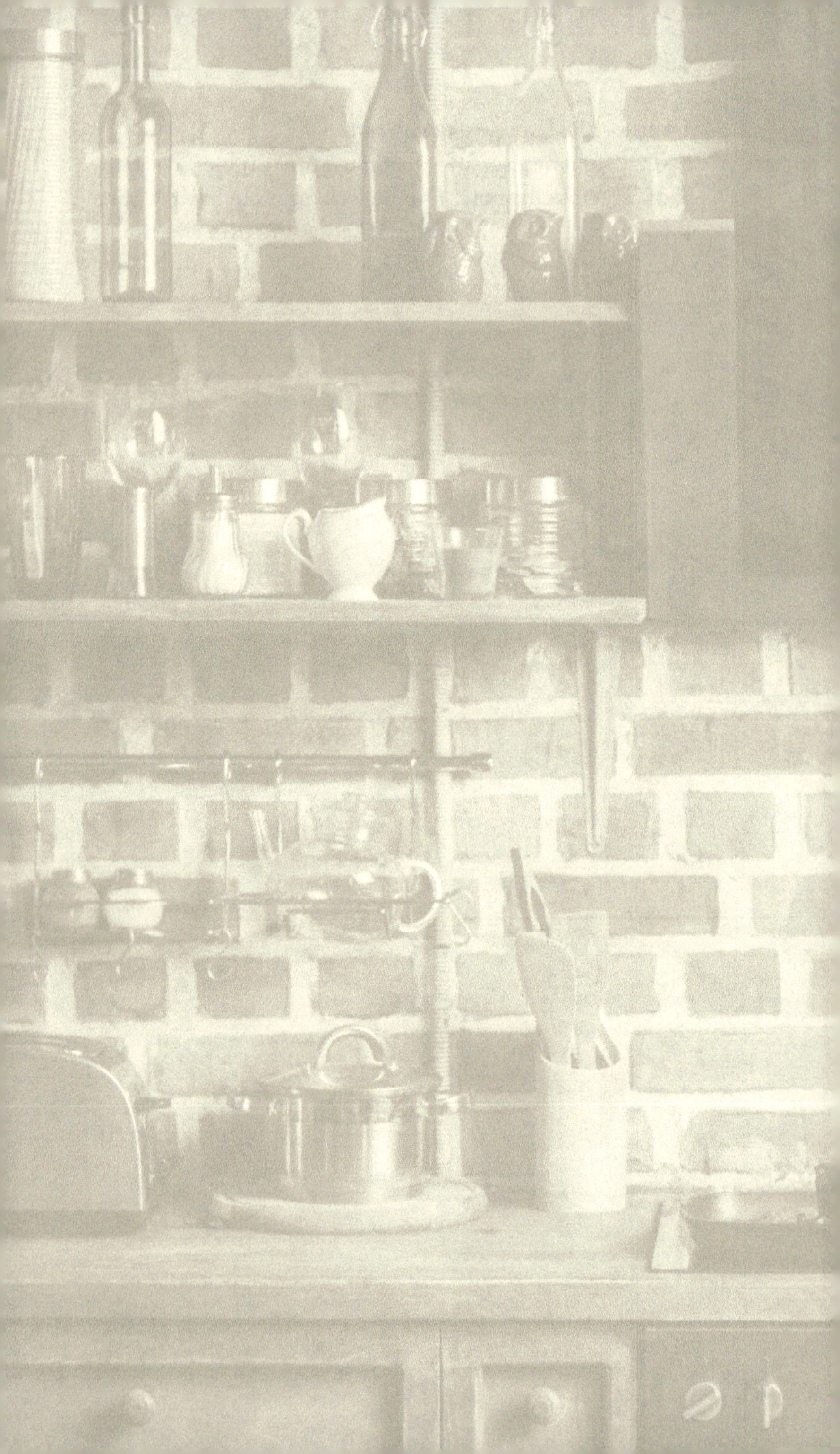

Chapter Twenty-Two

Later that morning, Nick painted the Adirondack chairs while I typed up some of Noni's stories on her desktop, which reminded me of the kind we used to have in our elementary school classrooms. In addition to the Lupo stories she knew, she talked about growing up on the farm, what it was like to be a teenager during the Depression, and meeting her husband Joe at a USO dance in 1944. I printed a copy of the file for Noni and emailed a copy to Nick and myself—maybe it wasn't my family, but I felt emotionally invested in the stories somehow.

After lunch, we said goodbye to Noni, and got on the road. It looked like rain, so we didn't put the top down on the convertible, and sure enough, after about ten minutes on I-75, it began to sprinkle, and then pour. Visibility was so bad, I wouldn't have blamed Nick for pulling over and waiting out the storm, but he just slowed down and stayed focused.

"Sorry. This ride home might take us awhile," he said without taking his eyes off the road.

"That's OK. I'm not in a rush to get back." Crossing my arms over my chest, I thought ahead to the task I was dreading—a pregnancy test. After we got back to Detroit, I'd leave right from the parking garage and stop at a drugstore on my way home. The thought of taking a test at my parents' house was pretty cringe-worthy, but I didn't want to do it at Nick's apartment either. I wanted to be alone. Maybe I could do it at the Devine Events office.

"Want to talk?" Nick glanced at me briefly.

"Not really..." I rubbed my hands up and down my arms. "I don't have anything new to say yet. I'm still...working through some things."

"OK. Do you want to stop at a store on the way home?"

I shook my head. "No. I'll take care of it."

He pressed his lips together, and I could tell he wasn't saying something he was thinking.

"What?" I pressed.

"It doesn't seem like you should be alone when you take it."

"I'll be fine."

"No, I know, it's not that. I mean it doesn't seem fair. For you to be alone."

I studied his profile carefully. His jaw was set at a stubborn angle. "Fair to whom, Nick?"

"To me."

"You!" My arms flew open. "How is it unfair to you that I want to take this pregnancy test alone? You're not my boyfriend."

"Maybe not, but I'm still the potential father. I want the answer just as badly as you do." He risked a sideways glance at me. "And I want the truth."

"What!" I exploded. "You think I'd lie to you about this? You're the liar in this car, Nick. I think we've established that this weekend. Thanks for the reminder." I turned away from him in a huff, crossing my legs toward the passenger door and staring out my window. *Unfuckingbelievable. Just when he starts to get under my skin again, he has to be an asshole.*

"Don't get mad, Coco. I'm trying to be honest here. You

know what? Women say they want men to talk about their feelings and be honest, but they don't really mean it."

"Are you fucking kidding me? I don't need to hear your feelings when you're insinuating that I'd lie about something like a baby."

"Wouldn't you? Even though you don't want it?"

"No, I wouldn't! But you're damn right I don't want it."

Nick exhaled like he was struggling to keep his temper. "You're trying to hurt me. I get it."

"Good." I felt a small victory in getting to him. A covert glance over my shoulder revealed white knuckles on the steering wheel.

"How many times am I going to have to apologize for the past, Coco?" His tone was aggrieved, as if *he* were the victim of injustice here. "I'm sorry. I never should have done any of the wrong things I did. But it was seven fucking years ago. Can't we move on?"

"I'm not looking for another apology because you hurt me in the past, Nick. I'm looking for one for what you said to me just now."

He was quiet after that, and I kept my eyes on the raindrops splattering down the window. All the way down I-75 we sat in icy silence, both of us hurt and angry, neither of us willing to apologize again. *This is why*, I told myself. *This is why it will never work. You're always going to throw the past in his face, and he's always going to play the martyr, make you feel like a bitch for holding a grudge.*

I didn't see any way out. And the only thing that could make this worse was a plus sign on that test.

By the time we pulled into the parking garage next to Nick's apartment building, my ire had mellowed. His must have too, because when he asked what floor I'd parked on, his voice was much softer than it had been the last time he'd spoken.

"Fourth floor." I directed him to where my Volkswagon was parked, and after pulling up behind it, he turned off the engine and put his hand on my leg.

"I'm sorry. I shouldn't have said that…about the test. You can take it alone if you want. Just let me know what it says." He opened the driver's side door, but I stopped him.

"Wait. I'm sorry too. I know this affects you almost as much as it affects me, and I know you have strong feelings about family."

"And about you." He met my eyes. "I love you. And I want you. But I don't want to live this way—being called a liar and an asshole for the rest of my life because of something stupid I did when I was twenty-two. I don't want every argument we ever have to circle back to it. I'm not that guy anymore, Coco. I'm not perfect, but given the chance, I know I could make you happy. Tell me what to do to get that chance."

"I wish I could, Nick. The truth is, I just don't know." I felt like crying again but managed to gulp it back. He nodded sadly and got out of the car.

After unloading my things from his trunk, I placed them in my back seat and turned to say goodbye. Nick stood a few feet from me. It felt like a few miles.

"I have to go to L.A. tomorrow. Back Wednesday. Just call me when…you know anything," he said.

"I will."

"And take care of yourself."

"I will." The tone of sad finality in his voice squeezed my heart.

Taking two steps forward, he kissed me on the cheek. "Thanks for staying the weekend with me. Let me know the details for the party next Saturday. I'll be there." Then he walked around the front of the Mercury, looking more morose than I'd ever seen him.

No—there was one other time I'd seen him that miserable, the night I'd broken things off because I thought he'd slept with another girl. The night he'd lied. The night he thought he lost me.

I'd believed that was goodbye forever.

Maybe it should have been.

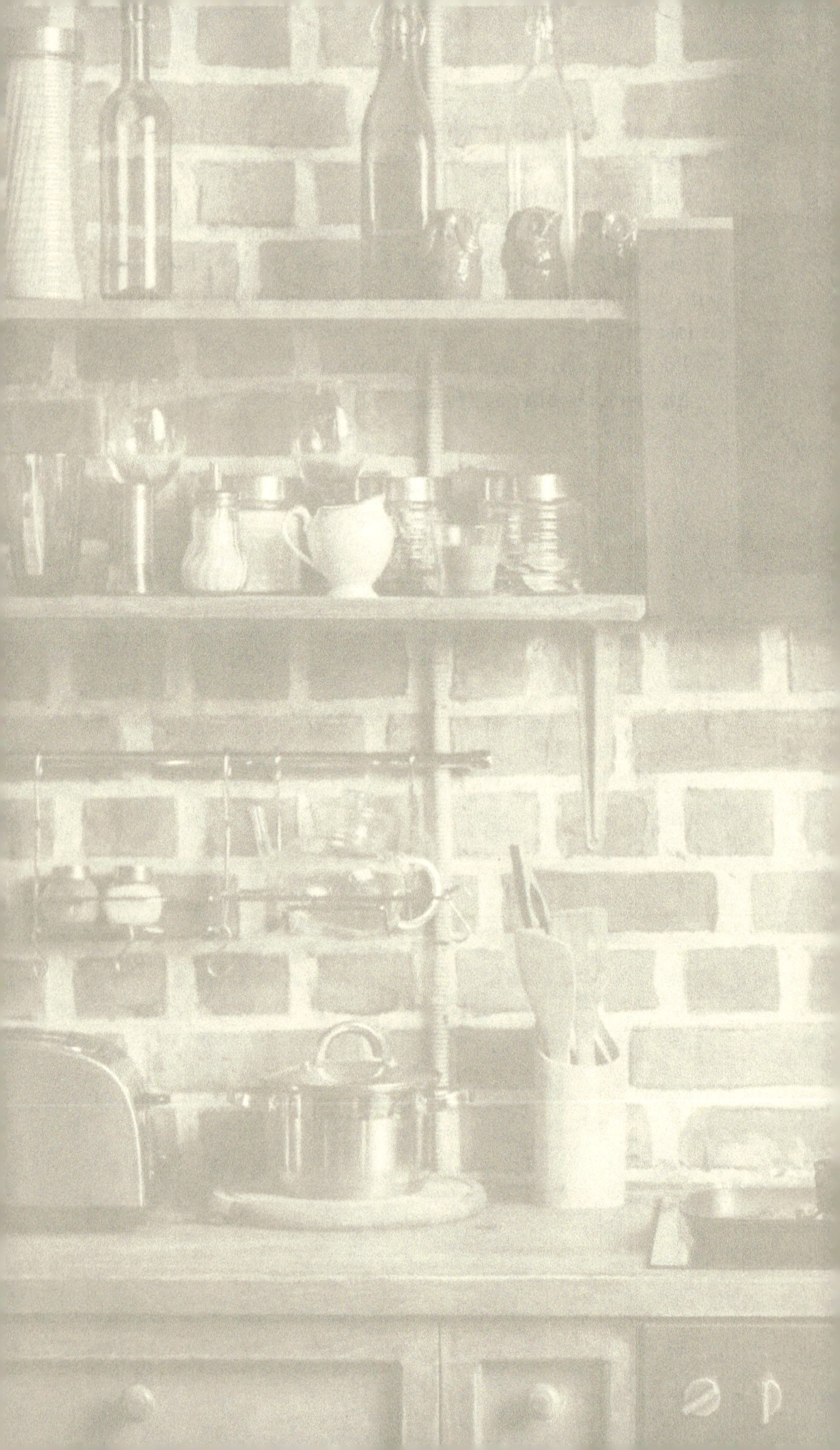

Chapter Twenty-Three

"What's it doing?" I sat on the edge of the tub in Mia and Lucas's bathroom, my hands twisting together in my lap.

Please be positive.

"Nothing yet." Mia and Erin stood at the vanity, both of them staring intently at the stick, like those people who can make objects move just by looking at them.

Please be negative.

"OK. Tell me when you see anything."

Please be positive.

"It's only been like thirty seconds—wait! Something happening!" Erin grabbed Mia's arms, and Mia grabbed Erin's back. They looked like a 6th grade couple at a middle school dance.

Please be negative.

"Oh, God, you guys. I'm a wreck. What is it?" Getting to my feet, I paced back and forth in front of the tub, terrified of either result.

"Hold on…" Mia's voice—was it hopeful or wary? I knew she wanted it to be negative.

And what if it was? Would I be relieved or disappointed? Why did I feel like I'd cry either way?

"OK, it's done." Erin and Mia looked at each other and turned to me.

"Holy shit." I felt woozy. I breathed in and out, touched my fingers to my temples. "OK, tell me. Am I pregnant?"

"No," Mia said. "You're not."

"Not according to this test," Erin added. "But you should probably take the second one in the box tomorrow to be even surer."

Exhaling, I closed my eyes and let my hands drop to my stomach. Not pregnant. Erin was right, and I would take the test tomorrow, but somehow I knew what Mia said was true. "I'm not pregnant." The word *pregnant* caught in my throat, and I struggled to choke back tears. They spilled over anyway. "I'm not pregnant," I sobbed.

"Oh, honey." Mia took me in her arms, and Erin wrapped us both in hers. "Are you sad or just relieved?"

"I don't know," I admitted as they released me. "Both, I guess."

"Come on in here. Erin, grab the tissues." Mia led me into her bedroom, spacious but cozy with its chocolate brown walls and king-sized bed mounded with colorful pillows. Photographs of Paris hung over the bed, and on her nightstand, Mia had a framed picture of Lucas and herself on the top of Notre Dame Cathedral. She sat on the foot of the bed, pulling me down beside her. "Speak."

"She's not a dog, Mia." Erin handed me the box of tissues and sat on my other side. "And let her catch her breath first."

"Sorry." Mia put her arm around me and squeezed. "I just hate seeing you this way. And I think talking will help. No more hiding things—I still can't believe you managed to keep your marriage and divorce secret to yourself."

I'd confessed the full truth to Erin and caught both of them up to speed before taking the test. "I know. I should have told you, but I made up my mind in Paris to forget he even existed." I plucked a tissue from the box and blew my nose. "Worked out really well for me, don't you think?"

"It did, until he came prancing back into your life. He should have just left you alone," Mia said loyally. "You deserve so much better."

I shook my head. "It wasn't like that. I sought him out, remember? He probably *would* have left me alone."

"I don't know," Erin hedged. "If he thought you were the love of his life, I don't see how he could have stayed away forever. I mean, why even come back to Detroit in the first place? He could have gone anywhere after winning Lick My Plate. Where was he before?"

"New York," I said. "He left for the Culinary Institute right after I left for Paris."

"He should have stayed there." Mia was grumpy about it. "I can't believe Lucas likes him."

"Everybody likes him." I threw up my hands. "I like him, for fuck's sake. I adore him! We have fun together and the sex, oh my God..." I flopped to my back and moaned in agony.

"That good, huh?" Erin asked.

"I can't talk about it. I'll cry again."

"So why not give him another chance? He said he was sorry, and it sounds like you guys are great together. Seven years is a long time."

I propped myself up on my elbows and looked at her. "Is that really you saying that, Miss This Is A Very Bad Idea? You're supposed to be my voice of reason here."

Erin laughed. "Where's the reason in holding a grudge for so long, especially against someone who makes you happy?"

"It's not that easy." I sat all the way up. "I don't know why, but I can't get over what he did."

"You don't have to." Mia patted my leg.

"But wouldn't you feel better if you did?" Erin persisted.

"Who wants to lug around all that bitterness? All that resentment?"

"I don't *want* to," I snapped. "But I don't know how to get rid of it. I was hoping this pregnancy would force me to do it."

"What?" Both of them stared at me, dumbfounded.

Realizing how crazy it sounded out loud, I lowered my voice. "I was sort of hoping I was pregnant, so that I'd be forced to forgive him and get back together. That way I wouldn't have to make the decision."

The looks on their faces told me what they thought of that plan. "Coco," Mia said, "I love you, but that's ridiculous. If you want him back in your life, then let him in, but I think we can all agree it's a good thing you're not pregnant."

"No, it's not!" I jumped up from the bed, whirling around to face them, arms flying. "It's not. You don't understand, I needed a sign, OK? I needed the universe to tell me what to do because I'm too messed up over him to think straight! This baby was supposed to be the sign, goddammit! The Fetal Forgive My Asshole Daddy And Get On With It sign! And now there is no sign and I'm back where I started and—stop laughing!"

Mia and Erin were trying hard not to smile but Mia's lips were smashed together tight and Erin's shoulders were shaking. "I'm sorry," Mia said, putting a hand over her mouth. "It's not funny."

I gave up the fight, my shoulders slumping. "You might as well laugh. Beats crying."

"Oh, honey, come on. You don't need a sign from the universe to tell you how you feel." Mia shook her head. "You are an emotionally intuitive person. Yes, you tend to act on impulse, but clearly in this case, you're not doing that. And we're proud of you. Now what does your heart say?"

Sighing, I dropped back onto the bed between them. "My heart is confused. And scared."

She nodded. "Love is terrifying. But remember when I called you from Paris because I was scared about how I was falling for Lucas?"

"Yes."

"Do you remember what you said?"

"'I'm jealous?'"

She laughed, nudging me with her leg. "No. Well, you might have. But you said everything happens for a reason, and that I just had to be willing to take a chance. I was never one to trust fate, but you helped me give myself permission to fall for him, not knowing what the end result would be."

"But Lucas hadn't hurt you in the past. Lucas was perfect," I grumbled unreasonably.

"No one is perfect, Coco. Lucas has his faults just like anyone, and he's nothing—*nothing*—like the man I thought I'd marry, but now look at me." She smiled, her face lighting up. "You helped me see that things don't always go according to plan, and that's OK. Life's full of surprises, right? Now I'm not saying Nick is the perfect one for you, and God knows I don't like what he did, but if you still love each other after all this time, well…" She shrugged. "That's a pretty powerful sign, in my eyes."

"Right." I took a deep breath. "Maybe I just need a little more time to get used to it…but I do love him, the cocky bastard." Mia's wedding dress caught my eye. It was wrapped in plastic, the hanger hooked over her closet door. "God, Mia. I can't believe you're getting married next weekend."

She grinned. "Me neither." Then she grabbed my leg. "Hey, maybe you'll meet the man of your dreams in France!"

Erin cleared her throat. "Excuse me, no. I insist that any dreamy man left in France go to me. You two have had your share."

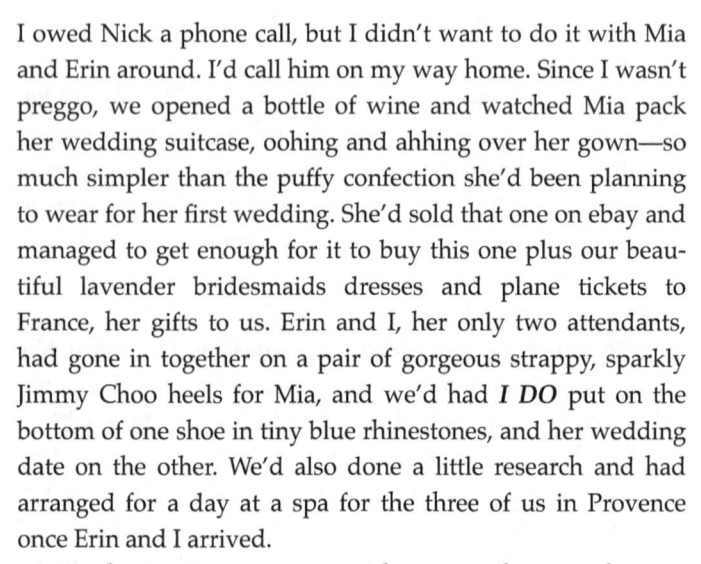

I owed Nick a phone call, but I didn't want to do it with Mia and Erin around. I'd call him on my way home. Since I wasn't preggo, we opened a bottle of wine and watched Mia pack her wedding suitcase, oohing and ahhing over her gown—so much simpler than the puffy confection she'd been planning to wear for her first wedding. She'd sold that one on ebay and managed to get enough for it to buy this one plus our beautiful lavender bridesmaids dresses and plane tickets to France, her gifts to us. Erin and I, her only two attendants, had gone in together on a pair of gorgeous strappy, sparkly Jimmy Choo heels for Mia, and we'd had *I DO* put on the bottom of one shoe in tiny blue rhinestones, and her wedding date on the other. We'd also done a little research and had arranged for a day at a spa for the three of us in Provence once Erin and I arrived.

Watching Mia dance around her room, happier than I'd ever seen her, I felt this lovely warm hum beneath my skin. She was going to spend the rest of her life with the man she adored, and she couldn't wait to get started.

Suddenly I thought of the story from Nick's family history, about the way his great-grandmother, the little one called Tiny with the red lips, had shown up at his great-grandfather's house to announce she loved him in the middle of Sunday dinner because she couldn't wait. I thought about the note we'd found with today's date on it—really, what were the odds of that? Probably a million to one.

So what was I waiting for? If you loved someone, you should say it, right?

The hum began to build into something more expectant as I realized I no longer wanted to wait either. Even though I wasn't pregnant, if Nick still wanted me, I wanted him too. I stood up, gripping my empty wine glass by the stem.

"Where are you going?" Erin asked.

"To see Nick," I said breathlessly. "I have to give him another chance."

Mia burst out laughing. "You decided that in the last twenty-five minutes? Now that's the Coco I know."

Grinning, I hugged her hard and then Erin too. "Thanks, girls. You're the best. I'll call you tomorrow."

"Have fun!" Mia yelled as I rushed out of her bedroom.

"But be safe!" called Erin.

"I will!" I took the steps down two at a time and headed for the back door. "Hi, Lucas. Bye, Lucas." I raced through the kitchen past Mia's handsome fiancée, who'd come home while we were upstairs and was preparing dinner.

"Hi, Coco. Where's the fire?"

"Grand Circus Park," I yelled without stopping to look back. I jumped into my car and drove downtown, frowning only once when I realized I was in sweatpants and a Detroit City Distillery t-shirt. My face was sort of puffy and tear-stained too, and I had no makeup on. *Oh, well. If he loves me, he loves me like this.*

I pulled into the parking garage next to his building, took the first empty spot I could find, and rushed up to Nick's apartment. By the time I got to his door, I was panting, elated at the way I was recreating a story from his family's past. I took a second to compose myself before banging on the door.

Nothing.

I knocked again.

Nothing. My heart rate slowed, and my shoulders fell slightly. He wasn't home? This wasn't supposed to happen. The guy has to be home when the girl shows up. Had Nick mentioned he was going out? Maybe he was at the restaurant? I knew how anxious he was about the test, so it didn't seem likely that he'd just take off somewhere without calling…wait, had I even checked my phone?

I dug in my bag and pulled it out. Sure enough I had two missed calls, a text, and a voicemail message from him. The text said **Hey, please call when you can**. The voicemail message was longer, and more disappointing.

"Coco, it's me. Listen, I just got a call that my event schedule changed and my agent booked me on a flight to L.A. tonight. I'll be back Wednesday, but I'll call you as soon as I can. And listen, I can't stop thinking about the other thing, so can you please let me know as soon as you can? See you soon."

Turning around to slouch against the door, I hit delete with more force than necessary, trying not to be too angry over this. After all, Nick was a "celebrity" now and he'd have "events" to do and flights to catch and people in his life that had to come before me. But how annoying that this one had to happen just when I was coming over here to give him a second chance. The date was today's date, not Wednesday's!

I was so aggravated I almost didn't listen to the voicemail from Angelina. But I figured nothing could put me in a worse mood than this, so I hit play and put the phone to my ear.

What she said had me sliding down the door until my butt hit the floor.

"Coco it's Angelina. Listen, the party's off. The whole fucking wedding is off. Lorenzo's a big asshole."

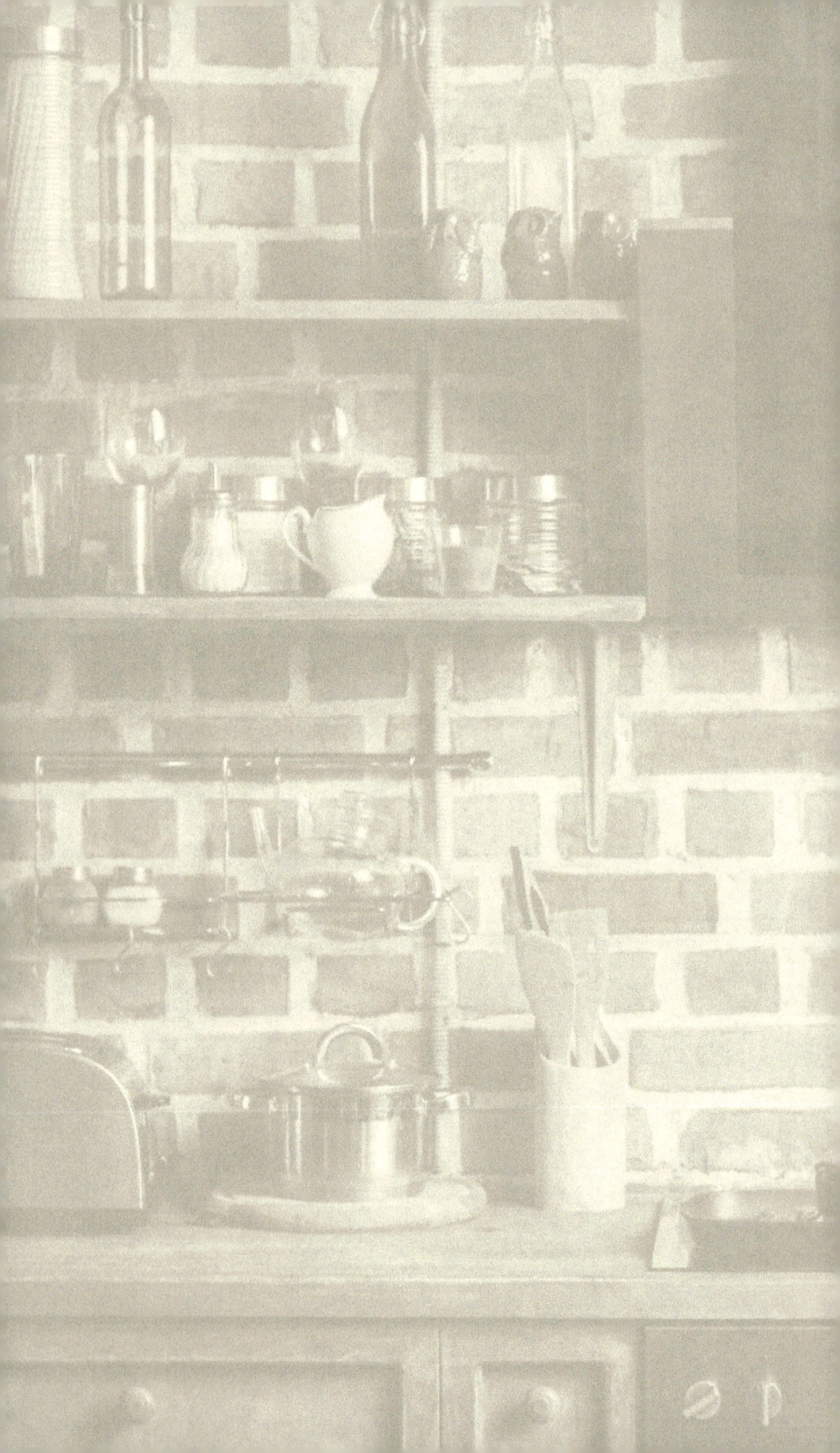

Chapter Twenty-Four

I listened to it three times, just to make sure I heard right. Then I called her. Maybe she was just being dramatic.

"Hello?"

"Angelina, it's Coco."

"Hi. The wedding's still off." She sounded stuffed up, like she'd been crying.

I bit my lip. "I heard your message. Are you OK?"

"No. I found out that he's been cheating on me with my slut cousin Christa. For months he's been fucking her!"

Damn you, Lorenzo. "So you broke up?"

"Hell yes, we did. And I'm not taking him back, neither. He can go fuck Christa if he wants to. Actually he can go fuck himself."

In the anise, I thought. "OK, well…are you sure? I mean, I don't think I'll be able to get deposits back from those vendors. It's less than a week away."

"I don't care. No party. I can't face anyone, I'm too humiliated."

Closing my eyes, I nodded slowly. *Goodbye, house.* "I'm sorry, Angelina. If you need any events planned in the future,

I'd love to work with you again." Not true, but what else could I say?

"All right. Thanks. Sorry about this." She sniffed.

"It's OK. You'll find someone better."

"Damn right, I will. Hey, is Nick Lupo available?"

"*No.*" Rolling my eyes, I ended the call and put my head in my hands. What the hell else could go wrong?

Back in my car, I called Nick, but it went straight to voicemail. I didn't want to leave the test results in a message, so I hung up and figured I'd try again later. At home, I brushed my teeth and curled up in bed, my phone next to me in case he called back. It was crazy how much I missed him sleeping beside me, when he'd only been there for the last two nights. I reached for my phone and texted him. **I miss you. Call me.**

But I fell asleep still waiting for the phone to ring.

The next morning I got ready for work, looking at my phone way more than usual. Normally I'm not someone who's glued to it, but my job makes it necessary to be available to clients and vendors even when I'm not at the office. By noon, I still had no call from Nick, and I figured with the late flight and time change, maybe he was sleeping.

Hey sleepyhead. Wake up. Let's talk.

After lunch, I tried calling again, and this time I left a message. "Hey, it's Coco. Just trying to reach you, so give me a call. The party this weekend is off, so don't worry about that. Thanks for saying you'd help out, though. And I'm glad we got to spend time together. Hope you arrived safely and that you're having a good time. Bye." That last part was kind of a lie—I didn't really want him to have a good time there. I wanted him to miss me the way I missed him.

By three in the afternoon, I was a little annoyed.

By five, I was angry

By six, I saw the pictures.

I was still at the office, and even though I'd managed to slay the dragon urge to Google him before, today was a different story. The dragon won.

I typed his name, hit enter, and sucked my lips between my teeth. In the news, it said at the top, and underneath the words was a photo of Nick with his arm around a pretty brunette, his lips pressed to her cheek. Gasping, I clicked on it. According to the gossip site that posted the photo, it had been taken two hours ago. And there were more.

Trying to remain calm, I clicked through a bunch of photos from the event, some kind of fundraiser with celebrity chefs cooking the food. I was hoping to see him with a bevy of different beauties, but it was always the same one. Apparently she was a chef too, a contestant on the current season of Lick My Plate.

And his ex-girlfriend.

My breaths came harder and faster, making my dress feel too tight in the chest. The photo captions did nothing to set my mind at ease.

Season One winner Nick Lupo cozies up to former flame and Season Two fan favorite Alex Rigler.

Sexy exes Nick Lupo and Alex Rigler turn up the heat in the kitchen.

Nick Lupo and Alex Rigler still sizzle. "She can lick my plate any time," he said.

My stomach twisted and churned—I felt the familiar old sickness I used to experience when Nick would flirt with other girls at parties and later I'd look through his texts to see if they were contacting him. Horrible, juvenile behavior that I never wanted to repeat. I knew gossip sites exaggerated things. But why hadn't he called?

Disgusted with him and myself, I closed the window

and packed up to go home. On the way, I called Mia and told her I'd been an idiot to think Nick was serious about me. After hearing everything that had happened since I left her house the night before, she said not to panic until I talked to him. And though she didn't say how glad she was that Angelina's party had been canceled, I could hear it in her voice.

By dinner that night, he still hadn't called, and I found myself stabbing my chicken breast with a fork instead of eating it.

"Something wrong?" Sitty asked, one eyebrow arched.

"No." I cut a bite and ate it, staring at my plate like a sullen teenager. Sitty said nothing further.

On Tuesday, Mia left for France, and Erin and I went out for a drink. Nick still hadn't called. She listened to me gripe about trusting him and being disappointed all over again, but told me not to jump to conclusions or overreact, which pissed me off. I wasn't overreacting! I was being fucking smart. Protective.

That night, I got my period.

When Wednesday came and went without a call, I deleted his number from my phone. I also emailed my real estate agent that I couldn't afford the house on Iroquois but I wanted to keep looking at things in my price range. Then I got out my Grass Widow Bourbon and took a shot before pressing Send.

Well, that's that. Goodbye, house. Goodbye, Nick. Goodbye crazy, stupid dreams.

Of course, on Thursday, he called.

I didn't answer.

I deleted his voicemails without listening.

I deleted his texts without reading.

More sickening familiarity.

On Friday, I didn't go to work, scared that he might try to find me there. He wouldn't dare show up at my parents' house, I figured, not after everything in our past. But I spent the weekend at Erin's apartment just in case.

Good thing.

When I got home on Sunday night, Sitty told me that not only had he come by on Saturday, but he'd stayed to have a little whiskey and water with her, and he'd told her a few things she thought I should know.

"He lost that phone, those things you're all attached to so much. He say it fell out on the plane to California and he never found it. He has a new one with a new number. I wrote it for you." She held out a yellow post-it with a phone number written on it.

"Not. Interested." I tried to bypass her and head up the stairs but she blocked my way.

"Why not?"

"Because he's not good for me, Sitty." The lost phone might explain why he hadn't called me from *that* number, but he could have found a way to reach me. And I'd made up my mind. Seeing those pictures and waiting around for him to call left me with a bad feeling. As far as I was concerned, I'd dodged a bullet.

"He loves you," Sitty declared.

"He said that?"

"What boy sits with someone's grandmother for two hours if he doesn't love her?"

True. Trying to think of an argument, I opened my mouth, closed it, and opened it again.

"You look like baby bird," she said. "And why do you dress like a painter?" She gestured to my sweats. "Last weekend you go with Erin with fancy underwear but this weekend it's rags."

I looked her in the eye. "I wasn't with Erin last weekend. I was with Nick."

She looked smug. "I know this."

"He told you?"

Her shoulders rose. "He did, but I already knew there was a boy involved."

I rolled my eyes. "Well, not anymore. We're done."

"Why? You don't like him?"

"I do like him. I love that asshole, in fact. But I'll have to get over it. He's never fought hard enough for me, Sitty. It's not enough for him to tell me or you that he loves me. I want him to show it. I want proof."

"What kind of proof?"

I sighed. "I don't know. I'd know it if I saw it. I'd feel it. Now can I please get by?"

She stepped aside and I passed her, but not before I saw her stick the yellow post-it in her pocket.

Christ, was she going to meddle in this? That's all I needed. I stomped up the stairs, changed into running clothes, and laced up my Nikes. "I'm going out for a run," I called from where I sat on the stairs.

"OK." Sitty's voice came from the kitchen. "You'll be back for supper?"

"Yes. In about thirty minutes." I stood up and stretched for a minute, then headed out the front door, ready for a good, hard sweat.

Three miles later, I came home exhausted and dripping to find a strange car in the driveway, an SUV I'd never seen before. It made sense when I found Nick Lupo standing on my front porch steps.

"Gotcha." He looked so good in his fitted black Burger Bar t-shirt I wanted to punch him with my newly corrected fist.

"Sitty," I muttered through clenched teeth before blowing a sweaty strand of hair out of my face. "She called you?"

He nodded. "She did. So can we please talk?"

"No." I narrowed my eyes, trying not to think evil thoughts about my grandmother. "Why would she do this?"

"I think she hopes I'll marry you. She kept asking me if I wanted a wife." He didn't even try not to smile.

"Oh, Jesus. I'm going to kill her." I attempted to get around him to the front door but he came off the steps and took me by the shoulders.

"Coco, please." His voice was low. "I don't even know if you're pregnant or not."

"You'd know if you bothered to call me this week."

"I know, I'm sorry. It was a rushed trip and I lost my phone and forgot my iPad at home. But I missed you like crazy. It's been hell wondering about the test results. Are you pregnant or not?"

I waited a beat, just to drag out the torture a little. "Not."

He registered the news, nodding slowly. "Well, that's good."

"Yes, it is. Now go away." I tried to shrug his hands off me and move around him, but he held on tight.

"No. You're going to stand here and listen to me."

"I already heard, Nick. You lost your phone while you were off on your rendezvous with your little hottie chef girlfriend. I saw the pictures online. She lick your plate?"

His dark eyes clouded with confusion for a moment, and he let go of me. "You mean Alex? She's not my girlfriend. She's a classmate from the Culinary Institute that's on the show now. She's dating another friend of mine, a chef I worked with in New York."

"Oh yeah? Well, why wasn't *he* her date for that event?"

"Because his name isn't associated with the show. I have to do a certain number of press events for the network, Coco, even if I don't want to. And she wasn't my date. We went as friends."

"Then why'd you say that, about how she can lick your plate anytime?"

"I never said that."

"I saw it as a photo caption!" Even I had to admit that sounded a bit silly, but I couldn't let it go. It *hurt* to see those things written about him.

"Come on, Coco." He rolled his eyes. "Those people just make shit up when the truth isn't juicy enough. Yes, we dated a little in the past, but it wasn't serious, and we certainly are not dating now. I support her on the show, that's all. Look, I hate that stuff too. But my contract is up at the end of the year, and I'll be done with it."

"Fine," I snapped, annoyed that he appeared to have a decent excuse for all those photos. "That still doesn't change the fact that you up and left in a heartbeat and didn't call me all week long! I get that you lost your phone, but *friends* have phones, Nick. And there are Internet cafes. Post offices. Fucking messenger pigeons."

"I'm sorry…I don't know what else to say. You're right, I should have tried harder."

"And you said you were going to be home Wednesday."

His cheeks colored slightly. "I had to do something else, and I didn't end up getting home until Thursday. I just figured I'd see you when I got back, but now I realize that's not good enough."

"Hell no, it's not. You don't fight hard enough for me, Nick. You never have." I tried to get around him again, but he grabbed my upper arms.

"Listen to me. I'm not perfect, and I don't claim to be. I'm going to make mistakes, and you will too. But I love you. And I know you love me. Give me another chance, Coco. Let me make things right."

I wanted to. Oh, how I wanted to. "It's too late for that."

He stared hard at me. And then, unbelievably enough, he smiled. "No. It isn't."

I blinked. "What?"

The grin widened. "It isn't. You're going to give me another chance. Maybe not right now, maybe not even tomorrow, but you will. Because we are good together, Coco. This is it for me, *and* for you. You'll see." He planted his lips on mine, and I was too stunned to resist, not that I'd ever resisted

Nick's kiss before. And this one was different somehow—I felt it from my scalp to my toes, a new charge in the air between us.

Then he let me go. He smiled at me, looking so happy I had to wonder if he was sane, and took off toward his car. It was the quickest I'd ever seen him move when he wasn't on a run.

"Wait," I said, flustered and hot in the shorts. "You can't just—what are you doing?"

He turned around, jogging backward a few paces. "I'm fighting for you!"

"From over there?"

He grinned and got in his car without another word.

"Oh for fuck's sake." Confused, frustrated, and totally turned on, I went in the house and slammed the door before screaming at it. "And stay out!"

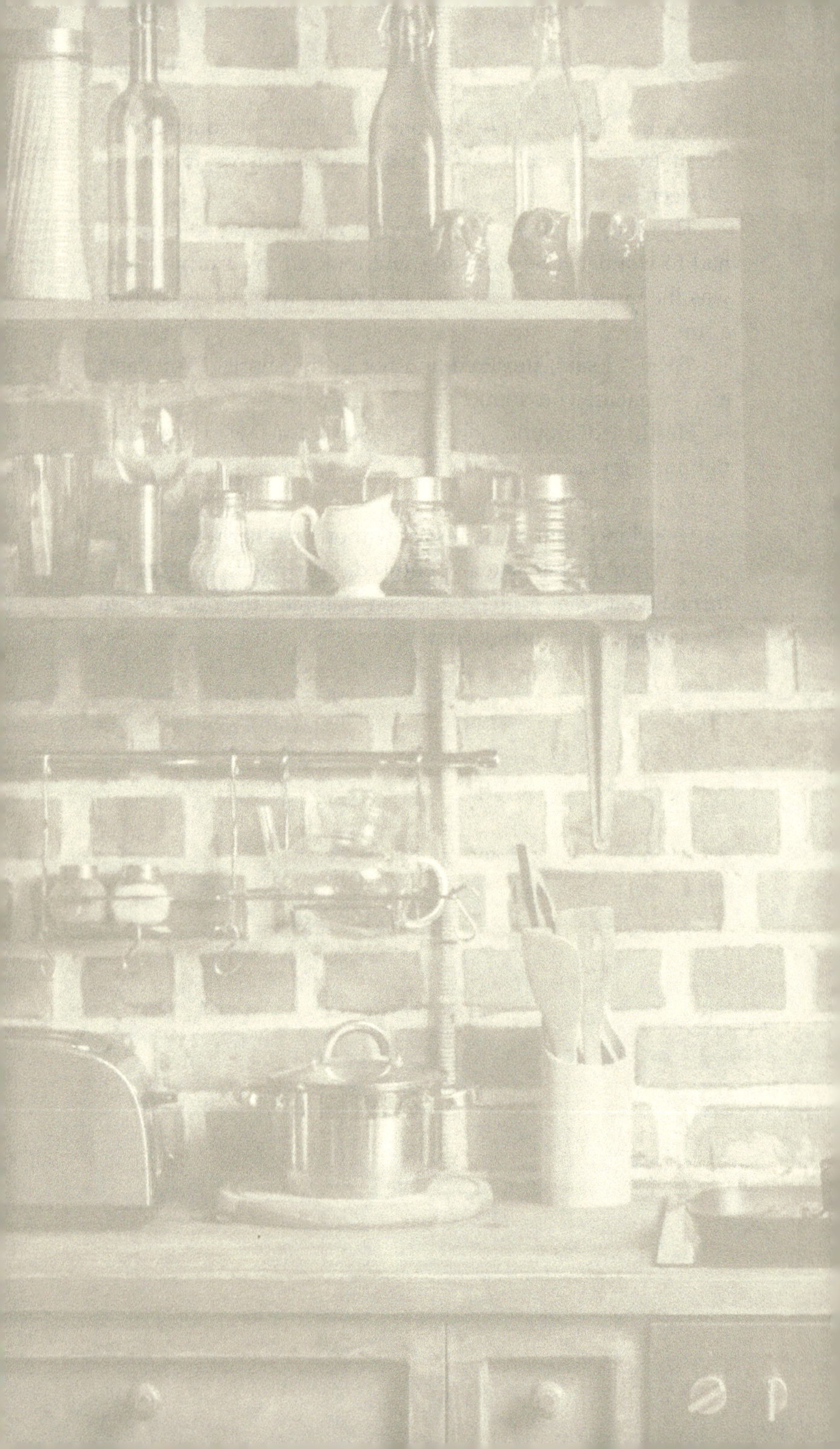

Chapter Twenty-Five

The next day, he sent me flowers at work. Two dozen breathtaking scarlet roses wrapped in green tissue paper, nestled in a box tied with a ribbon. The sight of them moved me a little before I came to my senses and blew a raspberry. *Big deal, he sent flowers. He's too late.*

I opened the card, which said, "There's a flower...I think she's tamed me..." It took me a minute to realize he'd quoted The Little Prince, which I had to admit won him a few points.

But not the game.

On Tuesday, he had lunch delivered to me from The Burger Bar, complete with a slice of cheesecake from the Astoria Pastry Shop, a Corktown bakery. The note said, "Wish I were there to have a picnic with you."

On Wednesday, he sent me a bottle of Auchentoshan Virgin Oak Scotch whiskey along with a card that read, "To my favorite virgin. Let's go to Scotland someday. Distillery tour?"

On Thursday morning I arrived at my office to find a tray of cinnamon buns on my desk, huge and warm and scenting the entire floor. Next to them, he'd scribbled a note on a piece of white printer paper. *Made these for you this morning. I miss you in my kitchen (and in my shower, my car, and my bed).*

I sank into my chair, dropping my laptop case at my feet. I'd like to say I considered giving the buns away or even throwing them in the trash, but of course, I dug right into one, savoring every sticky delicious bite and licking the icing from my fingers when I was done. After that I took the tray across the hall.

"You bake, too?" asked Lindsay Burns, one of the two interior designers whose offices were on the second floor. Eagerly she picked one up and took a bite.

"No. They were on my desk this morning. A little surprise."

"Oh my God." She crossed her eyes. "It's so good," she said with a mouthful. "Who made them?"

"Actually, my ex. He's trying to win me back."

"With food?"

I smiled ruefully. "He knows me. And he's a chef."

"Is he hot?" She took another huge bite.

"Yes," I said, sighing. "Ridiculously hot."

"He's hot and he cooks and he sends you food at work?"

"Yes."

"Hey, listen." She licked her fingers. "If you don't take him back, will you give him my number?"

"Sure…although I'm thinking about taking him back. But I have to make him work for it."

Lindsay nodded and polished off the rest of the bun. "Smart girl."

After taking the tray up to the third floor and down to the first to offer all the employees in the house a roll, I poured myself a cup of coffee and sat at my desk. Finding myself in a really good mood for the first time all week, I opened up my email inbox and started going through it. Mostly I had inquiries from brides, which were a good thing, but I also had a note from Linda, my real estate agent, with a few more listings in my price range. At the end of her email, she mentioned that the house on Iroquois had sold to the family who transferred here.

My heart fell. I'd known that would probably happen, but I still felt let down. Immediately I looked at my phone. I wanted to call Nick so badly—he was the only one who'd understand why I was so sad about it. I bit my lip...should I do it? I'd have to call Sitty and get his number, which was pretty pathetic. She'd probably gloat. But the phone was in my hand before I decided against it.

No. He has to come to me. Flowers and lunch and whiskey and cinnamon buns (damn, the guy understood me) were all well and good, but I still needed more. *What is essential is invisible to the eye.*

Still, on Friday morning, I woke up excited, wondering what today's surprise would be. And would he finally show up with it himself? The delivery guys were a nice touch and all, but I was ready to see him again, especially since I was leaving the following morning for France. Did he realize that? While I was in the shower, I tried to remember if I'd told him when I was going, and I wasn't sure I had. What if he was planning some big romantic dinner or something to cap off the week? Should I somehow let him know I wouldn't be around? Undecided, I left the house, half expecting to see a horse and carriage in the driveway ready to take me to work.

All day long I waited for the next offering. Each time the phone rang, I jumped. Each time I heard voices down the hall, my ears perked up. Every hour that passed had me scooting a little closer to the edge of my chair.

But the day passed, and nothing happened.

By five o'clock, I had to admit that he probably wasn't coming here. Maybe he was planning to come by my house tonight? Or maybe he'd already left something for me there. Smiling, I set up an out-of-office auto reply for the next week, tidied up my desk, and locked the door.

When I got home, though, there was nothing waiting for me. No flowers, no meal, no Nick. *Well, it's early yet. And maybe he had to work all day so he could get tonight off.*

I began packing for France, called Erin to remind her I'd pick her up at three tomorrow, and around eight, I gave in to my growling stomach and stuck a frozen pizza in the oven. Four slices and just as many glasses of wine later, I fell asleep on the family room couch with my phone clutched in my hand.

At some point, Sitty must have turned off the television, because the room was dark when I woke up. I checked the time—after two in the morning. Groaning at the crick in my neck, I stretched and rose to my feet. The wine had my head a little foggy, but as it cleared, I realized that Nick hadn't called. Or come over. Or sent me anything.

Well, fuck. What an anti-climactic finish to the week. And I was leaving in twelve hours.

After taking some ibuprofen, I went upstairs, brushed my teeth and fell into bed, missing him beside me like I had every night this week. Where was he? Was he thinking about me? Was this stupid of me to wait around when I wanted to see him so badly? Maybe it was. The next week of my life was all about Mia, but when I returned I'd reach out to him, even if I had to deal with Smug Sitty.

I drifted back to sleep, content for the first time all week.

The next day, I woke up at eight and took a run. My head ached from too much red wine the night before, but I made myself do it, thinking about all the tasty meals I'd eat in France this week. I hadn't packed any running clothes, but I planned to eat ALL the things.

After a shower, I put on a simple white cotton sundress that would be comfortable to travel in and added the final items to my suitcase. Mia had made me a list, of course, and I dutifully crossed off each item listed as I surveyed the contents before latching it shut. I had everything I needed. When I was ready to go, I looked longingly at the roses I'd brought home from the office. *Damn you, Nick. Why won't you call? Did you learn your lesson or not?*

I picked up Erin, grateful for her excited chatter about our trip and the wedding and the prospect of hot groomsmen or wedding guests. I needed the distraction. But eventually she asked, "How are things with Nick?"

"Fuck if I know." I settled into a chair at our gate. "He said Sunday he was going to fight for me, and then after all the hoopla last week, nothing. No surprise yesterday, and no phone call."

"Maybe he lost his phone," she said, laughing as she patted my arm.

"Ha. Right." I opened the bottle of water I'd just bought and guzzled it, still a little dehydrated from all the wine plus my morning workout. "Honestly, I have no idea what he's thinking. Half of me likes the anticipation and the other half can't stand the suspense. Are we back together or aren't we?"

"So you *do* want him back."

"Yeah. I do." I glanced at her. "Crazy?"

"Not at all. Especially since he gave me this to give to you." Pulling an envelope from her purse, she handed it to me and grinned. "I'm the messenger pigeon. He told me to say that."

Jaw open in disbelief, I screwed the cap back on my water and stared at the envelope. "What is that?"

"I don't know. But it's for you. He got in touch with me earlier this week and asked when we were leaving. Then he dropped this off at my apartment yesterday and told me to say nothing to you until we were here." Her green eyes lit up. "He's gorgeous. Gor-geous. Now open it. I'm dying!"

"Me too." Sliding my finger beneath the seal, I tore it open and pulled out a hand-written note.

Black ink on a white handkerchief.

I smiled as I began to read his small, neat printing.

Dear Coco, I'm sure the red lipstick had more effect, but my black pen will have to do. Just wanted to tell you I love you and I miss you and I hope the surprises made you happy this week. I want to make you happy every day for the rest of your life if you'll let me. See you soon. Love, Nick

"What does it say?" Erin demanded. "You're killing me!"

I read it again to myself before reading it aloud to her, struggling to get the words out when my throat began to close.

"God, that's so romantic," she gushed. "But what's with the handkerchief?"

I told her the story and she pounded the chair arm between us. "That's so cute!"

"It is, isn't it?" I fanned my face. "I think I might cry. God, I wish I could have seen him before I left. Why didn't he bring this to me himself?"

As I read the note again, a deep voice came over the loudspeaker at the gate. "Ladies and gentleman, may I have your attention please?" I was so swept away by my feelings, I didn't even realize the voice was familiar.

"Oh my God." Erin's hand gripped my wrist. "Coco."

"What?" I glanced at her.

"Look."

I looked up. Straight ahead, standing at the gate and speaking into the microphone (the man could charm anyone into anything, I swear), was Nick. And he was looking right at me as he repeated his request.

"Thank you," he said as the buzz in the terminal quieted.

"You see, I have to impress this woman over here." He pointed at me. "The gorgeous woman in the white dress."

Chills swept down my body. Heads looked back and forth from him to me, and a few people giggled in the crowd.

"I've been madly in love with her since I was nineteen, but I made a mistake back then. I lost her, and I didn't fight hard enough to get her back." The giggles quieted, and my stomach flip-flopped wildly. Tears filled my eyes. "But there's never been a day where I haven't thought about her and wished she were still mine." His voice cracked on the word "mine," causing the first tear to slip down my cheek. "And she told me to stop proposing to her out of the blue, but some habits are hard to break." He set the microphone down and walked toward me, and the silence of the crowd made my heartbeat deafening. I was frozen stiff in my seat. What the hell was he doing?

When he reached me, he got down on one knee, and gasps echoed through crowd.

Erin stood and backed away slightly, her hands over her open mouth.

When Nick pulled out a ring box, I put my hands over mine too.

"Coco," he said quietly, his dark eyes serious. "I married you before because I loved you enough to promise forever. And even though things went wrong, I never doubted you were the one. So I want to do it right this time. Maybe you think I'm crazy, but I think we've wasted too many years apart already. I want you back. I want you forever. Marry me again?" He opened the ring box, and my heart stopped. Inside was a gorgeous diamond and platinum ring in an art deco setting, a large emerald cut center stone surrounded by delicate filigree work.

"Oh my God," I breathed, my entire body shivering.

"It's a replica of the ring my Papa Joe gave to Tiny." Nick's eyes were shining too. "I wish it were the real thing, but my Aunt Vinnie wouldn't give it up."

"Oh, Nick." I wanted to do a dozen different things at once. Say yes. Kiss him. Hit him. Melt into a puddle. Jump up and down. Squeal. Tell him I loved replicas of vintage things. Hear him ask me to marry him again. But I couldn't do anything, could barely even breathe.

"What do you think?" he whispered.

I smiled. "I want sixty-seven years, at least."

"You'll have them. You'll have everything."

"Did she say yes?" called a voice from the crowd.

"Yes," I whispered to Nick. Then I let my head fall back. "Yes!" I shouted to the roof.

The crowd erupted in applause and Nick slid the ring on my finger. I blinked at it through tears before he pulled me to my feet and wrapped me in his arms. Whoops and whistles rang out as we kissed long and deep, Nick lifting me right off the ground.

When he finally set me down, Erin tackled me, alternating hugs with wide-eyed staring at my hand. Nick accepted handshakes from the crowd before giving Erin a kiss on the cheek. "Thank you. I couldn't have done this without you."

She fanned her face, which, like mine, was dripping with tears. "Me! What did I do?"

"Gave me the flight information. How else would I have been able to book a ticket?"

I grabbed his arm. "You booked a ticket?"

"I had to. They don't let people through security who don't. Not even handsome devils like me with a ring in his pocket."

I slapped his shoulder. "But are you really going? To France, I mean?"

"Of course I am. I can't miss the wedding." At my dumbfounded face, he grinned. "I got hold of Lucas and Mia yesterday to ask if they'd mind an extra wedding guest just in case you said yes. After I explained what I was doing, they made me swear up and down that we'd both be on that plane."

"Mia knew before I did?" I stuck my hands on my hips. I slapped his arm one more time before throwing my arms around him again. "Oh my God, I can't believe this." Burying my face in his neck, I breathed him in and held him there.

This was right. I could feel it.

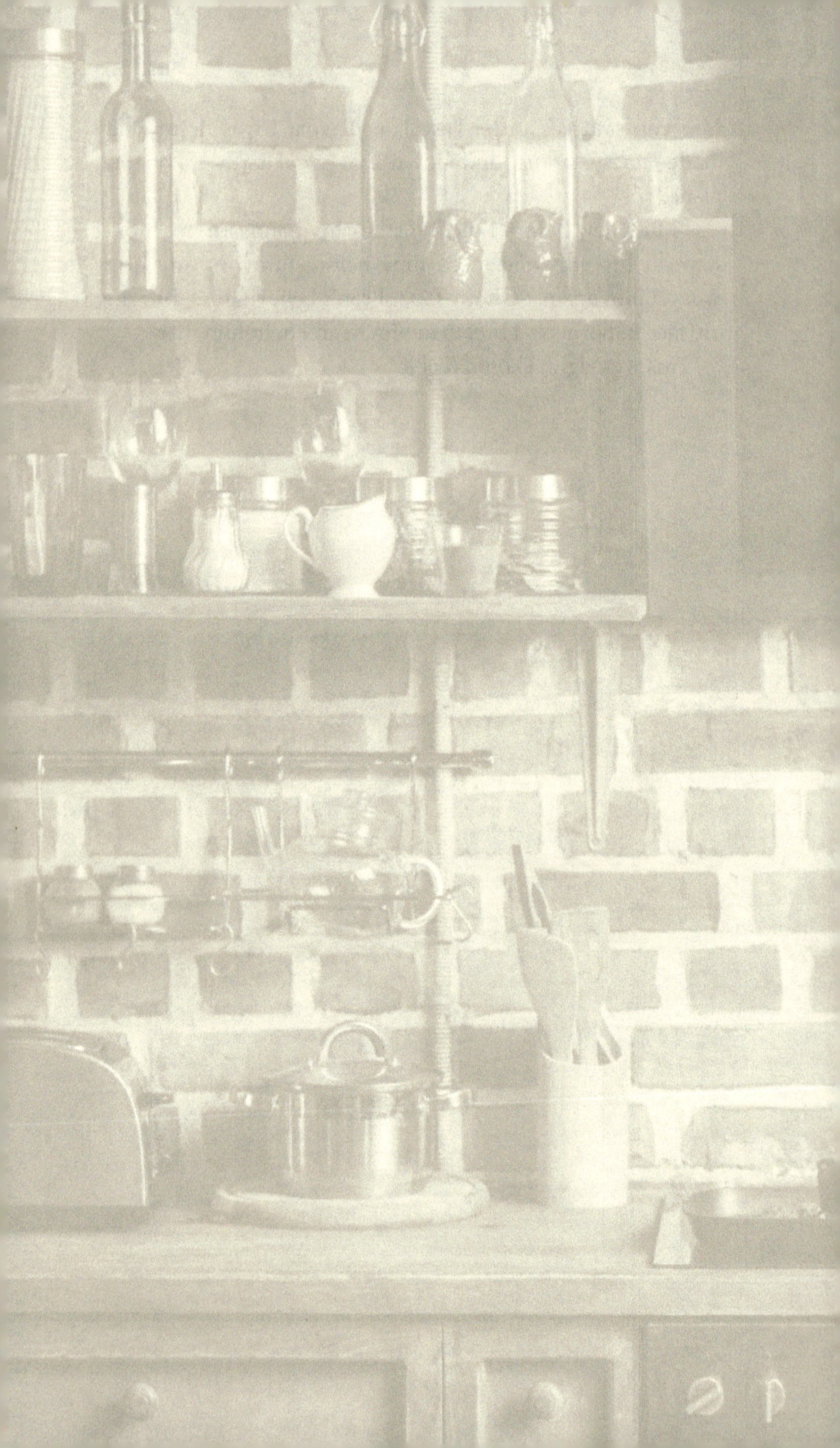

Chapter Twenty-Six

We arrived in Paris very early Sunday morning. Erin and I had planned to spend one night in the city, and we'd decided to splurge on a room at the Ritz since it was only the one night and we were splitting it. The rest of the week we'd be staying right at Lucas's family villa. Since Erin was in cahoots with Nick, he'd arranged for a second room at the Ritz, and Erin ended up having our original room to herself. She happily disappeared into the elevator when we arrived at the hotel, bleary-eyed with jet lag. She said she was so tired, she didn't think she'd even leave the room.

We didn't leave ours either.

Perhaps we should have. Perhaps it was sacrilege to have all of Paris waiting outside our windows, and me a history major, but the most romantic city in the world was doing a fine job casting its spell within our four walls.

Well, more if you count the bathroom. We did it in there too.

But the bed...oh, that bed. King sized, covered with crisp white linens and mounded with pillows, utterly inviting. As soon as the door was shut behind us, Nick swept me off my feet and carried me to it, our mouths drawn together as if by force. I threw my arms around his neck and kicked off my flats, exhausted but unable to stop myself from wanting him, now that we were finally alone.

He set me gently on the bed and looked down at me, nudging his shoes off. "Mrs. Lupo."

My eyebrows rose. "Not yet I'm not."

He grinned. "I know, just trying it out."

"I like it."

He stretched out on the bed, covering his body with mine. "Me too."

His weight on me was simultaneously too much and not enough. I reached up and pulled his lips to mine again, teasing them open, running my tongue along them, tugging at them with my teeth. "I missed your mouth," I whispered, hooking one leg behind him. "I love it so much."

"It's all yours."

My heart beat faster at the thought. "You know what I was just thinking?" I asked, letting him pull me up so he could work my dress over my head.

"What?" He tossed it to the floor, unhooked my bra, and slipped it from my arms. "I hope it involves my mouth on your tits, because that's what I was thinking."

I giggled and lay back as he lowered his lips to one breast and then the other and back again, like a kid who just unwrapped two awesome Christmas toys and can't decided which one to play with first. "No, but don't stop. I was thinking," I said, arching my back and running my fingers through his hair, "that I never even had time to change my name the first time around. And that might have been a good thing, because Coco Lupo sounds like a cocktail, not a person."

He lifted his head and looked at me. "I'd drink that cocktail morning, noon, and night. I'd get drunk on it."

"I'm sure you would." I moaned luxuriantly as his mouth worked its way down my chest to my belly. "Even so, maybe I'll hyphenate."

"My love." Nick straightened to unbutton and remove his shirt and then yanked his white undershirt over his head. "You can do anything you want. You can even keep your name if you want to, although I'd be really proud if you took mine."

In the soft morning light coming in through the windows, Nick had never looked more handsome. I loved everything about him, from the gray hair at his temples to the ink on his skin, to the heart that beat beneath my name. I reached up and touched it. "God, I love you. And yes, I'll take your name. I love your family and its history—I can't wait to call it mine."

He smiled at me. "I love that ring on you. The whole flight here, I kept looking at your hand."

"Me too!" I held it out between us. "It's so beautiful, Nick. I can't believe you had it made this week." On the way to Paris, Nick had explained that after flying in from L.A. late Wednesday, he'd driven overnight to Buffalo, where his dad's cousin Vinnie lived, the granddaughter of Tiny who had the ring. He'd taken a million photos of it, not trusting anyone else to take them. He wanted every detail right. Then he'd driven back to Detroit and gone straight to a jeweler, begging her to make a copy quickly. After hearing his plea, she agreed —and she also wanted permission to use his name, image, and the story for advertising.

"Wait a minute, I just realized something. You went to get the ring last week? You didn't even know if I'd take you back yet."

"Very optimistic of me, I know." He dropped his mouth to my belly again, shimmying down further. "But I wasn't sure what the test results would be, and I was sort of hoping the ring would win you over either way. Besides—Noni told me not to wait any longer, not if I knew this was what I wanted."

"I'm glad you didn't wait. I'm glad you surprised me that way. I think it means you know me too well." I ran my fingers through his hair. "We'll have a good story to tell now."

He slid my underwear down my legs. "Yes, we will."

"Nick," I said dreamily as he settled between my thighs, his lips planting soft kisses in a line straight south from my belly button. I propped myself up on my elbows. "I like the name Vinnie for a girl."

He picked up his head and looked at me. "Me too." Then he put his mouth on me and I forgot everything, even my own name.

Finally, we went deliciously, magnificently *slow*.

This morning he'd licked me into oblivion and then fucked me roughly from behind, both of us kneeling up against the headboard. Later I'd sucked his cock while he knelt over my face, finishing him off while he stood at the side of the bed and I hung off it, upside down. After room service lunch, we did it in the shower, my back up against the tile wall. Then we actually considered a walk outside, feeling quite proud of ourselves. But we'd fallen asleep before we were even dry, and now he was sliding inside me again, his face hovering above mine. It struck me then that every time since we'd gotten back together had been so rushed.

This was different. Now, those first frantic orgasms out of the way, we took our time.

Time, I thought as he moved inside me, his lips barely brushing mine. *We have time. We have each other. We have our past, but we have a future too.*

I opened my legs wider, tilted my hips to take him deeper, raked my nails slowly down his back. I was there again, that night he'd said we would go on forever, like the sky and stars, and I was here, writhing beneath him, our bodies connected and yearning.

"You were right," I said, digging my heels into his thighs.

"About what?" His cock pushed deeper, and he stayed there, moving against me in tiny, measured, rhythmic pulses.

"About the past. About forever. About us. Oh, God." I grabbed him, held him tightly to my body as everything around me splintered and the world was reduced to nothing more than my body, my heart, my soul, merging with his.

I'd never let him go.

"Well…what do you think?" Mia turned away from the full-length cheval mirror in the bedroom designated as the bridal dressing room at the villa and faced us.

"Oh God." Erin cupped a hand over her mouth. "I'm going to cry and ruin my makeup. You're so beautiful."

Mia's lovely pink lips curved into a smile. "Thank you."

I opened my mouth to say the same, but found my throat so tight I couldn't speak. She was beautiful, but even more than that she was happy. And considering it was Mia, she was remarkably calm. Her smile was serene, her hands steady, her shoulders relaxed. The room, with its large windows overlooking the olive grove, where everything was set up for the ceremony, was airy and suffused with sunlight, making her pale skin glow rosy and gold. She looked so peaceful, much more peaceful than I'd ever seen her look before anyone's wedding, let alone her own. Nary a hive nor hiccup.

"Oh, Mia, I'm so happy for you."

"Thanks. I'm happy for you too." Her smile widened. "I can't believe it, but I'm actually fond of Nick Lupo."

I laughed. "You're on cloud nine, you're fond of everyone right now."

"True."

"And this is *your* day—we can be happy for me when you get back."

Mia's lifted her chin. "If it's my day, then I get to feel anything I want—and when I look at you and see how happy he makes you, and how good he is to you, I feel all warm and fuzzy about it. And you can't stop me."

"OK, fine. You win. Be happy for me." I fussed with her hair a little, moving some loose strands off her face. She'd wanted to wear it down, so it was loosely knotted and spilling over one shoulder, echoing the lines of her elegant ivory chiffon gown. Sleeveless, the neckline dipped to a scandalously low V in the front (I could never wear anything like it, but Mia's smaller chest was perfectly suited for it) and all the way to the waist in back. There was beading at the top of each shoulder and around her slim waist, and the hemline was mermaid style. She hadn't wanted a veil, so nestled in her wavy brown hair were a few cream-colored flowers picked this afternoon from the villa's extensive gardens. Standing back to take in the full vision, I grinned at the way her little toes peeked out from beneath the hem in her sandals. "You're perfect. Absolutely perfect."

"Good, because I think it's time." Mia glanced out the window again and took a deep breath. "Looks like all the chairs are full, and I hear music."

"Are you ready?" Erin asked, reaching for her hand.

"More than ready." Mia reached for my hand, and squeezed. "Thank you for being here. I love you both so much."

Erin and I joined hands to complete our little circle. "We

love you too," I said. "Lucas is the luckiest man in the world. I can't wait to see his face when he gets a look at you."

The villa's front courtyard was set up for the reception, and Mia had chosen décor that echoed the colors of the Provençal landscape beyond it. Tables for eight covered with ivory or taupe damask cloths, sprigs of rosemary or thyme on each plate, centerpieces of lavender bouquets, and candles of various heights glowing in the twilight. Even the air smelled romantic—full of herbs and floral notes that made you want to drink it like honey. The day had been hot, but had cooled to a comfortable temperature, and a light breeze ruffled the tablecloths.

Behind the villa, beyond gardens of wildflowers and a row of lemon trees, twelve rows of chairs were set up on either side of a gravel path. At the end of the path, which was lined with votive candles, stood the Officiant, and beyond him, the olive grove.

Erin and I waited near the lemon trees with Mia's little half-sisters, who were serving as flower girls. Three guitarists strummed softly as Lucas's family was seated: his former movie star mother, a strikingly beautiful woman on the arm of her husband, a handsome man ten years younger; and his father, who resembled an older version of Lucas in a sort of shaggy-haired, aging-rockstar way. Next, Mia's stepfather and mother were seated, and finally, the groom and his two brothers appeared in front of the guests. They wore dark blue suits, white shirts and ties in a deep color Mia called *aubergine*.

I smiled when I saw how happy and handsome Lucas

looked, his usual scruff barely visible, his incorrigible dark waves tamed with some kind of pomade, possibly loaned to him by Nick. (Honestly, the man traveled with more hair products than I did.) Erin and I exchanged a quick smile and hand squeeze before she started up the dusty path, and I fought tears watching the pretty lavender dress float behind her. When she was halfway to the front, I began to walk up the aisle, praying my heels didn't sink into the gravel.

Immediately I sought Nick in the crowd, and my heart fluttered faster when I saw him smile at me. He wore a lightweight beige suit, white shirt and checkered tie, and his dark eyes shone with love and pride as he watched me. God, he was so handsome—for just a second I entertained the fantasy of taking a detour up his row and straddling him in his chair.

Mia's mother dabbed her eyes as I glided by, and then I locked eyes with Lucas, whose expression was adorably nervous and excited at the same time. I winked at him and took my place next to Erin. The music changed to something slightly more dramatic, and everyone stood in anticipation of the bride.

When she appeared at the foot of the path, murmurs and whispers floated through the crowd. *She's so beautiful, look how radiant she is, I've never seen her so happy...* I'd seen her only minutes ago, but as she came up the aisle on the arm of her father, she looked even more ethereal and lovely. Erin and I reached for each other's hands simultaneously and held on tight as Mia walked toward Lucas, her steps sure and determined, even in the gravel.

I glanced at Lucas, and a lump formed in my throat as I watched him touch a thumb and finger to his eyes, fighting tears, and then giving up and allowing a couple to fall. In contrast, Mia was bright-eyed and smiling when she reached him, and again I marveled at her grace and composure. *I hope I'm as relaxed and confident on my wedding day as she is.*

The service, conducted in both French and English, was only about twenty minutes long, simple but beautiful. Even the parts I didn't understand sounded like poetry. All too soon it was over, and Mia and Lucas were pronounced husband and wife. They kissed, and when Lucas lifted Mia right off the ground, the crowd erupted.

The guitarists struck a few buoyant chords, and the bride and groom took a moment to hug and kiss the wedding party before heading back down the dusty aisle, hand in hand, dancing and laughing and smiling as if they'd never stop.

Later, after dinner had been served and cake had been sliced, toasts had been made and dancing had begun, Nick took my left hand and squeezed it. We were sitting at a table near the dance floor watching Mia and Lucas sway gently in each other's arms, and I said a heartfelt prayer of thanks that everything she'd wanted for this day had come to fruition. Every detail had been perfect. Even the weather cooperated, cooling down even more as the sky darkened and a breeze picked up, carrying the scent of sunflowers and lavender across the courtyard.

"What a perfect day," I murmured. "I'm so happy for her. For both of them."

"Me too." Nick brought my hand to his lips and kissed the back of it. "Is this what you'd like for our wedding?"

I smiled sideways at him. "Maybe. What about you?"

"I like the idea of getting married outside, but I don't know about a destination wedding. That takes a lot of extra planning, doesn't it?"

"Yes," I lifted a glass of champagne to my lips. It fizzed in my mouth and down my throat. "So maybe something closer to home. The farm?" I set the flute down and looked at him.

He tilted his head from side to side. "Maybe. But there might be another place we like more. Let's wait and see." He played with my hand on the table, admiring the ring on my finger. "So what will your parents say?"

"They better say they're happy for me. Or else they're not invited." He laughed and tugged on my elbow, pulling me onto his lap. I went gladly, slipping an arm around his shoulders.

"Well, we know your grandmother will be glad about it."

"Definitely. She'll say all her novenas worked."

"She's going to take credit for this?" He pressed a kiss to my bare shoulder.

I rolled my eyes. "Probably. Somehow."

"Mmmm. You smell so good." He rubbed his lips back and forth over my skin, inhaling deeply.

Beneath me, I felt his cock coming to life, and it sent a jolt of arousal straight to my core. "Mmm. Think we can escape?"

"I know we can."

Sliding off his lap, I stood and let him lead me by the hand across the courtyard, away from the party, around the house and back toward the olive grove where the ceremony had taken place. We started out walking slowly, but as soon as we were out of sight Nick started moving faster. Soon we were running through the dark, slipping between rows of thick, curvy-branched olive trees. When we were deep in the grove, hidden from everything in the shadows of the moon, Nick turned and pinned my back to a wide tree trunk. "Lift up your dress."

Breathless, I hiked up the filmy skirt of my dress, under which I wore the skimpiest lace panties I owned. Without even bothering to remove them, Nick licked his fingers and reached between my legs, sliding them inside me.

"Fuck," I breathed, riding his hand as his thumb brushed

over my clit through the lace. Yanking at his belt and then his fly, I freed his cock and wrapped a hand around its thick, hard shaft, let my thumb play over the head. He groaned as a silky drop oozed from the tip and I swirled it over his sensitive skin.

Our mouths were open, close but not kissing, our breathing hot and labored.

"Nick," I panted. "I want it. Now."

"Yeah?" He fingered me deeper, before sliding his fingers out to rub hard, fast circles over my clit.

"Oh, God. Yes. Please." My legs were shaking.

He moved my panties aside and thrust into me, pushing me hard against the tree. On the second thrust, my feet left the ground, and I wrapped my legs around his waist. His hands moved underneath my thighs, gripping hard and spreading me apart. The small of my back jammed against the ridges of the bark with every powerful shove of his cock inside me.

"I love it," I breathed, clutching at his neck. "I love the way you fuck me. You make me come so hard."

"Fuck yes," he growled, going deeper. "I've wanted to get under that pretty dress all day."

I bit my lip, aroused beyond measure by his ferocious desire. I stifled my cries in his neck as he took me higher, my insides growing tighter and tighter around him. My entire lower body went numb for a moment, suspending me between pain and pleasure, between tension and relief, between a breath and a scream. Finally, his orgasm burst me wide open, and I gasped with every thrust of his cock inside my dripping, pulsing core.

"Jesus," I said a moment later. "I don't know how I'm going to walk."

"Good."

I dropped my head back against the tree and looked at

Nick's face in the silvery dark. "Maybe you'll have to carry me."

He kissed my lips. "Anywhere and everywhere. As long as you'll let me."

"Hmm. How about forever?"

He touched his forehead to mine. "Forever."

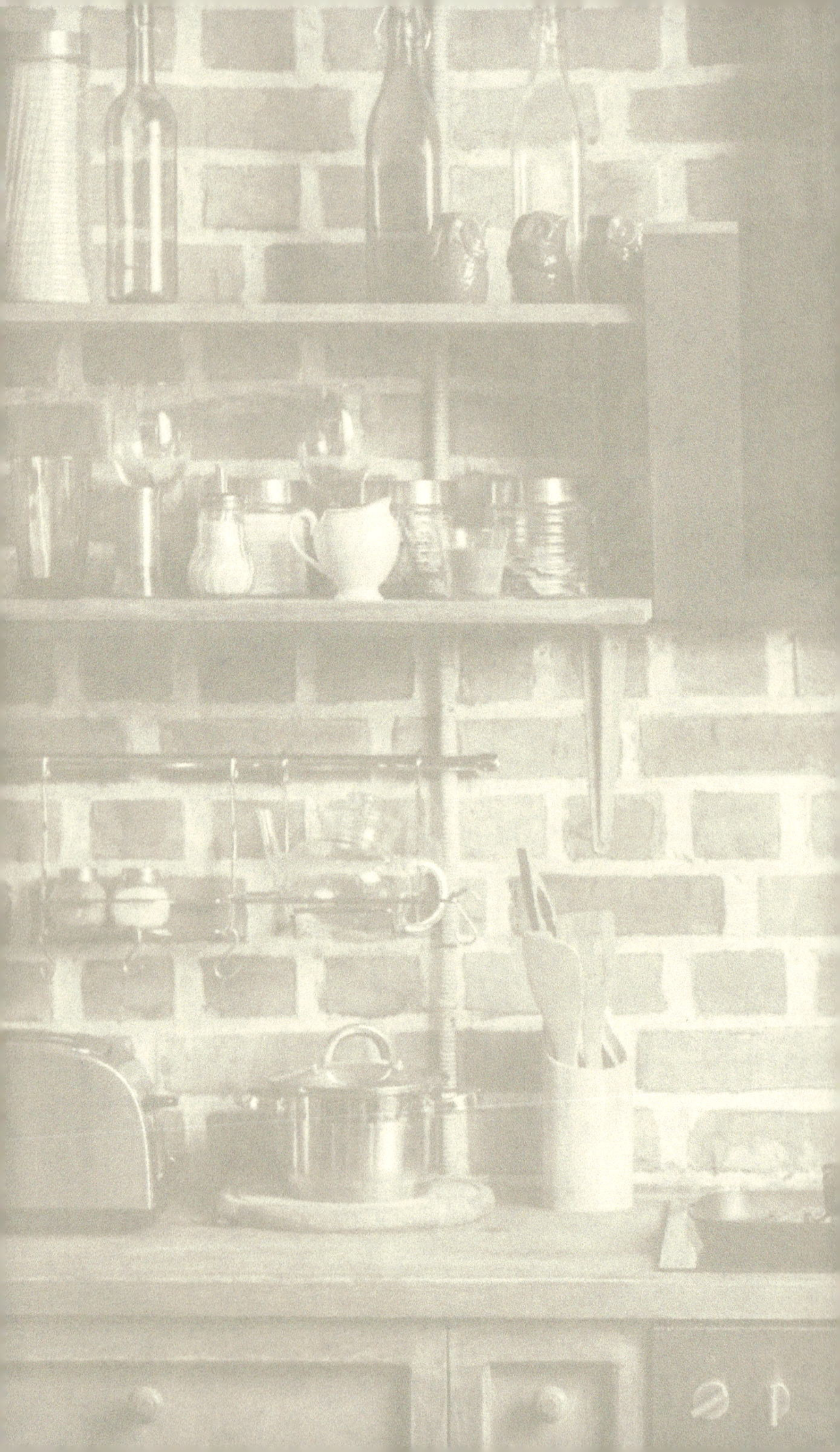

Epilogue

"Close your eyes." Nick's voice was soft, and his breath tickled my ear.

"Why?"

"I'm going to blindfold you."

"In my parents' driveway? In a convertible?"

"We'll start with that. Maybe later I'll do it somewhere else—if you behave."

I laughed. "I thought you were taking me out for ice cream."

"I'll still buy you an ice cream cone if you want one. But first I want to give you a birthday present."

"Now?" We'd only been back from France for about ten days, and my birthday wasn't for another month.

"I know it's early, but I saw this thing that I knew you had to have, and I just can't wait to give it to you."

"No complaints here. I love surprises." I clapped my hands. "What is it?"

He reached into the back seat and handed me a small black bag that said Shinola. "Look inside," he told me.

I peeked inside the bag and pulled out a photograph of

two Shinola bikes side by side, and a tiny box. I opened the box and took out a tiny little key. "What's this?"

"The key to the lock for your new bike."

"Really?" I grinned at him before studying the picture again. "How fun! And is that your bike next to mine?"

"Yes. Want to go pick them up?"

"Yes!" I glanced into the back seat. "But how are we going to get them home?"

"Leave it to me." He wrapped a soft scarf around my eyes and tied it at the back of my head. "Can you see?"

"Nope."

"Good."

He started the car and backed out of the driveway, and I imagined the stares he got driving around town with a blindfolded woman in the front seat of his '54 Mercury. And where the hell was he taking me? Were our bikes at the Shinola store? Wasn't that downtown somewhere? Why would he have to blindfold me for that?

I tried to figure out where we were headed by the number and direction of turns we took, but pretty soon I realized he was taking so many turns, he was trying to get me lost on purpose.

"What the hell?" I said, grabbing onto the dash. "You're making me carsick here."

He laughed. "Sorry, but you're too smart, cupcake. And this has to be a surprise. We're almost there."

In another five minutes, he slowed to a stop and turned off the engine. "You asked how we'd get our new bikes home," he said, "but they're already home." He untied the scarf and I pulled it off, anxious to see where in the world we'd ended up.

My jaw dropped, and I sucked in my breath before clapping a hand over my mouth.

We were in the driveway of the house on Iroquois. Every hair on my body stood on end.

"Nick, what is this?" My eyes roved over all the details I loved about the home, finally landing on the SOLD sign on the front lawn. "This house is sold."

"I know. I bought it."

"What?" I stared at him, unable to wrap my brain around this. "*You* bought it? But Linda said that family that transferred bought it."

"I know. That's what I told her to say."

I gasped and thumped him on the leg. "You didn't!"

"I did. Are you mad?"

I looked at the house again. "I should be, shouldn't I? I wanted to buy a house by myself."

"But that was when you were going to *live* there by yourself." He put his arm around me and pulled me close. "Now we're going to live here, together."

"Oh my God, Nick. I can't believe it." My heart was racing. "You said we should live in your apartment for a while, you big liar." In fact, I'd already started packing. The sooner I got out of my parents' house, the better. As expected, they'd been stunned at my engagement, but Nick hadn't made me face them alone. Together we'd told them how we'd realized after seeing one another again that we were still in love and wanted to be married, having already spent far too long apart. I'm pretty sure they thought we were crazy and foolish, but I didn't care. I'd never been more excited about my future.

"Had to keep you guessing." He kissed my head. "But that's all over with. And don't worry—I'll still let you do as much work here as you want to. I'll even show you how to work a hammer."

"Haha." I tipped my head to his shoulder. "God, you're an asshole. But I love you."

"I love you, too. And Coco, we're putting your name on the title as soon as possible. It's our place. I don't care who paid for it."

"Really? You mean it?" I looked up at him.

"Of course I do. It's you and me, cupcake."

Happiness bubbled up in me. "Hey, maybe if we get the backyard in shape by next summer, we can get married here!"

Nick dropped a quick kiss on my lips. "Good idea."

I slipped my arms around his waist, snuggling into the nook as we looked at the home where we'd build our future. *This is where I'll be every night for the rest of our lives.*

It would take a lot of work—both this house and this relationship—but I knew it would be worth it. Everything I needed to be happy was right here in front of me.

The End

Acknowledgments

Thank you to my husband and children for allowing me the time and space to write. I love you.

Author friends, you inspire me every day, and because of you I never feel alone in this endeavor. Thanks for letting me sit with you.

A million, trillion thanks covered in chocolate cake batter to romance bloggers and readers who spread the word about books. I wish I could name you all because I adore you so much. I am so, so grateful.

To my incredibly talented mentors, I hope someday to do for another author all the things you've done for me. I'm honored to call you my friends.

Finally, thanks to my readers, who have been so lovely to me in reviews, posts, and messages. I adore you.

About the Author

Melanie Harlow likes her heels high, her martini dry, and her history with the naughty bits left in. She's the author of the small town Cloverleigh Farms Series, the One & Only series, the After We Fall Series, the Happy Crazy Love Series, and the Frenched Series.

She writes from her home outside of Detroit, where she lives with her husband and two daughters. When she's not writing, she's probably got a cocktail in hand. And sometimes when she is.

Find her at www.melanieharlow.com.

Made in United States
Troutdale, OR
12/31/2023